MW01489053

Creating Partnerships with Parents

Creating Partnerships with Parents

An Educator's Guide

Donald C. Lueder

The Scarecrow Press, Inc.
A Scarecrow Education Book
Lanham, Maryland, and London
2000
Originally published 1998
Technomic Publishing Co., Inc.
Lancaster, Pennsylvania

SCARECROW PRESS, INC.
A Scarecrow Education Book

Published in the United States of America
by Scarecrow Press, Inc.
4720 Boston Way, Lanham, Maryland 20706
www.scarecrowpress.com

4 Pleydell Gardens, Folkestone
Kent CT20 2DN, England

Copyright © 2000, 1998 by Donald C. Lueder
Originally published in 1998 by Technomic Publishing Co., Inc.

The Technomic edition of this book was catalogued as follows by the
Library of Congress:
Main entry under title:
   Creating Partnerships with Parents: An Educator's Guide
Bibliography: p.
Includes index p. 269
Library of Congress Catalog Card No. 97-61844
Reprinted by Scarecrow Education
1-56676-583-8 (cloth)
0-8108-3926-1 (paperback)

⊖™ The paper used in this publication meets the minimum requirements of
American National Standard for Information Sciences—Permanence of
Paper for Printed Library Materials, ANSI/NISO Z39.48-1992.
Manufactured in the United States of America.

To my mother and father, whose total involvement made Creating Partnerships with Parents: An Educator's Guide *possible*

CONTENTS

Parent involvement is currently one of the buzzwords being bantered around by educators, policy makers, and legislators. In particular, the lack thereof has been cited as one of the major educational challenges facing this country. In a recent poll conducted by the U.S. Department of Education (USDOE), eighty-nine percent of the company executives who responded identified the biggest obstacle to school reform as the lack of parental involvement. Interestingly, the results from surveys of teachers, parents, and students reveal that they also recognize the need to engage many more parents in the education of their children (USDOE, 1995).

The seriousness of the issue has prompted federal and state policy makers to pass legislation designed to increase parental involvement. For example, the following has been added to the list of national education goals: "By the year 2000, every school will promote partnerships that will increase parental involvement and participation in promoting the social, emotional, and academic growth of children."

Involvement by the parents is mandatory in federally sponsored programs such as Head Start and Even Start, and in Title 1, Title VII, and PL 94-142 legislation. At the state level, in South Carolina, the Early Childhood Development and Academic Assistance Act of 1993 lists "increasing parental involvement" as one of its top priorities. The legislation requires all school boards in the state to develop parent involvement plans for their districts.

Yet, even with all of the attention that this issue has received and the pure sensibility of being involved, a great number of families are still not engaged in the education of their children. While educators and community leaders may recognize the need for more parental involvement, my experience is that they do not know how to go about getting it. And, often they are not sure what it is that they want to achieve when they are seeking more involvement by the parents.

My investigation of family/school/community partnerships began in 1986. For the past ten years, I have been visiting successful partnership programs and working with schools and communities to implement partnerships with families. *Creating Partnerships with Parents: An Educator's Guide* has evolved from my experiences with the schools and the results of my studies. It is a practical resource book for designing and implementing family/school/community partnerships.

Creating Partnerships with Parents is written primarily for superintendents, principals, curriculum coordinators, project directors, teachers and community leaders. In addition, I believe college and university professors will find the book useful as well as their students.

The Self-Renewing Partnership Model presented in this book is designed to help schools and communities to plan and implement family/school/community partnerships. Within the conceptual framework is a series of four intervention strategies called School/Community Collaboration Strategies. These strategies are used to reach out and work with the families. Programs, events, and activities (Best Practices) for implementing each School/Community Collaboration Strategy are described. Finally, a Strategic Partnership Planning System is presented as a comprehensive method for schools and communities to use in developing their family/school/community partnership program plan.

Creating Partnerships with Parents provides the reader with the "why, where, when, and how" of truly involving all families, especially the hard-to-reach parents, in the academic and social development of their children. Many families are "missing in action." I believe that the way to reach these family members is to create partnerships between the families, schools, and communities. Without such a collaborative effort, it is unlikely that the children will receive the teaching and support they need.

CHAPTER 1

Introduction: The Case of
The Missing Families

THE DILEMMA

Educators are faced with a frustrating two-pronged dilemma. First, superintendents, principals, and teachers are finding it exceedingly difficult, if not impossible, to reach many students in a meaningful way because they are coming to school with inadequate basic skills and knowledge. Further, these deficiencies are often accompanied with self-defeating attitudes. Second, educators have not found a way to gain the necessary support from the families to help avoid or solve these problems.

The flames of the dilemma are fanned by increasing social pressures resulting from the effects of such things as: unemployment, divorce, lack of health care, drug and alcohol abuse, violence, teenage pregnancy, and children with special needs. Unfortunately, as the pressures have increased the availability of resources has decreased. Simply put, the schools find themselves caught in a bind.

While educators generally believe more parent involvement is needed, they are not sure how to reach many of the families. Rutherford (1995) emphasizes this point when he states, "How to involve these parents [families] productively remains an open question, especially since few teachers and administrators have received training in working with parents [families]" (p. vi). He goes on to say:

> There is great interest from many quarters in helping parents become more actively involved in their children's education—as a right, a responsibility, and an unfulfilled opportunity. Although many educators and

1

2 INTRODUCTION: THE CASE OF THE MISSING FAMILIES

schools and some school systems have developed programs and practices to strengthen parent involvement in education, not all programs have succeeded in involving low income, racial and ethnic minority and limited-English proficient parents. Many such programs come and go. (p. vi)

In the past, superintendents, principals, curriculum coordinators, project directors, and teachers have been forced to use their intuition in a "hit-or-miss" fashion when they developed and implemented parent involvement programs. When designing programs, they picked from several traditional activities and events in hopes that one of them would work. They had no choice since there was no model or conceptual framework to follow. As a result, sometimes their efforts were successful, and other times they were not.

In an effort to respond to the dilemma described above, a model for involving all families in the education of their children has been developed. The Self-Renewing Partnership Model is a comprehensive method for designing and implementing partnerships between the families, school, and community. With this paradigm, the school and community reaches out to the families, which is radically different from the traditional parent involvement approach described in the next section.

Parents or Families?

Often the words "family" and "family member" are used in place of "parents" and "parent" when referring to the significant other(s) who are the child's caregiver and provider. I believe the new terminology more accurately reflects the realities of today's families, and the complexities of being involved in the child's education.

In many families, instead of the biological parent, or in addition to grandmothers, grandfathers, aunts, uncles, brothers, sisters, friends, etc., are the individuals impacting directly on the child's educational and social development. Therefore, terms like "family involvement, family resource center, and family/school coordinator" have emerged to indicate the new roles and responsibilities.

However, I also believe the words "parents" and "parenting" are generally understood and accepted. Therefore, these terms are used interchangeably with "family" to describe some of the programs and activities in the book (e.g., parent/teacher conferences, parent rooms, and parenting classes). When the word "parent" does appear, then, the broader context of "family member" is to be assumed. No matter what terminology is used, it is important to recognize and acknowledge that many different family members may be serving in the various roles that are encompassed in the difficult task of parenting.

THE TRADITIONAL PARENT INVOLVEMENT APPROACH

Typically, parent involvement programs have been essentially single-dimensional, with family resources flowing into the school for the purpose of supporting the school's curriculum, programs and activities. The families provide time, money, and expertise to help their children by being involved with the school, directly and indirectly.

Consequently, it's not surprising that when superintendents, principals, teachers, parents, and community leaders are asked to give examples of parent involvement, their answers are very similar. They cite such parent events and activities as serving as volunteers; acting as chaperones; working on fundraising drives; attending athletic, music, and theater events at the school; and participating in PTO meetings, open houses, and parent/teacher conferences. These programs and activities reflect the traditional "families supporting the school" parent involvement approach.

This approach is firmly ingrained in the cultures of our schools, and in many families. I can personally relate to this. Over the years, I have sold dozens of hot dogs and gallons of soft drinks at football games, and have attended countless numbers of band concerts, soccer matches, dance recitals and plays. And I have met with teachers, principals, and guidance counselors.

With all the fruit purchased to support the marching band, there was never any fear that anyone in my family, or in the neighborhood, would suffer from scurvy. After purchasing our daughter's remaining allotment of holiday wrapping paper, we had an abundant supply for years. This process was repeated again with the other kids, and we purchased more than ample amounts of candy, popcorn, and magazine subscriptions.

Most of us are intimately familiar with these activities. I am sure you can provide examples of your involvement and elaborate on your adventures. You would probably say you would gladly do it all again, and would argue that this kind of participation is very important to the child and the school.

All of this is true. However, the "families supporting the school" approach is only one aspect of being involved in the education of the child and does not do the job by itself. The traditional parent involvement approach suffers from serious limitations. If schools and communities continue to focus only on this approach, many families will not be involved, and their children will not receive the support and help they desperately need.

The Case of the Missing Families: A Systemic Problem

Usually, even in the best of situations, there is only a small group of families that is actively involved in the school. In schools where the teachers say they have great support from the parents, the percentage of families involved in the different events and activities usually hovers around twenty-five percent.

Typically, within this core of families, there is a smaller group that is involved in almost all of the programs and activities. Having these parents being so involved has both its pluses and minuses. On the plus side, these are the families that always respond when there are special needs. These are the parents who will help to develop the partnerships. However, often these families are perceived by other families as "controlling" the school, a perception that can keep some parents away.

These characteristics are indicators of the benefits and limitations of the traditional parent involvement approach. While it is great to have a group of families that you can depend upon to help and support the school, this kind of involvement does not solve the dilemma described earlier.

The many family members who are not actively involved at school are a concern, but their absence is symptomatic of a much larger problem. I believe the major parent involvement issue facing this country is that many parents are not engaged in the education of their children at home. It is this group of "missing families" that should be the focus of involvement programs. That is, when seeking greater involvement by the parents, the concentration should first be on the involvement in the home and then the involvement with the school.

Athough I do not have empirical evidence to support my claim, my contention is that the family's involvement with the school is an extension, or outgrowth, of the family's involvement in the home. Being involved at home is the basis for the involvement at school. Stated in another way, my hypothesis is: "Being involved with the child's education at home is a prerequisite for being involved at school."

Because parental involvement in the home is fundamental, it is understandable why research studies show that the parents' involvement in the home has a greater impact on the academic and social development of the child than their involvement with the school. This is why involving the "missing families" with the child's education in the home is essential.

Many children will not receive the needed parental support until the "missing" families are reached. To achieve this, the schools and communities must use a new approach. Currently, most calls for more parent involvement follow the traditional approach, concentrating mainly on ways to get the families to support the school. However, in order to solve the dilemma stated earlier, parent involvement programs must focus on increasing the families' involvement in the home *and* at school.

The Self-Renewing Partnership Model

The Self-Renewing Partnership Model presented here is a method for reaching and involving the "missing families" by creating partnerships between the family, school, and community. The goal of the partnerships is to create "learning communities" where families, communities and schools collaborate to provide the best possible educational opportunities and environments for the children. The nature and function of family/school/community partnerships are described and discussed in Chapter 3.

As mentioned, the Self-Renewing Partnership Model requires a shift in the way we have traditionally conceptualized the notion of parent involvement as it introduces a new outreach dimension for working with the parents. We can no longer think of parent involvement only as family members working with and supporting the school, the school and community must also work with and support the families.

Being involved in the child's education at home and at school is a complex task, and getting the families to be partners with the school and the community can be difficult. Usually, many barriers keep the families and the school apart, making many parents "hard-to-reach." The school, with the community's help, must work to overcome these obstacles (the barriers are described in Chapter 4). The outreach dimension of the Self-Renewing Partnership Model is designed to do this.

The Self-Renewing Partnership Model has two major dimensions that interact with each other: The "energy-out" component and the "energy-in" component.

The "energy-in" component expands on the traditional "families supporting the school" approach by specifying eight different roles the families have to play to be fully involved in the academic and social development of the children in the home and at school. These roles are called Parent Partner Roles. Some of the roles are directed at the school. Others are directed at the child, while yet others aim at the child and the school. The Parent Partner Roles include: Nurturer, Communicator, Teacher, Supporter, Learner, Advisor, Advocator, and Collaborator. The component is described as "energy-in" because the family's resources (time, money, and expertise) are directed at the school and at the child. The Parent Partner Roles are described and discussed in the next chapter.

The "energy-out" component is a series of intervention strategies that the school and community use to reach out and work with the families. It is this dimension that makes the Self-Renewing Partnership Model unique. The use of resources to reach out to the families is a new "direction" for involving parents.

The intervention strategies in the "energy-out" component, called School/Community Collaboration Strategies, are used by the school and community to create the collaborative relationships and to enhance the families' willingness and ability to play their Parent Partner Roles. The four School/Community Collaboration Strategies are: Connecting, Communicating, Coordinating, and Coaching. The strategies are progressive in nature and build on each other.

The strategies are implemented sequentially. First, the Connecting Strategy is employed to break down the barriers between the families and the school. The Communicating Strategy is then used to establish two-way communication flows. The Coordinating Strategy is implemented to get school and community resources to the needy families. Finally, the Coaching Strategy is used to enhance the family's ability and capacity to play their Parent Partner Roles. Whether all of the School/Community Collaboration Strategies are needed, or which one is emphasized, depends upon the families' conditions and level of involvement.

A separate chapter is devoted to each School/Community Collaborating Strategy (Chapters 6,7,8, and 9), including best practices, activities, events, and programs for implementing each strategy. The best practices have been gathered from successful partnership programs found in the United States and Europe.

Careful planning is required for a partnership program to be success-ful. Therefore, a Strategic Partnership Planning System has been de-signed to help superintendents, principals, project directors, community leaders, and teachers to develop and implement their programs. Using the system, family populations to be targeted are identified, appropriate intervention strategies are chosen, and best practices are selected and implemented. The Strategic Partnership Planning System is presented in Chapter 10.

SUMMARY

Using school and community resources to reach out to the families is not the norm. However, I believe this has to be done to involve the "missing families." Schools and communities must be willing to imple-ment intervention strategies to reach and work with the hard-to-reach parents in these families. It is vital that we involve all of the parents since the success and happiness of our children are at stake. Building partner-ships between the families, school, and community is what parental involvement should be about. By using the Self-Renewing Partnership Model to create family/school/community partnerships, the case of the "missing" families can be solved.

CHAPTER 2

Fully Involved Families: The Goal

Reaching out and helping all parents, or surrogates, to be involved in the educational and social development of their children is the major focus of this book. The Self-Renewing Partnership Model has been developed to help schools and communities to accomplish this goal by creating partnerships between the families, school, and community. The model uses intervention strategies to reach the parents and help them be fully involved in their children's education. But, what does it mean to be "fully involved"?

The concept of parental involvement held by many people is very narrow because it is based solely on the traditional "families supporting the school" approach. This limited perception is one of the reasons that so many families are "missing." Being "fully involved," on the other hand, means that the parents are engaged in the child's education in the home and at school. Partnership programs are based on this broader view.

To better understand the characteristics of the fully involved family, the specific roles that parents must be willing and able to play to be partners have been identified and are described in this chapter. These Parent Partner Roles include: Nurturer, Communicator, Teacher, Supporter, Learner, Advisor, Advocate, and Collaborator. Again, the word "parent" here refers to any family member or surrogate who is assuming the parenting roles.

Not surprisingly, many family members have difficulty knowing how and when to play the Parent Partner Roles, which helps explain why there are so many "missing families." Therefore, the function of the Coaching

Strategy in the proposed model is to help the families to enhance their skills and knowledge to play the Parent Partner Roles.

Because I am arguing for broadening the concept of parental involvement, I feel that it is important to explain the process I went through to identify the Parent Partner Roles. I hope by describing the process, I will give the reader a better understanding of the conceptual framework on which the Parent Partner Roles are based.

After grappling with this issue for a long time, as I went through the process, I was able to reinforce what "being fully involved" means to me. The identification of the roles entailed gathering data from students, educators, parents, and community members; reviewing the literature; and discussing the issue with colleagues who are working in the field of parent involvement.

PARENT INVOLVEMENT: WHAT IS IT?

It has been said, "If there is lots of agreement about the solution to a problem, then the problem must not be understood very well." This may be the case with the parent involvement issue. Calls for more involvement by the families are coming from many arenas across the nation (and the world, for that matter) and from leaders in corporations, legislatures, colleges of education, universities, public schools, and communities. However, many of those arguing for more involvement appear not to know or understand what it is they are seeking.

Anyone reading this would agree that getting more parents involved is a good idea, but we might not agree on the desired outcomes of the involvement. We need to be clear about what outcomes we want from the partnerships between families, schools, and communities. As the adage points out, "It is hard to get lost if you don't know where you are going." That is, we need to know where we want to go with the involvement.

As stated in the beginning of this chapter, I believe too many people are operating solely from the traditional "families supporting the school" approach without considering how parents influence their children both at school and in the home. As we plan partnership programs, we have to consider the many ways parents need to be involved in the child's education.

AN EXERCISE

The responses from a simple exercise provide good indicators of the desired outcomes of parental involvement. When thinking about this issue, I asked myself, "What are the things that families provide when they are fully involved in the academic and social development of their children?" I posed this question, in a slightly different way, to groups of students, educators and community leaders across the United States. These people were workshop participants, or members of the audience at some of my presentations. As I worked with these groups, I asked them to respond to the question, "What did your family provide you and instill in you that helped you get where you are today?"

Figure 2.1 is a summary of their responses. However, before looking at the answers, ask yourself the same question. List your outcomes on paper, or in your mind, and compare them with the answers presented in Figure 2.1.

Responses to the question: "What did your family provide you and instill in you that helped you get where you are today?"

Provided
- Love and nurturing
- Day-to-day necessities
- Stable and safe environment
- Financial support
- Psychological support and encouragement
- Advice and guidance
- Understanding, caring, and respect
- Monitoring and supervision
- Discipline and structure
- Exposure to new experiences and opportunities
- A good learning environment

Instilled
- Basic skills and knowledge
- Problem-solving skills
- A questioning of why and why not
- High expectations and standards
- Strong value system (e.g., responsibility, independence, perseverance)
- Respect for others and yourself
- Belief that education is important
- Work ethic
- Belief in yourself
- Sense of security

Figure 2.1 *A Summary of Desired Outcomes of Parental Involvement.*

The outcomes listed in Figure 2.1 are impressive. Hopefully, you can identify with many or most of them. If you can, it is likely that you feel your family was involved.

The responses correlate with the results of Reginald Clark's study of the characteristics of successful families. According to Clark (1983), these characteristics include: expressed valuation of schooling and expectations for school achievement, frequent discussions about school and positive reinforcement of school work and interests, a family climate that has regular routines and meal times, and a purposive use of time and space.

What makes Clark's study of particular interest is that he found these characteristics in single- and two-parent homes, and in poor and middle-class families where the children were doing well in school. There is no question that family structure and social economic conditions do impact on the children's social and educational development. However, Clark's findings suggest that strong parent involvement can overcome the negative effects of poverty and single parenting.

Obviously, if all children received the kind of support from their families that is listed in Figure 2.1, we would not be as concerned about getting more parents involved. Unfortunately, this is not the case. Many children are not the beneficiaries of this kind of involvement.

To help solve the "case of the missing families," we have to find a way to reduce the discrepancy between the amount and kind of support provided by many of the families, and increase the amount and kind of support that is needed for the children to be successful. The Self-Renewing Partnership Model, presented in Chapter 5, is a method for reducing the discrepancy and increasing the involvement of parents, especially the "hard to reach."

A BRIEF REVIEW OF THE LITERATURE

About the time that I began investigating the area of parent involvement, Anne Henderson, Carl Marburger, and Theodora Ooms's 1986 book *Beyond the Bake Sale* was published. These authors challenge the traditional view of parent involvement, suggesting even in the title of their book that the involvement of the parents is more complex than typically thought. They describe five basic parent involvement roles:

1. Partners: Parents performing basic obligations for their child's education and social development
2. Collaborators and Problem Solvers: Parents reinforcing the school's efforts with their child and helping to solve problems
3. Audience: Parents attending and appreciating the school's (and their child's) performance and productions
4. Supporters: Parents providing volunteer assistance to teachers, the parent organization, and to other parents
5. Advisors and/or Co-Decision Makers: Parents providing input on school policy and program through membership in ad hoc or permanent governance bodies

Figure 2.2 *Henderson, Marburger, and Ooms's Parent Roles in Education. (Compiled from Henderson, Marburger, and Ooms, 1986.* Beyond the Bake Sale: An Educator's Guide to Working with Parents. *Columbia, MD: The National Committee for Citizens in Education.)*

Partners, Collaborators and Problem Solvers, Audience, Supporters, and Advisors and/or Co-Decision Makers.

Their "Partners" role refers to the parents' basic obligations for their child's education and social development, while the "Collaborators" and "Problem Solvers" roles involve reinforcing the school's efforts and helping to solve problems. The "Audience" role entails attending their child's performances (drama, music, athletics, etc.) and the "Supporters" role refers mainly to volunteering in the schools. Finally, opportunities for parents to provide input on school policy and governance are addressed in the "Advisors" and "Co-Decision Makers" roles. The roles are summarized in Figure 2.2.

Also in 1986, David Williams, Jr., and Nancy Chavkin presented a list of roles that parents play when they are involved, including: Home Tutor, Audience, Co-Learner, Advocate, and Decision Maker. Some of the roles are similar to those described by Henderson et al. (e.g., Audience, Advisor, and Decision Maker). Both the Henderson et al. and the Williams and Chavkin categories are combinations of "at home" and "at school" roles, illustrating the cooperative relationship between the parents and the school. These roles are described in Figure 2.3.

Joyce Epstein (1992) has formulated a popular framework of six major types of involvement in a family/school partnership.

Originally, Epstein's typology (1987) consisted of five basic ways for parents and the school to be involved. Type 2, "The Basic Obligation of Schools," describes what the school does to communicate with the parents. Her other original four types of parent involvement were: The

Home Tutor Role: Parents helping their own children at home with educational activities or school assignments.

Audience Role: Parents receiving information about their child's progress or about the school. Parents may be asked to come to the school for special events (e.g., school play, classroom program, etc.).

School Program Supporter Role: Parents being involved in activities in which they lend support to the school's program and take an active part (e.g., classroom volunteers, chaperones for trips, collect funds, etc.).

Co-Learner Role: Parents being involved in workshops where they and school staff learn about child development or other topics related to education.

Paid School Staff Role: Parents being employed in the school as part of the school's paid staff (e.g., classroom aides, assistant teachers, parent educators, etc.).

Advocate Role: Parents serving as activists or spokespersons on such issues as school policies, services for their own child, or community concerns related to the schools.

Decision-Maker Role: Parents acting as co-equals with school staff in either educational decisions or decisions relating to governance of the school.

Figure 2.3 Williams and Chavkin's Home-School Partnership Roles. (Compiled from Williams and Chavkin, 1986. Teacher/Parent Partnerships: Guidelines and Strategies. Austin, TX: Southwest Educational Development Laboratory.)

Basic Obligations of Parents, Parent Involvement at School, Parent Involvement in Learning Activities at Home, and Parent Involvement in Governance and Advocacy. Later, the framework was changed to a typology of a "School and Family Partnership," and the word "families" is used instead of "parents." Also, Type 6, "Collaboration with Community Organizations" was added. Later, in 1995, this type was modified to read "Collaborations and Exchanges with the Community." These changes are much more than "cosmetic." The new terminology and content indicate the realities of today's family structures, and the idea that communities should be partners in the education of the children. Epstein's six types are presented in Figure 2.4.

Four of the six Epstein categories are things that the families do, or are responsible for, either at home or at school. The two "at home" types (Types 1 and 4) concentrate on the child's basic needs, creation of a positive environment, parent-initiated learning activities and child-initiated requests for help. Types 3 and 5, "Support for School Programs and Activities" and "Decision Making, Governance, and Advocacy" are the two "at-school" categories. Type 2, "The Basic Obligations of Schools," is one of two school roles, and this type deals primarily with communi-

Type 1: Basic Obligations of Families. Families are responsible for providing for children's health and safety, developing parenting skills and child-rearing approaches that prepare children for school and that maintain healthy child development across grades, and building positive home conditions that support learning and behavior throughout the school years. Schools help families develop the knowledge and skills they need to understand their children at each grade level through workshops at the school or in other locations and in other forms of parent education, training, and information giving.

Type 2: Basic Obligations of Schools. The schools are responsible for communicating with families about school programs and children's progress. Communications include the notices, phone calls, visits, report cards, and conferences with parents that most schools provide. Other innovative communications include information to help families choose or change schools and to help families help students select curricula, courses, special programs and activities, and other opportunities at each grade level. Schools vary the forms and frequency of communications and greatly affect whether the information sent home can be understood by all families. Schools strengthen partnerships by encouraging two-way communication.

Type 3: Involvement at School. Parents and other volunteers who assist teachers, administrators, and children are involved in classrooms or in other areas of the school, as are families who come to school to support student performances, sports, or other events. Schools improve and vary schedules so that more families are able to participate as volunteers and as audiences. Schools recruit and train volunteers so that they are helpful to teachers, students, and school improvement efforts at school and in other locations.

Type 4: Involvement in Learning Activities at Home. Teachers request and guide parents to monitor and assist their own children at home. Teachers assist parents in how to interact with their children at home on learning activities that are coordinated with the children's classwork or that advance or enrich learning. Schools enable families to understand how to help their children at home by providing information on academic and other skills required of students to pass each grade, with directions on how to monitor, discuss, and help with homework and practice and reinforce needed skills.

Type 5: Involvement in Decision Making, Governance, and Advocacy. Parents and others in the community serve in participator roles in the PTA/PTO, Advisory Councils, Chapter 1 programs, school site management teams, or other committees or school groups. Parents also may become activists in independent advocacy groups in the community. Schools assist by training parents to be leaders and representatives in decision-making skills and how to communicate with all parents they represent, by including parents as true, not token, contributors to school decisions and by providing information to community advocacy groups so that they may knowledgeably address issues of school improvement.

Type 6: Collaboration with Community Organizations. Schools collaborate with agencies, businesses, cultural organizations, and other groups to share responsibility for children's education and future success. Collaboration includes school programs that provide or coordinate children's and families' access to community and support services, such as before- and after-school care, health services, cultural events, and other programs. Schools vary in how much they know about and draw on community resources to enhance and enrich the curriculum and other student experiences. Schools assist families with information on community resources that can help strengthen home conditions and assist children's learning and development.

Figure 2.4 *Epstein's Six Types of Involvement. (Compiled from Epstein, 1992. "School and Family Partnerships," in M.C. Alkin ed.* Encyclopedia of Educational Research *(6th ed.). New York: Macmillan, pp. 1139–1151.)*

Creating Two-Way Communication: Parents and educators both have vital information to share. Educators share information with parents about children's progress in school; their expectations and hopes for the school and the children; and their curriculum, policies, and programs. Parents share information with educators about their child's needs, strengths, and background; and their expectations and hopes for the school and their child. Educators and parents listen to each other. Ideally, the result is parents and educators who are informed, who have created a negotiated set of joint expectations for children and the school, and who work together to create a school environment in which all can learn and feel successful.

Enhancing Learning at Home and at School: Parents contribute to children's learning by having high expectations, providing a setting that allows concentrated work, supporting and nurturing learning that occurs in school and elsewhere, and offering love, discipline, guidance, and encouragement. Educators develop curriculum and instructional practices and strong relationships with children that create conditions for optimal learning. Parents and educators develop an array of ways in which parents can be involved in and out of the classroom to enrich children's learning. Parents understand what is occurring in the curriculum and ways in which they can monitor, assist, or extend children's homework. Parents might function in the school as paid aides or volunteers, participants in educational activities offered at school for the family, or contributors to curriculum selection and enrichment.

Providing Mutual Support: Educators support parents by offering educational programs for them that are responsive to their interests and needs. Parents support educators in many ways, such as volunteering in the schools, organizing and planning activities, raising money, and attending functions (plays, sports events). Educators and parents build trusting relationships and arrange occasions to acknowledge and celebrate each other's contributions to children's growth. Increasingly, the school becomes the critical institution in the community for linking parents with useful health, education, and social services.

Making Joint Decisions: Parents and educators work together to improve the school through participation on councils, committees, and planning and management teams. Parents and educators are involved in joint problem solving at every level: individual child, classroom, school, and district.

Figure 2.5 *Swap's Elements of a Home-School Partnership. (Compiled from Swap, 1990.* Parent Involvement and Success for All Children: What We Know Now. *Boston, MA: Institute for Responsive Education.)*

cations. The other school role, "Collaborations and Exchanges with the Community," refers to the partnership between the school and the community.

Swap (1993) builds on Epstein's typology to arrive at four elements of a partnership between the home and school:

- creating two-way communications
- enhancing learning at home and at school
- providing mutual support
- making joint decisions

Home-School Communication: Communication serves as the foundation for all other home-school partnership activities. It involves the exchange of information between parents, teachers, and school that helps both school and family to assist the child in learning. This exchange of information needs to be done in a variety of ways to increase the opportunity for understanding. Communication is needed from both the classroom teacher and the site administrator to the parent. All parents should be contacted on a frequent and regular basis. Equally important, the school needs to develop effective communication channels for parents to communicate with teachers and administrators about their child, their hopes, aspirations, and ideas for their child and for the school.

Home and School as Supporters: Parents and teachers give basic support to each other. Parents express their support by attending to the basic needs of their children at home. This includes feeding, clothing, sheltering and attending to the health and welfare of their children. At school their support is shown through traditional activities such as raising funds for the school, attending open house or student performances, chaperoning field trips, conducting campus clean-ups, or organizing a book fair. Teachers support families by inviting and encouraging them to be an active part of the classroom and school activities. In addition, the school staff supports families through holiday food and clothing drives, special home visits and efforts to help families to find needed social services. These activities are ones with which both parents and school personnel tend to feel most comfortable. The school should set a goal to create a variety of support activities for parents and to have all parents involved in at least one support activity during the course of the year.

Home and School as Learners: Both the school staff and parents should have opportunities to increase their knowledge about how to work together. Parents need information about the school curriculum, school policies, and other aspects of school life as well as opportunities to increase their own parenting skills. Teachers need opportunities to increase their effectiveness in communicating with parents (including conferencing skills), in designing effective home learning and homework activities, and in involving parents, when appropriate, in classroom and school activities.

Home and School as Teachers: It is a crucial fact that parents are a child's first and foremost teacher. Schools provide the structured and professional framework to expand, complement, and support home learning as well as to teach children the content specific skills from kindergarten through twelfth grade. Parents need guidance and support on how to foster their child's formal learning at school. In addition teachers and other staff members need to explore ways they can work together with parents as mutual teachers of the child. Teachers have found that parents can assist as "teachers" in the classroom, and that teachers can be valuable assistants to parents in their homes by providing learning materials or through home visits.

Parents and Schools as Advisors, Decision Makers and Advocates: Parents, teachers, administrators and other school staff should have opportunities to work together to solve problems, to express their views, to influence other decision makers, and to be advocates on behalf of children. It is important to remember that parents who are willing to be advocates for their child or other children are not enemies of the school, but true friends. Many schools have established school site councils that involve parents and school staff working together. Active PTAs, with school staff involvement, also serve as valuable advocacy groups for students and the school. The number of individuals involved at this level will be small; however, those who are willing to fulfill this role need training, support, and encouragement.

Figure 2.6 Chrispeels's Parent Involvement Components. (Compiled from Chrispeels, Boruta, and Daugherty, 1988. Communicating with Parents. *San Diego, CA: San Diego County Office of Education.)*

The elements emphasize the reciprocal aspect of the collaborative relationship between the home and school. Figure 2.5 is a description of Swap's four elements.

Janet Chrispeels (Chrispeels, Boruta, & Daugherty, 1988) has also developed a popular typology of home/school/community partnership roles, built upon the earlier works of Lyons, Robbins and Smith (1983) and Epstein (1987). Chrispeels's typology first appeared in her *Home-School Relations Planner* (1985), which was revised as the *Home-School Partnership Planner* in 1987. Her parent involvement program components are: Home-School Communication, Home and School as Supporters, Home and School as Learners, Home and School as Teachers, and Parents and School as Advisors, Decision Makers and Advocates. A description of these roles appears in Figure 2.6.

In a discussion I had with Janet about parent roles, she emphasized the reciprocal nature of the home and the school roles. Later, she expressed this belief when she added the prefix "co-" to indicate these important interactions (Chrispeels, 1988, 1992). As a result, her five roles are now entitled: Co-Communicators, Co-Supporters, Co-Learners, Co-Teacher, and Co-Advisors, Co-Decision Makers, Co-Advocates. The typology forms a framework on which to build a home/school/community partnership. The prefix "co-" implies that both the school and the family perform these roles, sometimes together and sometimes apart.

The Reciprocal Nature of the Family and School Roles

I recognize that parents, teachers, principals, project directors, coordinators, community members, and so on, often play similar roles, for example, Communicator, Teacher, and Advisor. And, I agree that within a partnership many of the roles are reciprocal. However, I decided to separate the roles played by the parents from those played by the school for an important reason. I felt that by doing so, it would be easier for those who are responsible for planning and implementing the partnership programs to "zero" in on the roles to be played by the "targeted" families. That is, this focus makes it easier to decide which intervention strategy to use to reach out to the parents when creating family/school/community partnerships.

This is not to suggest that the roles that the school and community play in the partnership are not essential. Quite the contrary. These roles are crucial. In fact, the school and community are responsible for taking the initiative and implementing programs to build and maintain the relationships between themselves and the families. (Best practices for helping the faculty and staff to play these roles and implement the Self-Renewing Partnership Model are presented in Chapter 6, Connecting: Bridging the Gaps.)

PARENT PARTNER ROLES

Parent Partner Roles, as stated before, are the roles that family members must be willing and able to play in order to be fully involved in the educational and social development of their children. The eight roles are: Nurturer, Communicator, Teacher, Supporter, Learner, Advisor, Advocator, and Collaborator. Some of the roles are directed at the child, some at the school, and some at both the child and the school. The Parent Partner Roles are outlined in Figure 2.7.

As the titles suggest, existing research greatly influenced me as I delineated the roles the families needed to be able to play to be fully

---

Nurturer (Child-Directed): The function of the Nurturer Role is to provide an appropriate environment where the child will flourish physically, psychologically and emotionally.

Communicator (Child and School-Directed): The function of the Communicator Role is to establish and maintain effective two-way communication flows with the child and the school.

Teacher (Child-Directed): The function of the Teacher Role is to assist with the child's moral, intellectual, emotional, and social development.

Supporter (Child and School-Directed): The function of the Supporter Role is to be actively supportive of the child's at-school learning activities and the school's curriculum and other programs.

Learner (Child-Directed): The function of the Learner Role is to obtain new skills and knowledge that will help directly and indirectly with the child's educational and social development.

Advisor (Child-Directed): The function of the Advisor Role is to wisely counsel and advise the child concerning his or her personal and educational issues.

Advocator (Child and School-Directed): The function of the Advocator Role is to effectively and actively mediate and negotiate for the child.

Collaborator (School-Directed): The function of the Collaborator Role is to work effectively with the school and community to help study issues, solve problems, make decisions, and develop policy.

Figure 2.7 The Parent Partner Roles.

involved partners. In addition, I used the data from successful parent involvement programs and the responses from the previously discussed question: "What did your family provide you and instill in you that helped you get where you are today?"

The Parent Partner Roles are used as a guide when preparing to coach the parents. By knowing and understanding these roles educators can employ the best practices more effectively. That is, it is much easier to decide which intervention strategies to use when you know what outcomes you want to achieve. (Best practices for coaching the parents are presented in Chapter 9.)

THE PROGRESSIVE NATURE OF THE PARENT PARTNER ROLES

The Parent Partner Roles are hierarchical and progressive. That is, the roles build upon one another as the family involvement increases and develops. Thus, the role behaviors range from the more basic and fundamental (Nurturer, Communicator, Teacher and Supporter) to the more specialized (Advisor, Advocator, and Collaborator). All the roles are essential, as the "lower" order roles provide the foundation for the other "higher" level roles. Roles such as Advisor, Advocator, and Collaborator cannot be played unless the parents are able to play the lower level roles effectively. For example, to be a good advisor, a parent must know what is going on in the child's life in school (Communicator Role) and have established a learning environment in the home (Nurturer Role).

The family members are expected to play the lower level roles all the time, and only assume some of the high-level roles, such as Advocator and Advisor, when the need arises. Although the higher level roles are played less frequently, the parents must be prepared to assume them at the appropriate times. For example, family members need to be skilled in such areas as mediation, problem solving, advising, and conflict resolution to play the higher order roles.

In the following sections, the eight Parent Partner Roles are described and discussed, including examples of expectations and activities for each.

Nurturer Role (Child-Directed)

The function of the Nurturer Role is to provide an appropriate environment where the child will flourish physically, psychologically and emotionally. As such, the Nurturer Role is child-directed, concerned with maintaining positive learning conditions at home and the child's overall health, shelter, safety and behavior. The outcomes from this role form the foundation on which the Parent Partner Roles are played.

Expectations Associated with the Nurturer Role

- offering love, praise, and encouragement
- being understanding, caring, and respectful
- providing day-to-day necessities
- giving overall financial support
- establishing a stable and safe environment and a sense of security
- instilling a belief that education is important
- modeling a work ethic
- supporting the child's education by providing an appropriate learning environment

Examples of Activities Associated with the Nurturer Role

- establishing a daily family routine
- providing school supplies and equipment, medical examinations, vaccinations, and so on
- regulating TV use, including time and content
- scheduling and monitoring daily homework times
- responding to school's request for registration forms, schedules, report card signatures, permission slips, and other information
- monitoring the child's in-school attendance and behavior and out-of-school activities

Communicator Role (Child- and School-Directed)

The function of the Communicator Role is to establish and maintain an effective two-way communication flow with the child and the school. As such, the Communicator role is intertwined with all of the other Parent Partner Roles. The importance of being a good communicator has long been recognized by most scholars in the field.

The Communicator Role is a complex lower order role because it encompasses three major communication flows: communications between the family and the child, the family and the school, and the child and the school, while building on the Nurturer Role.

Although this role centers on the parents, we must not forget that in a partnership, the school and community must also communicate effectively with the family and the child. (Programs, activities, and events for helping the school to communicate effectively, with the parents are presented in Chapter 7.)

Expectations Associated with the Communicator Role

- communicating and listening effectively and accurately
- communicating with understanding, empathy, and high regard

Examples of Activities Associated with the Communicator Role

CHILD-DIRECTED

- communicating with the child about successes in school and home
- communicating with the child about problems and concerns
- communicating to the child the ways you can support him or her in programs and activities

SCHOOL-DIRECTED

- communicating with the school about what is going on in the child's school life
- maintaining continuous communication with the school about how you can support the child
- dialoguing with the school about the child's progress, strengths and weaknesses
- participating in productive parent/teacher or parent/student/teacher conferences
- responding promptly and effectively to letters and phone calls from school
- making timely and appropriate requests for information, assistance, and advice
- visiting the school regularly to talk with teachers, counselors, and principals
- participating in informal meetings with principal and/or teachers

Teacher Role (Child-Directed)

The function of the Teacher Role is to assist with the child's moral, intellectual, emotional, and social development. Few would disagree with the statement that, "The parent is the child's first teacher, and possibly, the child's most important teacher." The effect the family has on the child, especially in the early years, is dramatic and fundamental. It is essential, therefore, that the parents are able to teach the child in the home. However, many families need help to enhance their ability to perform this most important role.

Expectations Associated with the Teacher Role

- instilling in the child a strong sense of ethics, standards, and high expectations
- exposing the child to positive values, and character traits, such as respect, responsibility, and integrity
- teaching basic skills and knowledge
- initiating learning activities or responding to the child's requests for help
- developing in the child a belief in himself or herself

Examples of Activities Associated with the
Teacher Role

- reading to the child, reading together, and/or making sure the child reads at home
- working with the child on math, problem solving, and reasoning skills in the home during daily tasks and on family trips
- working with the child's teachers to coordinate classroom work with home-based learning activities
- exposing the child to various cultural, career, scientific, and historic sites, events, and programs

Supporter Role (Child- and School-Directed)

The function of the Supporter Role is to be actively supportive of the child's at-school learning activities and the school's overall curriculum and other programs. While the Supporter Role is both school- and child-directed, it is set in the context of being supportive in the school environment. Sometimes, the family's involvement is a combination of support for the child and the school. Playing the Supporter Role at school can be very active, for example, participating in open houses, volunteering, chaperoning, and so on, or more passive, such as, attending basketball games, band concerts, plays, etc. and visiting student art exhibits, science fairs, and so forth.

Expectations Associated with the Supporter Role

- supporting the child's participation in school activities, programs, and events
- providing support to the school for its curriculum, programs, activities, and events

Examples of Activities Associated with the Supporter Role

CHILD-DIRECTED

- attending school concerts, plays, award assemblies, sport events, and other productions
- visiting student art exhibits, science fairs, and other demonstrations
- participating in daughter or son dinners and dances, senior teas, ethnic suppers, and so on
- participating in classroom events, open houses, and PTA/PTO programs

SCHOOL-DIRECTED

- assisting teachers, administrators, and children in classrooms, or in other areas of the school
- participating in booster clubs and fund raisers
- chaperoning field trips and dances
- organizing and conduct campus clean-ups and beautification projects

Leaner Role (Child-Directed)

The function of the Learner Role is to obtain new skills and knowledge that will help directly and indirectly with the child's educational and social development. Parenting is a difficult task for anyone; therefore, it is important that the family members continually obtain new skills and knowledge. Parenting and learning are lifelong experiences. While the outcomes of the learning will benefit the child, new skills and knowledge also help the parents with their own development, growth, and life satisfaction.

Expectations Associated with the Learner Role

- enhancing skills and knowledge related to the parent partner roles
- obtaining knowledge and skills to enhance individual and family quality of life

Examples of Activities Associated with the Learner Role

- enrolling in parent education classes, continuing and adult education programs, and family center classes to improve general knowledge and skills in such areas as math, language, geography, educational issues, reading, and literature
- reading and studying materials on such topics as school curriculum and activities, basic skill development, family and student rights, college preparation, and dropout prevention
- participating in support groups and parent education workshops that focus on such topics as child development, parenting skills, alcohol and drug abuse, and teenage pregnancy
- learning about school board policies, and school rules and regulations

Advisor Role (Child-Directed)

The function of the Advisor Role is to wisely counsel and advise the child concerning his or her personal and educational situation. Since this is a higher order Parent Partner Role, the parents must be able to play the lower order roles first. For example, the family members and children need to be able to communicate with each other and have a trusting relationship. The parents need to truly *advise*, rather than telling the children what to do.

Expectations Associated with the Advisor Role

- being able to listen to the child's problems and concerns
- establishing a helping relationship with the child
- offering advice and counseling in an appropriate way

Examples of Activities Associated with the Advisor Role

- helping with personal concerns and problems
- assisting with curriculum and program issues
- advising about potential career paths and opportunities
- being familiar with the contents of the child's student records
- knowing and understanding the standardized testing process

Advocator (Child- and School-Directed)

The function of the Advocator Role is to effectively and actively mediate and negotiate for the child. Like the Supporter Role, the Advocator Role is generally played in the school environment. As the Advocator Role is a higher order role, the parents need to possess specific skills and knowledge to effectively play the role. In addition, they also need to be good communicators and supporters.

Expectations Associated with the Advocator Role

- being available to mediate and advocate for the child when needed
- being knowledgeable of school policy, curriculum, programs, and activities

Examples of Activities Associated with the Advocator Role

- helping to resolve conflicts, concerns and problems related to curriculum, programs, and activities
- reinforcing the proper enforcement of family and student rights
- monitoring the application of school policies and practices
- requesting copies of written school and school district policies
- advocating for curricular and operational policy and procedural reform

Collaborator Role (School-Directed)

The function of the Collaborator Role is to work effectively with the school and community to help study issues, solve problems, make decisions, and develop policy. The term "Collaborator" was chosen because it expresses the nature of the working relationship between the family and the school. Being a collaborator requires higher order skills and knowledge. This role is at the top hierarchy, building on all of the other Parent Partner Roles. Realistically, many family members will not play this role; however, if they chose to do so, they must be properly prepared.

Expectations Associated with the Collaborator Role

- entering into a collegial relationship with the school
- possessing the skills and knowledge to help with problem solving, program development, curriculum design, policy decisions, and so on

Examples of Activities Associated with the Collaborator Role

- participating in school improvement and community councils, school planning and management teams, special projects, and school committees where families have equal status with professionals and representatives from the community
- assist in reducing educational barriers
- monitoring health, library, and cultural services to make sure they are easily accessible to the school and neighborhood
- attending school board meetings
- serving on the school board and city council
- participating in (or organizing) family-family organizations
- appealing local school or school system decisions that are questionable or not understood
- being involved in curriculum activities
- influencing school policy
- participating on committees that focus on such issues as maintaining a safe environment in around the campus, bus safety, upgrading and beautifying the school building and

grounds, and establishing and maintaining high standards and expectations, quality programs, and extracurricular options.

SUMMARY

The Parent Partner Roles are the eight roles that the parents or family members must to be prepared to assume if they are to be fully involved in the education of their children. These progressive roles are separate, but interrelated—aspects of the complicated and elusive act of parenting. Because the roles build upon one another, on occasion, the family members play many roles during a particular event or activity. For example, at a conference between a parent and a teacher, the parent must be prepared to play the roles of Communicator, Supporter, Learner, and Advocator. Consequently, the parent needs to possess the skills and knowledge to be ready and willing to play the right role at the right time.

Learning to parent is an ongoing process. Just when you think you are "on top of your game," something occurs that causes you to wonder if you know anything at all about parenting. Fortunately, or unfortunately, this is the reality of being a parent, and this is why we all need help at times. The intent of the Coaching Strategy is to provide this help and allow parents to be fully involved in the education of the children.

By creating partnerships between the families, school, and community, we can provide enriched learning and supportive environments for the children in the home and at school. The nature and function of family/school/community partnerships are discussed in the next chapter.

CHAPTER 3

Family/School/Community Partnerships: A Solution

Recently, the African proverb, "It takes the whole village to raise a child," has been used to bolster arguments for greater cooperation between the families, school, and community. While overused, the proverb does express the intent of a family/school/community partnership. As mentioned, I believe that partnerships between the family, school, and community can involve all parents and solve "the case of the missing families" introduced in Chapter 1.

Family/school/community partnerships are fertile environments for collaboration and provide the families with ideal settings for enhancing and playing their Parent Partner Roles. As suggested in the proverb, the partnerships are based on the notion that *everyone* is responsible for the education of the children, and by working together, all children will have a better chance to be successful. In the partnerships, the resources, or "energies," of the various stakeholders are aligned so everyone is making a contribution to the common goal of learning. However, for the "whole village" to be involved requires a concerted, sustained, collaborative effort. Family/school/community partnerships don't just happen. They need to be planned, formed, and cultivated.

This chapter explains the nature and function of family/school/community partnerships, and how these relationships benefit not only the children, but all parties involved. In Chapter 5, a comprehensive model for designing and building the partnerships is presented. Later chapters, in turn, describe and discuss the strategies for implementing the model. But, the first step in planning a partnership program is to have a common understanding of what a family/school/community partnership really is.

WHAT IS A FAMILY/SCHOOL/COMMUNITY PARTNERSHIP?

A family/school/community partnership is a collaborative relationship between the family, school, and community designed primarily to produce positive educational and social effects on the child, while being mutually beneficial to all other parties involved. As the definition suggests, the concept of partnerships between the family, school, and community is more far-reaching and complex than such interactions as "home/school relations" or "community/school cooperation." These latter terms are rather general and informal, while the idea of a "partnership" connotes a more defined coalition or alliance and suggests a formal, or informal, "contract" between the family, school, and community.

The partnership philosophy of collaboration and cooperation between all parties is more comprehensive than the underpinnings of the traditional parent involvement approach. As indicated earlier, parent involvement programs have typically focused primarily on the family's involvement at school with the intent of gaining support for the school's curriculum, activities and programs, such as volunteer activities, PTA/PTOs, open houses, and so on. Family/school/community partnerships, on the other hand, have a much broader focus, encompassing the families' and the school's involvement in the child's education both at school and in the home.

The partnerships should not be seen as ends in themselves, but as a means for the families, school, and community to work together to enhance the academic and social growth of children. Thus, the partnerships are more of a process based on a collaborative and helping attitude and belief system than a product. They are "environments" for people to help each other, so they can help the children.

A family/school/community partnership offers the parties involved the opportunity to effectively play their individual roles and fulfill their responsibilities. As such, they are "learning communities" where the families, community, and school can concentrate on the sources of the educational and social problems, rather than merely symptoms. Problems such as low achievement, poor attendance, dropouts, misbehavior, teenage pregnancy, and drug abuse are symptoms of more deeply rooted social and family issues like poverty, dysfunctional family relationships, lack of health care, and poor parenting skills and knowledge.

I believe that most social problems will ultimately be solved through education. Therefore, it is imperative that we work together on doing the right things in the right way.

Rutherford (1995) supports the idea of collaborating, arguing that a number of forces have increased our awareness of the need for more formal connections between families, schools, and communities. These forces include the national concern for families and parents; the lack of adequate quality preparation for children prior to entering school, especially in families who are not proficient speakers of English; the recognition that schools and communities cannot do it alone and that they must join forces; and the commitment and "calls for action" from policymakers for parent and community involvement in education and the strengthening of home learning (Rutherford, 1995, p. vi).

I agree that the factors Rutherford lists have affected our awareness of the need for partnerships. However, his use of the word *commitment* when referring to the attitudes of policymakers may be overly optimistic. I don't believe the policymakers have a full understanding of what is involved in establishing a partnership.

Creating partnerships with families is a complex task, especially with the hard-to-reach parents. Those asking for more involvement by the parents must recognize that it will take a long-term comprehensive effort by the school and the community for this to happen. When planning a family/school/community partnership program, therefore, it should be kept in mind that formation of collaborative relationships usually requires changes in organizational and family cultures. This takes time. Someone asked me one time, "How long do we have to work to involve the parents?"

I answered, "Forever!"

Collaboration is the concept that underlies a family/school/community partnership. Webster defines collaboration as: "to work jointly with others." *Roget's Thesaurus* lists terms such as: cooperation, willingness, joint effort, synergy, and team work when referring to collaboration. However, even these words do not fully describe the close working relationships that are characteristic of family/school/community partnerships.

The relationships in a family/school/community partnership are built on trust, mutual regard, caring, and shared beliefs. Therefore, they are usually deep and complex. The collaborative relationships are formed on the assumption that education is a shared responsibility and that all partners are "equal" players. "Equal," in this case, means that each

---

"It Takes the Whole Village to Educate a Child"

As mentioned earlier, this African proverb has been used repeatedly to express the need for greater cooperation between the families, school and community. Most would agree with the statement; however, this kind of collaboration is not common. To make changes of this kind requires a comprehensive plan that involves all the stakeholders: stakeholders who are committed to making a change for the better.

I am reminded of a TV news program that reported how a small community within the city was trying to bring "themselves up by their bootstraps." Some women were excitedly describing how they were going to change their community. They were wearing T-shirts with the proverb printed across the back.

While I applauded their cause and efforts, I also worried that they would soon become frustrated and disappointed due to a lack of understanding of the complexities of this kind of change. Without involving the major stakeholders in a comprehensive plan, they will likely fail. The Strategic Partnership Planning System (SPPS) presented in Chapter 10 is a method for getting the kind of involvement and commitment needed to make a partnership program work.

---

partner contributes in major ways to the success of young people, and that everyone has a say in determining the path to the common goal of learning. While education is still considered primarily to be the domain of the school, in a partnership, it is recognized that the family possesses unique strengths, resources, and expertise that can have a positive impact on the learning process.

Joyce Epstein and Lori Connors (1995), when addressing the question, "What do we mean by parent involvement?," suggest the idea of a partnership better expresses the shared interests and investments of families and schools in the children. A partnership emphasizes that both the families and the school must share the responsibility for the children's education. They state:

> The broader term [family/school/community partnership] recognizes the importance and potential influence of all family members, not only parents, and all family structures, not only those that include the natural parents. Moreover, the term allows students to join the partnership. . . . The term makes room too, for community groups, individuals, agencies, and organizations to work with schools and families and to invest in the education of children whose futures affect the quality of life in the community. (p. 140)

One of the goals of the Self-Renewing Partnership Model is to increase the family members' ability and willingness to play their Parent Partner

Roles. Although some parents may need help, and even seek help, they do not want to feel they are being "fixed." Even the most distressed families have strengths and a sense of pride. Efforts should be made not to patronize or demean family members as we work to increase their involvement and to increase their capacities to be partners. This is why the intervention strategy for helping the families to enhance their skills and knowledge is called the "Coaching" Strategy.

Educational excellence is a hollow goal if it does not promise and expect equity. Until recently, the concern for equity in education has been taking second place to the concern for educational excellence. You cannot have excellence if it is not for everyone.

I'm reminded of a family education program that forcefully expresses the goal of equality and independence, rather than co-dependency, in its vision statement. Their guiding philosophy is, "If you have come here to help me, you are wasting your time. If you came because your liberation is bound up with mine, then let us work together" (Rioux & Berla, 1993, p. 314).

BUILDING ON FAMILY STRENGTHS

Involving the families in the learning process, especially in the home, makes perfect sense since more than eighty percent of a student's time is spent out of school. Families have a great untapped capacity to work with their children at home in many ways, as well as to assist the schools with their programs and activities. A major strength is that the parent (or surrogate) is the child's first teacher, which provides for an almost unlimited opportunity to teach, model, and guide. Families know their children better than anyone else, having intimate knowledge of their needs, skills, and talents. Most families also have a keen interest in their children's future and want them to succeed; as a result, they want to be involved in the education of their children.

Efforts to engage the families should focus on their strengths, not their weaknesses. Unfortunately, when attempts have been made to involve the families, at times, the focus has been on the latter. Although many families have problems, the school and community must not use a deficit approach when working with them. Metaphorically, we must concentrate on the "doughnut, not the hole."

We need to work with the faculty and staff to alter any preconceptions they might have about the inadequacies of parents. For example, any idea of "them against us" must be dispelled and replaced with a "win-win" attitude to ensure that the teachers and families benefit from the partnerships. As a result, when developing a family/school/community partnership program, those involved need to believe that:

- The probability of higher student achievement, as well as more excitement and joy in the classroom and at home, is greater when this kind of learning community is created.
- Even though the child is central to the relationship, engaging the families and community in the education of their children will not only help the children, but the family, school, and community as well.
- When the families and community work collaboratively with the school, everyone should find their roles less stressful, more productive and more rewarding. There will be fewer conflicts and problems.

PREVENTION RATHER THAN THE CURE

Many of the benefits from the partnerships are visible and respond directly to a need; for example, workshops, food pantries, and tutoring. However, most of the benefits for the teachers and principals are more indirect and preventive in nature, including reduced stress, increased morale, and greater feelings of accomplishment. Throughout, the idea is that by having a good working relationship between the family, school, and community, fewer problems will arise. And if problems do arise, they will be more easily solved and addressed.

As the auto mechanic on TV says, "Pay me now, or pay me later." If we do not reach out and connect with all families to solve some of the problems now and help the children, we will be faced with even bigger problems later. As a result, it will take some "selling" for teachers, principals, counselors, and community leaders to buy into a "pay now, so you won't have to pay later" model. This is not easy because our culture tends to want immediate results: along with a 100% guarantee. The Connecting Strategy chapter includes best practices to prepare the faculty and staff for the partnerships.

A Word about Empowerment

All teachers want to help the kids, but they also would like some help for themselves. Teachers and principals need to feel they are more effective, productive, happier, and less stressed when the families are working closely with the school (naturally, you would hope the families feel this way as well).

As you seek to empower parents, you also need to provide an opportunity for teachers to increase their control and decision-making over events and conditions of their work life. Teachers need to feel supported and empowered to reach out to the families. Usually, they are not anxious to add this responsibility unless they feel they are seen as responsible by the principal. Most teachers are not willing to share decision making with the parents unless they feel they have authority to make decisions themselves. Schools operating successful partnership programs and school improvement projects usually have faculties and staffs that feel strong, secure, and empowered to make important decisions about their work and personal life. They are eager for more information and resources that would help them to enhance the academic and social development of the children.

A downside to this is that all too often as more responsibilities are added to the teachers' already overloaded schedules, nothing is taken away. As one tired teacher remarked, "I'm not sure that I can stand much more empowerment."

We need to be cognizant of the additional loads that are being placed on the faculty and staff to prevent them from becoming overwhelmed. If involving the families just means more work for the teachers, it is unlikely that the partnership will flourish. Best practices need to be implemented to free up the teachers and staff to perform their partnership tasks. As much as possible, it is important to build opportunities for collaboration into the school day rather than after hours. Of course, the addition of a family/school/community coordinator to assist the faculty is most welcome.

THE POLITICS OF PARTNERSHIPS

Understanding the political aspect of partnerships is a key to forming and maintaining relationships with the different parties. It may seem strange to link politics with partnerships since family/school/community partnerships are characterized by trust, caring and positive regard. The mention of "politics" immediately conjures up thoughts of bureaucratic sludge, red tape, waste, and corruption. While it is true that generally the word "politics" is associated with negative outcomes, in this situation I would like us to think about the political process in a generic way.

Back in 1936, Laswell defined politics as: "who gets what, when, and how." This is a good straightforward definition and fits the political context of a partnership. We are all motivated by self-interests to get what we want. If the term "self-interests" seems a bit harsh, then the word "needs"can be substituted. However, I maintain that the act of influencing others to meet our self-interests is what the political process is about.

While this may sound very manipulative, meeting our self-interests by influencing others is inherently neither a positive nor a negative act. For example, if you have a good relationship with your "significant other," then each of you is meeting some of your self-interests through the relationship. When this occurs, you would say that you have an enduring partnership. And, the partnership will last as long as both of you continue to feel that your self-interests are being met.

With family/school/community partnerships, the phrase in the definition, "to produce positive educational and social effects on the child, while being mutually beneficial to all other parties involved," relates to the political process. While the child's self-interests are the main focus of the partnership, the other parties also wish to have some of their self-interests or needs satisfied. For the partnership to be effective and long lasting, therefore, the relationship must meet some of the needs of the parents, teachers, principals and community members as well as the child's.

We may initially be able to get educators, community leaders, and family members excited about entering into a partnership, but it will be hard, if not impossible, to keep them actively involved and committed if they do not see some direct payoff for themselves. To illustrate this point, I often use a popular liquid diet advertisement as a metaphor. The advertisement guarantees that you will lose weight if you, "drink a delicious shake for breakfast and lunch" and "eat a sensible meal at night." My guess is that many people follow the first direction, but not the second. As a result, the diet program "does not work" for them because they did not adhere to both requirements. Likewise, in partnership, the self interests of all stakeholders have to be addressed for the relationship to work. In other words, if the child's needs are met, but not the self-interests of the other parties, the partnership will suffer.

Therefore, knowing and understanding the political process is important when planning, implementing, and maintaining a family/school/community partnership. It is essential that we identify the self-interests of all the parties: the child, families, school, and community. We need to ask ourselves: "What are the things, in addition to the concern for the children, that will influence the different parties to be active partners?" Determining what the different stakeholders want and need will help decide what strategies to use to create and build the partnerships.

Lareau and Benson (1984) found that differences in family/school relationships are not related to the amount of interest parents have in their children's educational achievement; rather, they appear to stem from social and cultural characteristics of the families and the way the schools respond to these characteristics. This is why it is important for schools to "do their homework" and determine the needs of the different family populations.

The self-interests of the families vary greatly. Meeting the self-interests of some families and getting them to be partners is not always complicated, however. Letting them know you care and that you would like to work with them may be enough to get them involved. In these cases, something as simple as a phone call or a personal note may be sufficient to influence their self-interests. In other instances, incentives such as food, door prizes, child care, and transportation are effective in helping to bring the families to school for conferences, parenting meetings, open houses, and so forth. All of these strategies should send the message, "You and your needs are important to us."

For many of the "missing" families, getting them to be partners with the school is more difficult. Many hard-to-reach parents feel alienated and disenfranchised from the school and with society as a whole. As a result, strategies evolving from a well-organized plan will need to be implemented to bridge the gaps between the families and the school. In order to involve these families, best practices such as neighborhood meetings and home visits must be used to overcome the barriers and meet their self-interests.

Some families face severe problems, such as lack of food or clothing, health issues, drug abuse, and so on. These problems will have to be solved before the families affected are able to focus on their children's educational needs. For these parents, the adage, "It is difficult to think about swamp control when you are over your waist in alligators," comes to mind. It is difficult for these families to be thinking about the future of their children when they are trying to survive the day. The school can use the Coordinating Strategy to help the families to apply for food stamps and other social programs, find a job, and so on.

The need to provide programs to help families in these situations is analogous to the problem that necessitates having a free student breakfast program at school. Besides the humanitarian reason, the educational argument for having the program is that if the kids are hungry, it is hard for them to concentrate on learning. The breakfast program eliminates a barrier. With the needy families, once some of the pressing concerns are taken care of, the parents can be influenced to focus their attention on the children's social and educational needs. The Coordinating Strategy chapter (Chapter 8) presents examples of programs and activities to get community resources to the families in need.

Unfortunately, if we do not reach out to the underserved families, a typical parent involvement program can actually widen the gap between the "haves and have nots." Many traditional parent involvement programs and activities are oriented toward the middle class, thereby missing the other segments of the community. Many families feel that they do not fit in with the core group of parents that are "controlling" the programs. The Self-Renewing Partnership Model presented in Chapter 5 is designed to involve all families, but it is especially useful for reaching and empowering the underserved parents.

THE BENEFITS OF A FAMILY/SCHOOL/COMMUNITY PARTNERSHIP

As we develop partnerships, we need to be clear about the positive outcomes for all the stakeholders. The following is a summary of positive outcomes that can be expected from partnerships between the family, school, and community.

Benefits to the School

- better communications between school and home
- improved student behavior
- enhanced social and interpersonal relationships between students
- greater acceptance and understanding of students and families from other cultures
- reduction of in-school violence
- better working conditions for faculty and staff
- improved attitudes and relationships and better communication between teachers and families
- greater family participation in school programs and activities

- schools being more accessible and user-friendly to family and community
- more family/school activities
- families viewing the school and faculty/staff more favorably
- families having a feeling of ownership, belonging, and inclusion concerning the school

Benefits to Students

- increased achievement and motivation
- more positive attitude toward school and school work
- higher quality and more appropriate homework
- increased attendance
- decrease in dropouts, suspensions, and discipline referrals
- better relationships with family
- improved feelings about self

Benefits to the Family

- increased empowerment and education
- improved family life and closer relationship with children
- greater community/school support of families
- better communication between home and school
- increased understanding of school's curriculum, programs, and activities
- increased knowledge about how to help the child
- greater opportunities to engage in learning activities at home
- greater opportunities to work closely with teachers
- more consistent expectations, practices, and messages about homework and home learning activities
- increased access to schoolwide resources such as, family resource centers, homework telephone networks, home visits, classes, and workshops
- greater opportunities to shape important decisions that enhance their child's chance for success in school

Benefits to the Teachers

- improved morale

- more positive teaching experiences
- greater feelings of accomplishment and success
- more support, appreciation, and trust of families' judgment
- fewer discipline problems
- more responsive students
- less stress and frustration
- greater awareness of family perspectives and less stereotyping of students and their families
- higher expectations of students
- closer relationships with students

Benefits to the Administration

- improved relationships with students and family
- fewer family complaints
- better use of limited resources to address the critical need of linking home and school
- increased communications from family members about the child that is not available in any other way
- greater family/community support for school bonds and needed school improvements.

SUMMARY

Since a family/school/community partnership is based upon mutual trust, caring, and respect, the school's organizational culture must exhibit these characteristics if it is going to effectively develop and nurture partnerships with the families. If the faculty and staff feel that their efforts are appreciated and are convinced that their suggestions and recommendations will be thoroughly considered, they are more likely to be willing to reach out and empower the parents. When the partnerships are working, the school will be more responsible to the families and the families more responsible to the school and, ultimately, the children will be affected positively by this alliance.

Do family/school/community partnerships sound like Camelot? Are the outcomes too idealistic? Not really. I have seen the partnerships work and they are effective and energizing. The Self-Renewing Partnership

Model presented in Chapter 5 is designed to help schools and communities create these collaborative relationships whereby all parties are fully involved in the academic and social development of the children.

However, many barriers have to be overcome to create and maintain effective family/school/community partnerships. The following chapter describes and discusses the sources of barriers that keep families and the school apart.

CHAPTER 4

Barriers: Gaps to Overcome

All too often when schools attempt to involve the parents, they get little or no response. The teachers and principals conclude the family members just don't care and that the parents are not interested in being involved. As a result, the schools, which are already overburdened, tend to give up trying to involve the families. It is easy to understand how the educators would reach this conclusion. However, the results of my research (Lueder, 1989) indicate that the opposite is true. Most families care about the future of their children and are interested in their children's education. But, what is keeping many of them from being more involved then? Why are there so many parents that are "hard to reach"?

Often, there are barriers between the parents and the school that need to be overcome before a family/school/community partnership can be created. Such barriers can be family-based, school-based, community-based or a combination. One of the functions of the outreach dimension of the Self-Renewing Partnership Model presented in the next chapter is to reduce the gaps between the families, school, and community. The present chapter discusses the sources of the barriers that can keep the families and the schools apart.

FAMILY-BASED BARRIERS

Several family-based barriers can separate the parents from the school. Some sources of these barriers are psychological (e.g., apprehension, fear, alienation), while others are physical (e.g., time, distance, lack of child care). Lack of skills and knowledge, especially with hard-to-reach parents, can also cause a major barrier. While such things as lower socioeconomic conditions and divorce are factors in making some parents "hard to reach," Clark's (1983) research cited earlier indicates that these are not always causal variables. I believe the following barriers are the major contributors to gaps that may exist between the families and the school.

Psychological Barriers

Many family members don't ask the school for assistance or information because they are not connected with the school. These families feel intimidated and perceive the schools as unapproachable and threatening. In fact, it is not unusual for families, especially those living in distressed communities, to mistrust and fear the schools. These reluctant and hesitant parents are among those who have been deemed to be "hard to reach."

The psychological gap between the school and the family can be exacerbated if the family members experienced failure in school themselves. Usually, parents' attitudes toward school are rooted in their own educational background. Not only do they distrust the school, they try to avoid an environment where they had a bad experience. What makes it even worse is that the parents see their experiences repeated with their children. The family members assume the school will also "fail" their children if the school "failed" them. This self-defeating outlook adds to the parents' sense of alienation from the schools and increases the barriers.

Physical Barriers

Many families would like to take a more active role in the education of their children, but their home situation is such that they are struggling to just keep things together. They do not believe they can find more time, resources, or energy to do more. As they deal with their busy schedules, problems, and other pressures, involvement in the education of children gets pushed aside. In fact, for some parents, making sure their children make it to school is a major accomplishment.

Physical barriers, though more common in low-income homes, are not limited to poorer families. Often the lack of time and energy is a problem for middle- and upper-class households as well, especially when the parent or parents are working outside the home.

Lack of Skills and Knowledge

A large number of family members lack the skills and knowledge necessary to be fully involved parents. Many of the "hard-to-reach" parents would like to be involved, but they don't know what to do. Educating children is a complex and difficult task and often families have not been prepared to assume the different Parent Partner Roles.

The need for more skills and knowledge varies greatly among families. For example, some families may only need information about the nature and function of upcoming conferences and meetings, while others may be seeking classes in conflict resolution or adolescent behavior. Yet, other families may need training on how to help their children with learning activities at home, or want help with issues like nutrition, communication, discipline, drug abuse and teenage pregnancy.

The "hard-to-reach" families are often hit with a combination of barriers. For example, parents may feel disconnected with the school and also be inadequately equipped to play the roles necessary to be fully involved in the educational and social development of their children. Some families may be faced with severe problems and not know where or how to get help. For these reasons, it is so important to understand the family needs, cultures, and concerns. With this information, appropriate intervention strategies can be selected and implemented.

NORMATIVE BARRIERS (FAMILY-, SCHOOL-, AND COMMUNITY-BASED)

Some barriers that prevent partnerships from forming between the families, schools, and communities are rooted in long-standing beliefs and perceptions about the roles of parents, teachers, principals, and community members. Some see education as the sole responsibility of the school. They see the role of the families and community is to support the school's curriculum, programs and activities. The traditional approach to parent involvement is based on this perception.

Seeley (1985, 1989) contends that this belief has caused a "delivery system" mentality wherein the schools believe, inaccurately, that they should be the only providers of educational services. The result is a sort of "isolationalism" from the families and the community. In turn, the families' reaction to the delivery model is to adopt a "delegation model," where they feel they do not have to, and are not expected to, be involved with school. These attitudes are clearly self-defeating and lead to barriers.

When education is seen as delegated to one party, as opposed to being a collaborative process, gaps between the families and the schools will develop. One result of this isolationalism is that when problems occur, the parents tend to blame the teachers whereas the teachers are apt to blame the parents. This creates a "no-win" situation for the families and the school, but especially for the children.

Lightfoot (1978) suggests the history of home-school relationships indicates that families and schools are inclined to be adversaries because of the nature of the relationship: Parents focus on their own child's needs, while the school has to be concerned with the needs of all the children in the school. Consequently, there is a "natural pull" between what the parents feel the school should be doing for their child and what the school feels it can do for all the children. Lightfoot argues that schools avoid dealing with this potential conflict by adopting brief, ritualized encounters when they do have to involve the parents. Such activities as open houses and PTA meetings are cited as contrived events that are advertised as opportunities for a partnership, but are actually organized in such a way that little or no authentic interaction can occur. These traditional events can be refined to reflect the partnership philosophy, however. These changes are discussed in the Communicating Strategy chapter (Chapter 7).

While I agree that "isolationalism" does exist in many settings and that certain norms are setting the families and schools apart, I do not believe these conditions are inherent in the relationships. The relationship between the school and the families does not have to be adversarial. Most families and schools want to work together, but they may need help in doing it. I have worked with schools to help form partnerships based on a trust, respect, and mutual regard. Such partnerships have been very effective. However, any negative attitudes and beliefs have to be dealt with first.

If true partnerships between the families, school, and community are to occur, the different parties need to perceive that education is everyone's responsibility. For this to happen, the principal and teachers must actively pursue family participation. Both the families and the school must agree that they have a common goal, which is to educate the children. Comer (1980) says: "Rather than considering work with parents an extra burden, schools should think of it as an opportunity to educate students and parents at the same time. A school has an opportunity to help children learn in the classroom when it helps parents develop skills" (p. 144).

While I agree with Comer, getting the faculty and staff to reach out to families is sometimes difficult. As a result, it is often necessary to work with the faculty and staff to help them understand and accept the concept that: Having the families as partners will not only help the children, it will also help them.

If data suggest that some parents are uncomfortable with the school, the faculty and staff need to look at themselves and determine how accurate the families' perceptions are. Specifically, they should determine if there are things the school is doing, or not doing, that is keeping the parents and school apart.

It is important to keep in mind that even if you find that the parents' perceptions are inaccurate—that in fact, the teachers and principals do want the parents in the school, the parents' perceptions are still real to them. As a result, the families' perceptions need to be changed to bring about participation.

There is another normative barrier that is more subtle. As indicated in the previous chapter, many parent involvement programs are based on a middle-class value system, and as a result, may create barriers in and of themselves.

Rich (1988) believes that all parents want the best for their children but that some do not feel comfortable participating in the traditional school activities. Henderson (1987) points out the disparities between values, attitudes, expectations and behaviors of poor minority families and the middle-class values, attitudes, expectations and behaviors that are enshrined in most schools. For some families that feel that they do not fit into the system, some parent involvement program can actually increase the gaps.

The school can implement programs to reduce the gaps between social classes, however. By bringing the families, teachers, and principals together, the sense of estrangement is reduced and the school environment becomes far less threatening and more conducive to learning for both students and parents.

SUMMARY

The various barriers that are preventing family involvement causes problems not only for the children, but for the school and community as well. The children are the "messengers of our future" and we cannot afford to lose them. It is increasingly apparent that the school and community must assume the responsibility of helping many of the families to create appropriate home environments and to enhance the skills and knowledge needed to play the different parenting roles. Otherwise, we have little chance of being able to support and educate all children. The Self-Renewing Partnership Model presented in the next chapter has been developed to help the schools and communities meet the challenge of overcoming barriers and involving all families.

CHAPTER 5

The Self-Renewing Partnership Model: Energy-Out and Energy-In

The Self-Renewing Partnership Model is a powerful conceptual framework for creating partnerships between families, school, and community. The model differs radically from the traditional parent involvement approach, described in Chapter 1. Whereas the primary goal of most traditional programs is to increase family support for the school's curriculum and program, the goals of the Self-Renewing Partnership Model are more focused and comprehensive. That is, the purpose of this model is to fully involve all of the families in their children's education *both in the home and at school.* Figure 5.1 is a diagram of the Self-Renewing Partnership Model.

The model has two dimensions that interact and build on each other. These dimensions are labeled "energy-out" and "energy-in" to indicate the directions that the resources flow. The energy-in dimension encompasses the eight Parent Partner Roles. It is called "energy-in" because as the families play their parenting roles, their resources (time, money, expertise, etc.) are directed *in* at the children and *in* at the school. This component is an expansion of the traditional "families supporting the school" approach. However, more resources from the fully involved parents are flowing to the school, and much of the energy is concentrated on the child.

The energy-out dimension is composed of a series of intervention strategies, called School/Community Collaboration Strategies. The school, with the support of the community, uses these strategies to reach *out* and work with the families. It is the energy-out dimension that makes the Self-Renewing Partnership Model unique and effective. With its

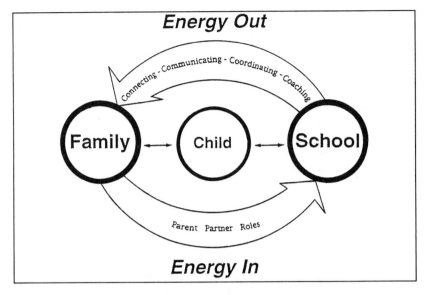

Figure 5.1 Self-Renewing Partnership Model.

function being to reach out and help get the parents involved, it is the energy-out dimension that "jumpstarts" the partnership process. It cannot be emphasized enough that reaching out to the parents is the key to finding and involving the "missing families."

THE RATIONALE FOR REACHING OUT

As mentioned throughout this book, we can no longer think of parent involvement only as "families supporting the school," but must think of it also as "the school and community supporting the families." This outreach approach is supported by other authors as well. For example, Coleman (1991) argues that because of changes in the family structure, it is necessary for the school and community to help some parents to develop their capacity to perform their parenting roles. He contends that when the United States was more of an agrarian society, the extended family was a characteristic of the farming community. Now with over two-thirds of the mothers in the outside workforce and family members living in many different cities, there is less "social capital" available to support and develop the children.

Nancy Feyl Chavkin (1995) also supports the idea of reaching out to the families. She says:

> Educators are realizing that they can't do it alone. Districts cannot fix the problems of health, hunger, and unemployment, but they can collaborate and help students and families get services. . . . Districts need to have a common vision that emphasizes reaching out to parents and the community and using the resources within the home and community to help students. Any vision that does not include reaching out to the families and communities is a limited vision that is failing to look beyond the school building at the needs of the whole child and the community. (p. 82)

A SHIFT IN PARADIGMS

Reaching out to the families is not the norm in most schools and communities today. As indicated earlier, the outward flow energy is a radical change from the traditional approach to parent involvement. Consequently, for the energy-out dimension to work, the involvement of the families must be viewed in a different way.

The term "paradigm shift" has been used recently to describe major changes in the way people perceive an issue or condition. A paradigm is your view of the "world" based on your personal frame of reference. Paradigms provide a way to organize a large amount of data in order to identify relationships and give meaning through context. According to Covey (1992), a paradigm is "your scheme for understanding and explaining certain aspects of reality." He contends that if we want to make major changes, we need to shift our paradigm and perceive the issue in a totally new way.

To accept that reaching out to families is a necessary step to create partnerships, especially with hard-to-reach parents, the schools, communities, and families must make a shift in the way they think about themselves and their mission. Teachers, counselors, principals and community members must believe that they need to be involved with such activities as home visits, neighborhood town meetings, parenting classes, family resource centers, and support groups.

This means that we have to embrace a new paradigm and have to give up our present one. We have to be convinced that the old model is not working before we are willing to accept a new one. It is difficult to convince people to give up their current way of thinking, especially if it requires the use of scarce resources (time, money, etc.) to treat the sources and not the symptoms.

For example, in most schools and communities, we know that we can do better; yet, we are not completely dissatisfied with what is happening now. Therefore, we are reluctant to reject the present model and go through the process of introducing and accepting a new one. Developing new roles and relationships can be very frightening, so we tend to hold tight and not change.

Sometimes it is easier to make educational changes in distressed schools and communities because it is clear that the old model isn't working. In these situations, the teachers, principals, community members, and families are more apt to be willing and eager to find a different way to help the children and themselves.

A "Light Bulb" Experience

An encounter I had with a principal in California helped clarify the "energy-out" dimension and the need for a paradigm shift. A school district asked me to provide staff development training for their Chapter 1 (now Title 1) Family/School Coordinators. Since I was in the district already, the superintendent suggested that I meet with his principals and share my parent involvement ideas and research. I agreed, and we gathered in a large lecture room. Right after I was introduced, a principal in the back of the room stood and said, "What could you possibly tell me about parent involvement that I don't already know. I have a terrific parent involvement program at my school."

I responded, "I'm not sure I can tell you anything that you do not already know. Would you share with me what you are doing at your school?"

He told how he was able to get many of his parents to come to school and do volunteer work. They helped supervise students in the classrooms and cafeteria, copied materials and answered the office telephone.

As he described his program, a "light went on." His concept of parent involvement was very different from mine. He thought of parent involvement only as family members coming to school to help. Whereas, I perceived parent involvement as much more than that. For me, parent involvement meant the family members were actively engaged in the education of their children at home and at school.

It became clear that to accept the energy-out dimension, he would have to abandon his traditional parent involvement approach and embrace the concept of family/school/community partnerships. After introducing the notion of partnerships and having further discussions with him after the meeting, I sensed that he was interested in trying to help his school and community to make the shift.

THE EVOLUTION OF THE ENERGY-OUT DIMENSION

The energy-out dimension and the intervention strategies (School/Community Collaboration Strategies) have evolved over a period of time. The genesis of the outreach concept occurred early in my investigations of parental involvement and the idea gradually matured into a conceptual framework for creating partnerships between the families, school, and community.

My parent involvement research began in 1987 as the Tennessee General Assembly had appropriated a million dollars for a statewide parent involvement initiative. (It is difficult to imagine that much money being appropriated now.) In the fall of 1986, eleven different parent involvement models were implemented at seventeen sites in distressed communities throughout Tennessee. In the spring of 1987, the State Department of Education hired me to evaluate their parent involvement programs. They were interested in knowing which models, if any, were working.

I was contacted in February and was asked to have the evaluation results available by May as the Department wanted to be able to report to the legislature before the end of their session. Because of the short turnaround time and the lack of baseline data, about all that could be done was to "count noses," and ask the families how they felt about the programs. Although limited, these data can tell you a lot about the programs.

What I discovered was that all the programs were "working." The families were participating in events and activities, and felt the programs were helping them and their children. These findings were somewhat surprising since the prevailing wisdom was that it would be very difficult, if not impossible, to get the families to participate. The results showed the parents were concerned about the education and future of their children, and that they wanted to get involved, thereby dispelling as myth the common belief that families in distressed situations don't care about being involved (Lueder, 1989).

Although compelling, the evaluation results nevertheless did not reveal "why" these programs were working. Obviously, something was happening that helped to get the parents involved. To better understand why these families were participating, four of the model programs, each with a strong parent education component, were selected for further study. The program sites were located in very diverse settings, ranging from urban inner city to very remote rural.

After revisiting the sites and gathering data related to their operation and outcomes, it was evident that all of the programs had a similar characteristic: They were using some of their resources to reach out and work with the families. Rather than being an explicit objective of their programs, it appeared that the outreach aspect resulted from trial and error. This discovery created the "aha" that sparked the formation of the energy-out component and the development of the Self-Renewing Partnership Model.

When I visited other successful programs around the country, I found that most were reaching out to the families in some way. I need to interject that I had to be selective in the programs I decided to visit because projects with an outreach dimension are not easy to find. When you do find them, they are generally "little pockets of success" in a school or a center within a school district. The innovative programs are usually limited to a single location. There are some exceptions, however. For example, the San Diego, Nashville, and Omaha schools have implemented district-wide programs.

The few outreach programs that exist have emerged from someone's intuition and perseverance in the absence of a conceptual framework. That is, individuals with missionary zeal have developed the programs using a hit-or-miss approach. Even though they did not have a plan, the principals or directors, and their staffs recognized, up front, that the families needed help, and it made sense to them to find a way to reach out to the parents. The School/Community Collaboration Strategies that are presented in the following section fill this void and provide a comprehensive way to reach out and develop partnerships with the families.

School/Community Collaboration Strategies: The Big C's

As stated earlier, the Self-Renewing Partnership Model differs radically from other parent involvement models because of its "energy-out" dimension. The dimension is composed of a series of progressive intervention strategies called School/Community Collaboration Strategies. The four strategies are: Connecting, Communicating, Coordinating, and Coaching. The school, in cooperation with the community, uses the various strategies to overcome barriers between the school and the families, build collaborative relationships, and help the parents to play their Parent Partner Roles. Specifically, the School/Community Collaboration Strategies are used to make connections, develop two-way communication flows, and coordinate needed services and resources. Once collaborative relationships are established with the families, the Coaching Strategy is used to involve and empower the family members by enhancing their parenting skills and knowledge. The following is a summary of the functions of the School/Community Collaboration Strategies.

The Connecting Strategy is designed to:

- prepare the school and community to reach out and connect with the families
- create an inviting and helpful school environment where the family members and faculty/staff can comfortably interact with each other
- overcome any psychological or physical barriers that might be preventing the families from working with the school
- begin to build collaborative relationships with the families
- initiate two-way communication flows between the families and the school

The Communicating Strategy is designed to:

- establish two-way communication flows between the families and the school
- continue to build collaborative relationships with the families
- begin to increase family and community support for the school's programs and activities

The Coordinating Strategy is designed to:

- increase family awareness of availability of school and community services and resources
- ensure that school and community services and resources are accessible to all families in need
- facilitate the creation of new services and resources
- organize family and community resources to help support the school's curriculum and programs

The Coaching Strategy is designed to:

- enhance parents' ability and capacity to effectively play the parent partner roles
- enhance the parents' general sense of well-being, knowledge, and skill level

The functions listed under each of the strategies are also the objectives of the family/school/community partnership program. When the program is planned (see Chapter 10), these objectives are used to develop the Partnership Action Plan.

THE PROGRESSIVE NATURE OF THE SCHOOL / COMMUNITY COLLABORATION STRATEGIES

Like the Parent Partner Roles, the School/Community Collaboration Strategies are progressive. That is, the strategies build upon each other. For example, you need to be "connected" with the families before you can communicate, and you have to be communicating before services and resources can be coordinated. Before parents can be coached, barriers need to be overcome and a collaborative relationship needs to be established between the families and the school.

Therefore, when forming partnerships with the families, it is necessary to ascertain the characteristics of the targeted family groups and to determine the source and magnitude of any barriers that may exist. After this, the appropriate strategies are selected and best practices are implemented. The procedures for choosing the Collaboration Strategies for a particular situation are presented in the Strategic Partnership Planning System chapter (Chapter 10).

In the following chapters, each School/Community Collaboration Strategy is described and discussed, including an array of best practices that the school and community can use to implement the strategies.

THE "SELF-RENEWING" PHENOMENON

The interactions between the energy-out and energy-in dimensions result in a "self-renewing" system. When the energy-out dimension (The School/Community Collaboration Strategies) impacts on the families, the energy-in dimension (Parent Partner Roles) becomes more active and effective. Because of the school's intervention, the parents are more involved with the children's education in the home, and with the school, through parent education workshops and classes, parent/teacher conferences, open houses, volunteer programs, and curriculum committees.

The interaction between the energy-out and energy-in dimension is a synergistic relationship. This means that by interacting the two dimensions generate more energy than originally existed; the whole is greater than the sum of its parts. As the school and community reach out and empower the families, the families become more "energized" and direct more of their resources toward the children and the school. And, as the family's energy-in dimension is enhanced, it strengthens the collaborative relationship between the school and community and creates more power for the school's energy-out dimension. This power increase in the energy-out dimension results in more energy going out and impacting on the families.

Thus, the term "self-renewing" is used to indicate the synergistic relationship, or "integrated circuit" between the two components. When a family/school/community partnership is working effectively, it perpetuates itself. All parties, the families, school, and community that are empowered by the collaborative relationships are continually "renewed."

While all parties in the partnership benefit from the "energy loop," we must keep in mind that the ultimate beneficiaries of the partnerships are the children. The partnerships are not ends in themselves, but a means to impact on the educational and social development of the children.

SUMMARY

It is my firm belief that if all children are going to receive the kind of help and support they need we must assist families to be fully functioning parent partners. This is why I am advocating that schools and communities use some of their resources to reach out to the families and create family/school/community partnerships.

As families learn to play their Parent Partner Roles, the children will receive the needed support at home and the schools will receive more support from the families.

To enhance children's academic and social development, more parents must become partners with the school and more schools and communities must become partners with the families. The families have to be connected with the school; two-way communication flows must exist between the school and the families; and parents must be empowered to play their Parent Partner Roles, both at home and at school. The School/Community Collaboration Strategies described in the following chapters have been designed to help the schools and communities to reach out and create partnerships.

CHAPTER 6

Connecting: Bridging the Gaps

CONNECTING	COMMUNICATING	COORDINATING	COACHING

Unfortunately, it is common for the schools to invite the families to participate in meetings, conferences, and activities and then only have a few family members show up. When this happens, it is easy to understand why teachers and administrators get the impression that the families are not interested in being involved. In reality, however, the reason the families are avoiding the school is not that they do not care—instead, many parents do not feel "connected" with the school. And they are not making connections because of psychological or physical barriers that are blocking the way.

As discussed in Chapter 4, there are many different sources behind the barriers that are causing gaps between the families and the school. Many families do not get involved because they are anxious, apprehensive, and even fearful about dealing with teachers and principals. In some cases, family members feel so "out of place" that they are disenfranchised from the school and society as a whole. For other families, logistical barriers such as conflicting work schedules, lack of child care, and no transportation prevent them from getting involved.

On the other hand, schools may also be creating barriers. School-based barriers can result from impersonal or demeaning behavior by the faculty and staff; an overwhelming, complex bureaucracy; or faculty and staff not knowing how to work with families.

I cannot emphasize enough that traditional parent involvement programs are often ineffective because they are implemented without large segments of the family populations being "connected." As a result, these "hard-to-reach" parents do not respond to the school's "messages" and are not impacted by the programs. By reaching out and letting the families know that schools care, are willing to help, and would like to work with them, the chances of creating a partnership improve dramatically.

As stated in the previous chapter, the School/Community Collaboration Strategies are progressive and hierarchical, with the Connecting Strategy being the most basic intervention. The connections between the school and the families provide the foundation for the other three School/Community Collaboration Strategies. Collaborative relationships are created by making connections, establishing two-way communication flows, coordinating resources and services, and coaching the families.

Connecting with the parents is the first step in forming family/school/community partnerships. Therefore, the Connecting Strategy is designed to:

- prepare the school and community to reach out and connect with the families
- create an inviting and helpful environment where the families and faculty/staff can comfortably interact with each other
- overcome any psychological or physical barriers that might be preventing the families and the school from working together
- begin to build collaborative relationships with the families
- initiate two-way communication flows between the families and the school

CONNECTING BEST PRACTICES

The following sections present best practices that the school can use to implement the Connecting Strategy. To help the reader find and select appropriate best practices, the programs, activities, and events are grouped around the following categories:

- creating user-friendly schools
- group connecting
- one-on-one connecting
- preparing the faculty and staff to reach out

The best practices in the first three categories are intended to overcome family-based barriers, whereas the practices in the last category are directed at school-based barriers. The programs, activities, and events described in the "Creating User-Friendly Schools" are the most general, while the best practices in the "One-on-One Connecting" category are those that can be targeted at the hard-to-reach families.

Since the process of making connections with the families is developmental and incremental, in some cases, several best practices may be needed over a period of time. Also, the degree of "disconnection" that parents feel varies from family to family. Consequently, some best practices are directed at specific family populations while others are more general in nature and intend to reach the families that are "on the verge" of being connected.

Making connections with the hard-to-reach families is usually difficult, requiring a sustained comprehensive effort. For these more "disconnected" parents, programs and activities will have to be implemented to overcome negative feelings such as alienation, fear, and helplessness. It is important to be patient when attempting to make connections with "hard-to-reach" parents. It takes time and a sustained effort to build good working relationships with distressed families.

The intent and purpose of the interventions must be clear when choosing the best practices. A particular best practice can serve several purposes, so the outcomes depend upon what is emphasized as the practice is being used. For example, a telephone call is an effective connecting best practice when the emphasis is to overcome barriers and initiate a relationship. However, if a family is already "connected," the emphasis of the call is on building the relationship and conveying useful information. The formation of relationships is a dynamic process and the facilitator must decide what to emphasize as the relationship "unfolds."

The best practices listed under the other School/Community Collaboration Strategies can be adapted to help make connections. For instance, several of the parent education topics described in the Coaching Strategy chapter are of great interest to parents. When selecting connecting best practices, therefore, first peruse the best practices described in this chapter and then look at some of the practices presented in the other chapters.

Creating User-Friendly Schools

Making the school environment as welcoming, inviting, and helpful as possible is an important "bridge" to connect the faculty and staff with the families and the community. A school is a complex bureaucracy and can easily be perceived as impersonal and threatening. Every effort should be made to make it easy for the families and community members to interact with the faculty and staff and to have access to resources and services. The explicit and implicit message to the families and community should be: "You are welcome, you are important to us, and we want to work with you to educate your children."

Welcome Signs

At many schools, the first thing families read when they come to school is the statement: "All visitors *must* report to the office."

This stern message can be a real "turn off." As negative as this phrase may be, some signs are even worse. Below is an example of a "welcome" sign displayed in an elementary school:

> Warning! City Statute 548 requires that all visitors to a public facility report immediately upon entering such a facility to the office or director of such building stating reason for entry and business to be transacted. Violators are subject to a $500 fine or six months in jail. Welcome to your school.—Source: *Vital Connection*, San Diego Schools

Some might argue that the negative signs are necessary for security reasons. Certainly, security is important, but I doubt if negative signs are very effective.

When discussing this issue with groups, I facetiously tell them that when I travel, I stop by schools to sell drugs and abuse teachers. When I arrive at the school, I immediately go to the office and sign in. I make sure that I let the principal or secretary know where I will be "selling and abusing," so as not to miss anyone. Of course, the point here is that the individuals for whom the negative signs are intended, like drug dealers and loiterers, will not heed the notice anyway.

Since the parents and community members are the ones who usually see and read the signs, why not display a more positive message such as:

> Welcome, families and other visitors.
> To better serve you and the students,
> please come by the office so we can help you.

This notice sends an inviting message to the families, while also requesting that they stop by the office. Most visitors understand the need for security and have no problem being asked to check in at the office. The positive signs will give parents and visitors better feelings, perceptions, and expectations about the school and their visit.

Nice Welcoming Gestures

Some outreach gestures made by the faculty, staff, and students at two schools that I visited made a very positive impression. For example, when I arrived at the Montgomery Junior High School in San Diego, California, and at the Hoover Elementary School in Buffalo, New York, the following message was taped on the front door and displayed at other locations around the schools:

Welcome
Dr. Don Lueder
from
Winthrop University
South Carolina

What a nice surprise to see the signs. The greeting made me feel very welcome and special. It also let the learning community know who was visiting and wandering around their school.

Parent Parking Spaces

Providing reserved parking spaces for parents is not only a convenience, but a strong symbolic gesture that says to the family members, "You are important and we value you." Think of the message you are sending when on a rainy day parents find a space marked for them, so they can park near the door and not get wet.

If you have limited space and need to allocate parking for other visitors, then label the spaces, "Parents/Visitors." You can get a lot of goodwill from this "parking" practice.

Office Manners

Observe how secretaries and other staff members greet family members on the phone or in person. Think about the kind of impression they are making, and whether they are being helpful.

Emphasize the importance of being responsive and caring. Point out they are usually the first school officials that the parents and other visitors come in contact with. I have found that I learn a lot about a school's culture from the way I am greeted when I arrive at the office.

Also, remind the teachers and staff that how they greet and interact with families and visitors in the hallways and other school areas is equally important. Visitors' perceptions of the school's curriculum, programs, and faculty are often based on the first interaction they have with someone at the school.

Big Jim

In a school in San Diego the custodian's picture is displayed in the lobby. Under his picture is printed, "Big Jim Says . . . ," followed by several positive educational reminders for the students and families. I was told that Big Jim is a significant and respected person in the lives of the students, faculty and staff, and families. His words and presence send out a strong message that education is important and that everyone is a partner in the education of the children.

Coffee and Tea Connections

When parents and visitors arrive at the school for a meeting or conference, have coffee, tea, or soft drinks available. Serve the beverage in cups or glasses bearing the school's collective vision, mission statement, or logo. Not only is this a symbolic gesture about the importance of the visit, it is also an opportunity to promote the school's commitment to education and the families.

School Maps

It is important to have a school map at the school's entrances showing how to get to the office. How many times have you arrived at a school and wandered around trying to locate the office?

Partnership Policy

Display the school's family/school/community partnership policy in the lobby and around the school. Print copies of the policy and disseminate it widely to the families and the community. The policy is an official announcement of the school's commitment to family involvement.

If you have no policy, bring community leaders, school faculty and staff, and family and community leaders together to develop one. Attempt to reach a consensus about the importance of reaching out and involving all families. Present the proposed family/school/community partnership policy to the school board, school improvement council, school management and planning team, the PTA, and so on, for their approval. Make it a policy for everyone.

A Family Doorbell

At a middle school located in a distressed community with a high crime rate, the doors of the school were locked during and after the school day. Soon after the family/school coordinator began working at the school, she noticed that when the parents came to the school they had to pound on the door to get in. Usually, it took a long time before anyone responded, and sometimes, the family members just gave up and left.

Since it was felt necessary that the doors stay locked, the coordinator worked with the school's principal to install a doorbell that rang in the office. Different staff members are now responsible for answering the door in a friendly and helpful manner. Installing the bell removed one of the physical barriers that was keeping the family from being part of the school.

Family of the Month

A picture of the "Family/Families of the Month" can be displayed as part of the school's lobby program. Faculty, staff, and community members can nominate families based on partnership activities the parents have been involved in with the child or the school.

One caution, while this is a nice way of acknowledging involvement by the family, there can be a downside if it becomes too competitive. The activity should not resemble a "lawn of the month" contest catered to a few. Recognizing several families at a time and nominating families from all segments of the population can prevent elitism and a feeling that only middle-class values are emphasized.

Photo Books

Place photograph albums in the lobby, main office, and parent room for families and visitors to browse through. Such albums consist of pictures of partnership events and activities, in and out of the classrooms, such as volunteering, celebrations, awards, social events, and meals. The albums maintain a pictorial record of important and interesting activities where students and families are involved. Family members and children love to see themselves in the albums. When possible, send copies of pictures to the families and the local newspapers.

Office Decor

Like the school lobby, the office must be inviting and welcoming. For example, the school and partnership missions should be posted, along with examples of student art and photographs. Appropriate posters related to teamwork, success, and cooperation can also be displayed.

Down with Counters

The high counter that shielded the office staff from the students, family members, and other visitors was taken down at one high school. Removing this barrier was a dramatic symbolic move that sent a strong message to the family and community members that we are working together as partners.

Welcome Wagon

To make the families more comfortable with the school, a committee of parents and community volunteers created a "welcome wagon" support program. The welcome wagon members act as hosts/hostesses during registration times and on the first days of school when the pre-kindergarten and kindergarten students and their families arrive. The welcome wagon committee also schedules "connecting" events at different times of the year to create a positive school environment. This is also a good service for families and students who are transitioning from elementary to middle schools.

Underwear Link

Matt Benningfield, principal of the Dann C. Byck Elementary School, has used an effective best practice for many years to connect with new mothers in the neighborhood. When a baby is born, he sends a congratulation card attached to an infant-sized undershirt. The bottom of the shirt is pinned shut and is filled with brochures and other information about the school and community services, as well as materials about parenting, home learning, and other topics. The undershirt provides an innovative link with the school from birth and invites the parent to be a partner from the start.

Best Buddies

A student version of the welcome wagon group is a program called "Best Buddies." Students volunteer to act as school ambassadors at programs and activities, greeting families and visitors and providing directions and tours. At one school, the best buddies helped family members when they came to school to register their children. The student volunteers directed the family members to appropriate places and answered questions.

A Best Buddies program is very useful when students and families are moving from elementary to middle school or from middle to high school. The students are great "connectors" with the families and the activity is a learning and an enjoyable experience for them.

Parent/Family Centers

Establish centers or rooms in the school where family members can come for information, support, and training. Some schools use the term *parent center*, others use *family center*. The latter term acknowledges the whole family's involvement and indirectly welcomes grandparents, aunts, uncles, siblings, and other relatives. No matter which term is used, the families should feel that the facilities are available for everyone.

As you would guess, the centers are great places for family members to gather for a cup of coffee, soft drink, and a doughnut. The centers provide an environment that helps make connections and form a community. In some distressed situations, the family center serves as a community center or "safe haven."

In a well-equipped center, books, audio- and videotapes, games, puzzles, telephones, computers, copying machines, software, and other materials are available for the family's use. Some schools even provide kitchens, laundry rooms, and sewing machines. Schools can approach businesses, industry and service groups for donations to buy equipment, supplies, and software. A section describing the use of the centers to coordinate services and resources for needy families is presented in Chapter 10.

Self-Help Workshops and Classes

A variety of parent education programs and activities can be offered to make connections and meet a variety of family needs. For example, high school diploma equivalency, literacy, English language, and adolescent psychology classes are popular. The events do not need to be limited to school-oriented topics, but can focus on such concerns as daycare, recreation, personal health, drug abuse, crime, and violence. A large portion of the Coaching Strategy chapter (Chapter 9) is devoted to parent education best practices designed to enhance the families' capacity to effectively play their Parent Partner Roles.

Styling and Profiling

At an elementary school in Nashville, the parents were invited to volunteer to be "clients" for a cosmetology class at a nearby comprehensive high school. The students needed somebody to practice on for haircuts, styling, permanents, hair coloring, and manicures. The parents could fill this need. The parents loved to have their hair and nails done, and were eager to volunteer. The activity was directed at the self-interests of both parents and the cosmetology students. As a result, connections were made with the families and the students got their clients.

Coupon Exchange Center

A place in the school can be set up for parents, faculty, and staff to exchange food, service, and other product coupons. Everyone places coupons that they don't want in a box and also look through the supply to see if there are coupons they can use. Parent volunteers can sort through the coupons, categorize them (e.g., food, drinks, cleaning supplies, paper goods, etc.), and possibly put them in separate boxes. Otherwise, a class can be asked to organize the coupons as a project, or the task could be part of a parenting class in nutrition, budgeting, filing, or reading.

The coupon center can be established simply by putting a box in the main office, guidance office, or parent center. Usually, the teachers' lounge is not a good spot if you want the families to use the coupon exchange center as a gathering place.

Field Trips

Invite parents to go along with their children on field trips to libraries, fire houses, TV and radio stations, newspaper offices, airports, hospitals, court houses, police stations, parks, museums, factories, and so on. Some family members may never have visited many of these places. They will be anxious to go, and it will be a good learning experience for everyone.

Connecting with Feeder Schools

As students transition from one school to another, it is important for the families to be oriented to the new school. In some cases, parents do not even know where the new school is located. In Nashville, kindergarten students go to school in their neighborhoods, but busing begins with the first grade. At one inner-city school, the parents were putting their kids on a bus and had no idea where the children were going. The school was located about eight miles away and the families had never visited the school. Most families did not have transportation and they did not know how to get to the school if they did have a means to get there.

To solve this problem, orientation meetings were scheduled at the "feeder" school and the families were transported to the new school. Family members toured the building, met with teachers, guidance counselors, and principals, and had an opportunity to ask questions and share their concerns.

School Vegetable Garden

A way to make a connection, build support, and provide lessons in cooperation, giving, health, and nutrition is to plant a school vegetable garden. Family members, students, teachers, principals, and other staff members all work together to plan, plant, cultivate, and harvest the garden. Students from the vocational agriculture or science classes can be asked to be involved in organizing the garden as part of a class project. Informal sessions on nutrition, cooking, and botany can also be presented.

Usually, there is a plot of land on the school grounds or nearby in the neighborhood that can be made available for a garden. In one school neighborhood, the land under some electric power lines was used.

Everyone shares the crop. Sometimes the garden is large that there are enough vegetables to be given to senior citizens living at home and to nursing homes. Not only are the recipients pleased and grateful, but sharing the harvest is a demonstration of the collaborative spirit.

School Flower Garden

A variation, or addition, to the school vegetable garden is a flower garden. Not only do the participants get fresh cut flowers for their use at home, but flowers are given to "shut-ins" and senior citizens, hospitals, and retirement and nursing homes. Local garden clubs or horticulture classes can be asked to help with planning the garden.

Opening School Facilities to Families

Adopt a "community school" philosophy, where the school is believed to be for everyone's use. Arrange for the school facilities to be available to families for recreation, classes, support groups, and other meetings. Libraries, media centers, gymnasiums, and pools are open to family members after school and during weekends. Not only will the family members feel connected by using the facilities, they will also take "ownership" for the school. If school funds are not available for supervision and other costs, businesses and service clubs can be asked for their support by volunteering time to work with the family members and to raise funds.

Group Connecting

Logistics

Being flexible in the location and timing of group events can overcome some of the physical barriers. Providing transportation and child care is also helpful. The following are a few logistical suggestions:

- The events can be held at school or in the community at churches, community centers, hospital cafeterias, and so forth. The location of the social activity should depend upon where the families live, how comfortable they are with the school, the availability of facilities, and so on. Be flexible and plan accordingly.
- Provide name tags so it is easier for the family members and the faculty and staff to meet each other. Sometimes, when making up name tags for the families, or asking the family members to, include the child's name or have the family members list their names as Cindy's Mom or Danny's Dad, or whatever is appropropriate.
- Use a sign-in sheet to get the parents' names, addresses and telephone numbers. Let them know that the information will be distributed to all the families so they contact each other if they wish. The school uses the data for follow-up communication.
- Give inexpensive door prizes. The prizes can be a variety of new and old items, tickets, food, and so on. Small educational

games or toys make excellent prizes. Local businesses are often willing to donate items for prizes. Also, teachers and community volunteers probably have potential prizes ("White Elephants") stored in their closets, dressers, and so forth, just "waiting" to be donated.

Social Events

Social events are an excellent way to make connections and build relationships with the families. The events are opportunities for the faculty and staff to "bridge the gap" by interacting informally with the families. Fun and relaxation should be the focus, with little or no business conducted. Hopefully, the next time a family member sees a teacher or principal they can reminisce about the fun they had.

"BREAKING BREAD"

Having a meal together has traditionally been a wonderful means of connecting in most societies. There are an almost unlimited number of ways that food can be used to bring the school and families together. In most cases, the school and community can host these events at little or no cost to the families as businesses and service clubs are usually willing to help with the cost of such events. Once families are connected and involved, the school, community and family members can plan the events together and host such things as Thanksgiving Day luncheons and Christmas brunches as part of their partnership activities. Examples of social events that are food oriented include:

- spaghetti dinners—Spaghetti dinners are quite inexpensive to prepare and serve and are also an easy meal for the cafeteria staff to fix.
- pizza parties—Most families like pizza. Pizzas can be ordered or prepared at school.
- potluck or pass-the-dish suppers—Families come to the event with a dish-to-pass (e.g., casseroles, sliced meats, vegetables, salads, etc.). The entrees are set out on large tables to make a buffet. The school supplies drinks, dishes, silverware, and so forth. Usually, the families bring one of their favorite dishes and the results are fantastic.

- ethnic dinners—These are similar to potluck suppers, but in this case families bring foods native to their cultures to share with others. If facilities are available, family members can even prepare the food on-site. The event is a learning experience for the children and other families.
- community breakfasts—The school hosts a breakfast on a teacher workday for families, faculty, and staff. This early morning get-together is a good way to start the day.
- ice cream socials—Almost everyone loves ice cream and these events have been around for a long time. Besides having a selection of flavors, an area for making your own sundae is provided with nuts, chocolate syrup, whipped cream, and so on.
- dessert night—At this event, families, faculty and staff bring dessert dishes to share. The school supplies coffee, tea, and so on.
- cookie swap party—Similar to the Dessert Night event, homemade cookies and cakes are brought to the party to be shared with other family members, teachers, principals, and staff. This offers the families an opportunity to "show off" their favorite cookie. Milk, coffee, and tea are provided by the school.

A Holiday Buffet

Berryhill Elementary School in Charlotte, North Carolina, has been hosting an annual Holiday Candlelight Buffet Luncheon for more than thirteen years. The luncheon is not only a celebration of the holiday season, but a celebration of the learning community.

The cafeteria staff prepares the food for the children, family members and friends. The luncheon is served from 10:00 A.M. to 1:00 P.M. The price for the buffet is the same as on a normal lunch day ($2.00 for adults and $1.35 for children). As usual, the children on free lunch eat at no cost. Entertainment is provided by the students.

The luncheon has become a tradition for this lower socioeconomic community and there is always a large crowd of family members and visitors. The Holiday Buffet is seen as a major connecting best practice for the school.

FAMILY PICNIC

A great way to build a learning community is for the school to host a family picnic. This can be a "Back-to-School" event where the families, faculty, and staff come together for an evening of informal fun. The picnic provides an opportunity for the families and children to interact with the teachers, and sometimes their families, outside the classroom setting. Usually, no formal school "business" is conducted, but tables can be set up where families can pick up information on parenting and social issues, family handbooks, the school curriculum, extracurricular programs and home learning activities.

How much the school can provide in food and supplies will depend on the intent, situation, and funding. Generally, the purpose of the picnic is to bring people together as a "bonding" experience and most families are "connected" to some degree. Sometimes, the school supplies the drinks and paper goods, while the families bring their own food.

If the event is being staged primarily to connect with hard-to-reach families, the picnic should be free, or very inexpensive. Transportation and child care are also provided. The picnic is a symbolic gesture to the families that they are important, and that you would like them to be partners with the school. Businesses, service clubs, and industries are usually willing to help with the cost.

PLAYING TOGETHER

The school can host a variety of events and activities to bring families and faculty and staff together to have a good time. Parents and children observe the faculty and staff in different roles and see them as "real" people. By having fun together, the families and teachers are more comfortable with each other. The following are some suggestions for "playing together" activities:

- movie night—Videos appropriate for the whole family are shown in the school's auditorium or cafeteria. Films are rented that are fun and have a positive message. Families are encouraged to discuss the meaning of the movies with their children at home. Pop corn and soft drinks are provided.
- sock-hops—Families, faculty, and staff come together for an old-fashioned sock hop in the school's gymnasium or cafeteria. Music from the fifties is played with a teacher, family member, or community volunteer acting as a DJ. Everyone is encouraged to dress according to the times (e.g., poodle skirts, peg pants, etc.). Light refreshments are served.
- bingo parties—Bingo parties are held in the school's cafeteria. Faculty and staff usually have small "treasures" tucked away in

closets that can be used as prizes. Local businesses and store owners can also be approached to donate prizes.

- yard sale/flea market—Families, faculty, and staff are invited to bring in items that they would like to donate for a school yard sale or flea market. As with the bingo parties, industries, businesses, and stores are usually also willing to make donations. Entertainment can be provided by the school's band and chorus, groups of students, and community groups. The school makes a little money for future partnership activities while everyone has a good time.

- spring fling or fall festival—The PTA, School Improvement Council, or other groups organize a school festival or fair for the families and community. Games and activities are arranged for the children and adults, and student art exhibits, band concerts, dance demonstrations, and chorus presentations can also be part of the event. Food and refreshments are available. Sometimes, the fair can be combined with a chicken barbeque or spaghetti dinner.

- community feast and auction—Tickets are sold in the community for the feast. In addition to the food, a live and silent auction is held. Items to be auctioned are donated by businesses and individuals. One community holds this event as part of the July 4th weekend celebration.

- an angel happening—This is a traditional fund-raising project at a Family/School Christmas Bazaar. A local craft maker makes ceramic Christmas tree angels especially for the annual event. Each year, the angel is a little different. Families, students, and teachers take advance orders for the angels. The community members look forward to purchasing the annual edition of the Christmas angel each year.

- faculty/student basketball game—Scheduling a basketball game between the faculty and the students is a good way to connect with the families. Families like to see their kids perform and it is a good time for all.

- some other events—Once the school and families start to organize events for the learning community, they can also schedule such things as hay and sleigh rides, fishing and hiking trips, and so on.

> ### A Halloween Carnival
>
> A Halloween Carnival that is held each year at an elementary school in Nashville demonstrates the developmental and progressive nature of the School/Community Collaboration Strategies. The school is located in a community where previously there was little or no family involvement. The families did not feel connected with the school. Most of the family members had not done well in school themselves and were hesitant to be involved.
>
> During the first year that the school had the carnival, the teachers organized games and contests for the students. The activities were noncompetitive and the students were not pitted against each other. All the students who participated were winners. The families were invited to attend and some of the family members came and watched.
>
> The second year, the family members were asked if they would like to help with the games and activities. Several family members volunteered to assist the teachers. The family members were instructed about the noncompetitive nature of the games and contests and how everyone would be "rewarded" for doing their best. The parents were connected and began to communicate with the teachers.
>
> By the third year, more and more families were involved with the Halloween Carnival and by the fourth year, the families organized and conducted the carnival themselves. As the families became more and more involved, the teachers were able to coach them about responsibility, planning, cooperation, and decision making. As a result, the carnival became a "win-win" partnership experience for the students, families, and teachers.

NEIGHBORHOOD MEETINGS

- family neighborhood forums—Family forums or town meetings are held in the neighborhood to discuss partnership activities and other family and school issues. The location of a meeting is dependent upon how "disconnected" the families are. If the families are unsure about the schools, it is best to select a neutral or a "home" location where the families usually gather in their neighborhood. For example, a community center or church may be a better place than a nearby school or housing office if the families don't feel comfortable with schools or the housing authority.
- education Sunday parent pledge programs—Presentations are made at churches and synagogues seeking community support and family involvement. After the presentations, the family and community members are asked to "pledge" in writing to encourage learning and success for the children.

- neighborhood parent-teacher conferences—At times, regular parent-teacher conferences are held in the neighborhoods. This is especially important if the neighborhoods are not near the school as is often the case when busing is involved. Depending upon the type and size of the meeting, it can be held at community centers, the housing office conference area, churches, synagogues or other places of worship, youth centers, hospitals, factories, union halls, laundromats, and even a nearby school. A special section on conducting parent-teacher conferences is included in the Communicating Strategy chapter (Chapter 7).

Fast-Food Connections

A school decided the best place to hold a connecting meeting was at a location where the families "hung out" a lot. It was determined that a majority of the families frequented a certain fast-food restaurant in the neighborhood. The school made arrangements with the restaurant to host a meeting. Parents and children attending the meeting ate for free, as the restaurant and the school split the cost. To help foster the connections, the principal and teachers put on restaurant uniforms and served the families. The meeting was a huge success.

One-On-One Connecting

For some family populations more intensive one-on-one best practices are necessary to make connections. Three best practices are very effective when attempting to make connections with hard-to-reach families: personal letters, telephone calls, and home visits.

While the activities are similar in intent—to overcome barriers and to begin to form a collaborative relationship with the parents—they differ in the level of intensity and personal contact; that is, the letter is the least intensive and the home visit is the most. A personal letter may work with families that do not feel alienated, but for the parents who are feeling very "out of place," a face-to-face visit is probably necessary to make connections.

When working with the "disconnected" families, always keep in mind that your primary focus is to overcome the barriers and to initiate a collaborative relationship. Establishing a communication flow is important, but first you have to be connected. When making connections, build on the family's strong points. All families have strengths and a sense of pride even though they may be living in poverty or be poorly educated.

The following section presents guidelines for composing letters, making telephone calls, and conducting home visits. The guidelines apply whether you are reaching out to the families, by mail, over the phone, or in person.

Guidelines for Letters, Telephone Calls, and Home Visits

THE INITIAL CONNECTING ATTEMPT

- Begin the letter or conversation by telling a little about yourself.
- Be prepared to say something positive about the child.
- Emphasize how much you want to work with the student and the family.
- Ask about the child's special interests, pets, hobbies, sports, and other outside school activities.
- Explore if the child has any special needs that you could help with.
- Inquire about the child's likes and dislikes.
- Check to see if you have the student's correct birthday because you would like to do something special that day.
- Let the family know that they are welcome to come to school and give them a time when you are available to visit with them.
- Give them information about when and how you can be contacted and ask the same of them.

FOLLOW UP TO THE INITIAL CONTACT

Once you feel that you have some rapport with the family members and have some understanding of the child, you may be able to begin to focus on some school-oriented questions and information. This is the beginning of a communication flow. Guidelines for implementing the communicating best practices are presented in the next chapter. However, since the connecting process blends into the communication process, some suggestions are presented in this chapter as well. Therefore, once a connection is forming:

- Ask about the family's expectations of you, the school, and the child.
- Inquire about the responsibilities the child has at home.

- Tell the family how you manage your classroom.
- Ask how you can help with the child's learning at home.

When talking with families, either over the phone or in person, you may have to lead the discussion, ask questions and bring up different topics because the families may not know what or how to ask. Besides information about their children and the classrooms, parents usually want to know:

- What is the policy on homework, discipline, attendance, and so forth?
- What is the cost for lunch and breakfast and how do you apply for reduced cost or free meals?
- Will my child be going on field trips?
- How are teachers and principals hired?
- Who decides on the curriculum?
- What extracurricular activities such as band, chorus, theater, and athletics are offered?
- What resources are available at the school such as nurses, guidance counselors, social workers, psychologists, and so on?

Do not expect to cover everything in one encounter. Remember that you can accomplish only so much with one letter, phone call or home visit, especially with "disconnected" parents. Try to create the expectation that you will be communicating with the family on a regular basis through home visits, telephone calls, letters, and conferences.

COORDINATING RESOURCES AND SERVICES

Sometimes, telephone calls and home visits, usually one visit, allow you to informally assess the family's condition and need level. For example, during a home visit, you may become aware of family problems such as extreme poverty, drug abuse, alcoholism, child abuse, divorce, and teen pregnancy. When some trust is established between you and the parent, the school and community will be able to help by coordinating services and resources and providing information and support.

Connecting Letters

While providing some information, letters are primarily intended to overcome barriers and to begin building build trust and mutual respect. The letters should stress to the families that the faculty and staff feel that they are important and that the school cares. Formulate the letters using the guidelines presented at the beginning of this section. Additional suggestions include:

- Keep the letter short and to the point. Long letters are not very effective and some parents may have difficulty reading.
- Make sure the parents can read English. If not, send letters written in their native language.
- Emphasize how much you are looking forward to working with their child and the family.
- Let the family know they are welcome at school, and how to contact you for a visit.
- Encourage the family to contact you if they need information or have questions.

Connecting Telephone Calls

Positive telephone calls from school are not very common, especially to families with students at the middle and high school levels. Therefore, your call will come as a surprise to most of the families. If the parents feel disconnected from the school, the phone call may be viewed with some suspicion. Therefore, make sure telephone calls are upbeat.

With families that feel alienated and disenfranchised, a telephone call may not be enough to make a connection. A more intense one-on-one best practice like a home visit may be required.

The Connecting Home Visit

Home visits are probably the most effective best practice for making connections, especially with the most "hard-to-reach" parents. While time consuming and labor intensive, visiting families in their home is a strong indication of your concern, caring, and commitment. This personal one-on-one practice, if conducted properly, demonstrates that you want to work with the parents, as partners, to educate their children.

It would be great if all families were visited by someone from the school, especially the child's teacher. However, I recognize that conducting home visits is very labor intensive, so this intervention may have to be limited to the most "disconnected" families. However, I encourage you to extend this practice to as many of the families as possible.

Home Visits as "Vehicles" for Other Interventions

While home visits are an excellent connecting best practice, they are also useful events for implementing all of the School/Community Collaboration Strategies. Home visits can serve as "vehicles" not only for making connections, but for engaging in two-way communications, coordinating needed services and resources, and conducting parent education activities. This latter use of the home visit, to enhance the families' skills and knowledge to play their parenting roles, is discussed in the Coaching chapter (Chapter 9).

It is very important to be clear about the intent of a home visit, especially when it is being used to connect with the families. The operative word for the visit is "collaboration." The objective is to make connections and to initiate a relationship that is based on trust, mutual respect, caring, and understanding. Therefore, the visitor's attitudes and assumptions about the families are crucial.

First, we must assume that most families are interested in their children's education and want them to succeed. Second, we must believe that under the right conditions most families are willing to work with the school. So, if the families are not involved and are "missing," the reality may be that while there is a desire by the parents to be involved, certain barriers are preventing them from doing so. Consequently, the home visit is an important intervention strategy for beginning to overcome these barriers.

Families shouldn't feel that you have come to "fix" them. As we work with the families, we need to be careful not to, unintentionally, patronize or demean. All families, even the most distressed, have strengths. We must build on the strengths and attempt to eliminate the weaknesses. This can be tricky when the family is feeling alienated and disenfranchised from the school. However, it has been my experience that with a genuine caring effort, combined with perseverance, connections can be made and collaborative relationships can be established with most families.

Some may think that families, especially those with meager means, do not want school and community people coming to their home. I have found just the opposite. Most families, when approached in a helpful way, realize the visitors are interested in them and their children. Actually, most families welcome and look forward to the visits. Once they get over the surprise of the school and community reaching out to them, family members seem to enjoy having teachers, counselors, principals and community people visit their homes.

When Are You Going to Visit My House?

I was working with the faculty at a school located in a distressed community in Nashville to determine the effects of home visits. The teachers were going to visit one half of the students' families. The half that was not visited would serve as the control group.

We quickly abandoned the study when the kids from the control group came to the school, all excited, asking when the teachers were coming to visit them. Making connections and establishing relationships with the parents was far more important than the research, so the teachers made visits to the homes of all the students. Even though we did not conduct the study, the reactions of the kids who were not scheduled to be visited indicated the positive attitudes toward the home visits.

PLANNING AND CONDUCTING HOME VISITS

When trying to connect with the families via a home visit, remember that the parents are not accustomed to having teachers, family/school coordinators, school social workers, program directors, and other staff members from the school coming to their homes. Since nonthreatening visits from people in authority are not the norm, the visits must be personal and upbeat. Use the guidelines at the beginning of the chapter when forming what information will be shared and what questions asked during the connecting visits. In addition to these important guidelines, the following are some suggestions for preparing and making home visits:

- If the family has a telephone, call to let them know that you would like to come by to get acquainted. Ask when it would be convenient to visit. Be flexible and adjust to the family's schedule when making the appointment.
- Mail or send appointment cards home with the child stating the date and time of the home visit. The mission statement, collective vision, or parent involvement slogan can be printed on the cards.
- Include a magnetic note holder when sending out an appointment card or making a visit, so the family can post the information on the refrigerator door. Have positive messages printed on the note holders like those on the cards.

- Dress in good, but casual clothes when visiting the families. In the United States, strangers appearing in the neighborhood wearing formal business attire, especially in lower socioeconomic neighborhoods, are often perceived as threatening social agency officials or religious salespersons.
- If you are offered something to drink or eat, if at all possible, accept it. Refusing an offer of hospitality may send the wrong message.
- If you are uneasy about making the home visit because of the conditions in the community where the families live, it is a good idea to take someone with you and go during the daytime. Making a visit when you are anxious will not be as effective. Even though the families are living in a distressed community, most family members are law-abiding citizens and feel "caught" in these conditions.
- Wear an identification button or tag indicating who you are and what school or program you are with. The identification badges will let the families and neighbors know who you are and help them remember your name. Try not to make the tags too official or institutional.
- Have "door hangers" prepared with a message such as: "I came to visit you. Sorry that I missed you." Include your name and telephone number and ask the parent to call. The door hangers are used when you made an unscheduled stop and the family was not home, or if the family was not home for an appointment. Making connections with the family is sometimes difficult, so and you need to use a positive approach and be persistent.

Once connections are made and relationships have been formed with the families, the home visit can focus on parent education. For example, the family members can be shown how to read to their children and use home learning activities. Some home visit programs lend or give books, educational toys, puzzles, games, and materials to the families.

As part of the home visit, the child's development in understanding and expressing language, use of small and large muscles, self-help and social skills, and so forth, can be assessed. An educational and social profile is constructed for the child that indicates strengths and weaknesses. The profile is used for designing appropriate learning strategies for the child at home and in school. Best practices for coaching the parents during home visits are described in Chapter 9.

A CAUTION

Not all faculty and staff will perceive home visits as an opportunity to connect and work with the families. Some teachers will be reluctant to make home visits and see them, at best, as a required inconvenience if forced to make them. I remember talking to a group of middle-school teachers and when I mentioned home visits their eyes rolled and glazed over. Making home visits in the middle school is not the norm. However, as tough as it may be to convince some teachers about the importance of connecting with the hard-to-reach parents, efforts must be made for the visits to occur. It is helpful if the faculty is involved in the partnership program planning process described in Chapter 10.

Certain federal programs such as Title I Prekindergarten, Even Start, and Head Start require that the teachers conduct home visits. Of course, the reason home visits are mandated is that many of the families who are eligible for these projects are not "connected" with the school and are not involved with the education of their children.

I believe this is very positive legislation; however, the effects may not be positive if the individuals conducting the visits don't have the appropriate skills, knowledge, and attitudes. For example, one of the purposes of the required visits is to provide the family with information about the program that they are participating in and have them sign various forms and documents. While this is an important and necessary aspect of the visits, some teachers see this as the primary and sole purpose. This is unfortunate because if the visitors arrive as "officials" from the school or agency only to get the families to comply with an impersonal bureaucratic requirement, the gap between the home and the school may become even wider. The parents may sign the forms, but an important connecting opportunity will be lost. Therefore, faculty and staff need to be advised and instructed on how to make home visits. Such training should emphasize that making connections with the families and developing positive working relationships with the school is the primary purpose of the home visits.

Preparing the Faculty and Staff to Reach Out

As stated in Chapter 4, some of the barriers that prevent partnerships from forming between the families and the schools result from long-standing beliefs by the faculty and staff about the roles of parents, teachers, principals, and community members. That is, some teachers and administrators may not perceive that the school should be reaching out to the parents.

Therefore, in many schools, the faculty and staff will have to be convinced that by using the Self-Renewing Partnership Model to build collaborative relationships with the families their lives, and those of the children and parents, will be better. The following best practices are presented as ways to prepare the faculty and staff for this paradigm shift.

Family/School/Community Partnership Planning Sessions

One of the most effective ways to prepare and orient the faculty and staff to reach out to the families is for them to be involved in developing a family/school/community partnership program planning process. The Strategic Partnership Planning System that is presented in Chapter 10 is a process for shared belief development, mission identification, goal setting, and intervention strategy selection. Using the system, the participants decide "where they want to go" and "how to get there."

Need Assessments

It is important to do your "homework" before attempting to reach out to the families. As part of the planning process, data are gathered to learn about family needs and self-interests, cultures, attitudes, and values. These data can be gathered by surveying the families in person, by telephone, or asking them to respond to a questionnaire.

The need assessment can also identify barriers such as time, transportation, and child care constraints. The results of the need assessment are helpful when deciding on goals and objectives, and which intervention strategies are most likely to be most effective.

Family Surveys

The survey questions evolve from the concepts underlying the family/school/community partnerships. The questions should be short, simple and to the point. People usually do not respond to long complicated surveys, whether in writing or verbally. If you use mailed surveys, make it as easy as possible to respond. Enclose a stamped envelope or construct the questionnaire in such a way that when completed, it can easily be folded and stapled together, and dropped in the mail. Another format is to use a postcard for a short survey.

Family Interviews

The return rate from mailed surveys is often low, especially if the targeted population feels disconnected. Therefore, instead of mailing the surveys to the families, data can be collected through parent interviews conducted at grocery and convenience stores or at open meetings in the neighborhood. If the school has a PTA/PTO and School Improvement Council, the members can be asked to help with the data collection.

The interview questions should try to identify both family strengths and weaknesses. If the community is feeling alienated, it may be difficult to get much in-depth information, but it is a start. Even finding out if there is a psychological gap between the family and school is important information.

Family Focus Groups

To obtain information about family needs, desires, and culture, invite a small group of parents to breakfast, lunch or for coffee to meet with the principal and one or two teachers. During the family focus group meetings, family members share their perspectives about their children, the school, and educational issues. Similar meetings for community leaders can also be organized.

If the families are not comfortable about coming to school, or if it is inconvenient, the meetings can be held in the neighborhoods at community centers, churches, businesses, and similar locations. Once the families feel connected, the family members may want to meet at the school occasionally, or on a regular basis. Try to respond to the families' desires about location and times. The intent is to gather information, but it is also a way for the families to feel connected and to want to be involved with the school.

Neighborhood Bus Tours

In some settings, faculty, staff, parent representatives, and community leaders are not familiar with the environments where the families live. Many of the teachers have never been in their students' neighborhoods. This is especially common in districts with extensive busing.

To prepare teachers to reach out to the families, organize school bus tours of the neighborhoods. The tours can be scheduled during workdays or just before the children arrive to begin the school year. The tours can be part of the teachers' inservice training. The bus rides are a quick and easy way to increase awareness and understanding, and provide new perspectives about the students and their families. The bus tours can begin to answer such questions as:

- What are family's and children's views of the world?
- How do the families live?
- What do the children do in the neighborhood?
- What are kids good at?

After the bus tour, a debriefing session is conducted so the participants can share their perceptions, raise questions, and make suggestions for additional connecting plans. Later, more intensive best practices, such as neighborhood forums, and home visits, can be used to make connections and gain a more in-depth understanding about the families.

The Deluxe Neighborhood Tour

A way to make the tour of the neighborhood even more effective is to include a luncheon with family members. Contact the local clergy and see if they would be willing to host a luncheon for the teachers and some of the families in their neighborhood. By having a meal together, teachers and parents will have an opportunity to get to know each another, ask questions, and make connections. The cost of luncheons can be covered by donations, grants, neighborhood groups, or the school district.

Parent Involvement Conference

Organize a conference for community and family leaders, teachers, counselors, and administrators to discuss ways to create family/school/community partnerships. Spotlight successful family involvement practices operating in other schools to help stimulate action. The conference can raise awareness and set the stage for using the Strategic

Partnership Planning System (Chapter 10) to develop a partnership program for the school.

COMMUNICATING: BUILDING ON THE CONNECTING STRATEGY

The best practices presented in this chapter are implemented to overcome barriers and make connections. Once connections are made, the focus shifts to establishing two-way communication flows between the families and the school. The programs, activities, and events described in the following chapter are ways that the school can form the communication flows.

CHAPTER 7

Communicating: Establishing a Flow

CONNECTING	COMMUNICATING	COORDINATING	COACHING

You know the "oh oh" feeling you get when you look in the mailbox and find a letter from the Internal Revenue Service (IRS). Unfortunately, many people get that same sinking sensation when an unexpected letter arrives from their child's school. The reason for this negative reaction is that communications from the school typically range from cool and impersonal, to negative and threatening. This may be what is occurring now, but it doesn't have to be this way.

It is overly optimistic to expect that we will have warm feelings toward the IRS, even if they start sending out thank-you notes. However, I do believe the "oh good" reactions can replace the "oh oh" responses we have toward school correspondence. This will happen if two-way communication flows that emphasize the positive are established between the school and the families.

Certainly, all communications between the school and the families cannot be positive. At times, there will be problems and concerns that have to be addressed. However, if collaborative relationships built on positive communications are in place, when problems do occur, they are more likely to be resolved in a positive manner. Information is the currency of power, and the sharing of power builds relationships. Trusting relationships between the families and the school will be the foundation for problem-solving where the teachers support families, rather than blame. And, the parents will be doing likewise. By working together, the parents will feel like "insiders" rather than "outsiders" in the educational process.

Parents want to know what is happening in school and how their child is progressing. While being as positive as possible, it is important for the school to be honest and "tell it like it is." The families want specific information about how they can help at school and at home. It is important for the families to learn how the operation of the school works, so they can "plug in" and be partners. Jane C. Lindle (1989) found that the most enhancing factor in home/school relationships was the "personal touch": the teachers and principals who take a personal interest in their children.

As discussed in the previous chapter, families must be connected with the school before the parties can communicate effectively. Connecting best practices are used to reach out to the families and to begin building relationships. After these connections are made, communicating best practices are employed to establish a two-way communication flow and to strengthen the collaborative relationships between the school and the families. Once a collaborative relationship is developed and a two-way communication flow established, the school and community can implement the Coaching Strategy to enhance the families' ability and willingness to play the Parent Partner Roles. Therefore, the Communicating Strategy is designed to do the following:

- Establish two-way communication flows between the families and the school.
- Continue to build collaborative relationships with the families.
- Begin to increase family and community support for the school's programs and activities.

Linking Family/School Coordinators with Teachers

When establishing two-way communication flows make sure there are linkages between all parties. Communications need to flow between the families and the teachers, families and children, and teachers and children. If the school is fortunate enough to have a family/school coordinator, it is important to focus on the communication flow between the coordinator and the teachers. This is a most important relationship and it is sometimes forgotten.

COMMUNICATING BEST PRACTICES

The programs, activities, and events that are described in this chapter focus on ways to establish effective two-way communication between the families and school. However, many of these best practices can also improve communications between parents and children, and teachers and students. For a family/school/community partnership to be effective, there needs to be good communication between all parties.

Depending upon the family and school situations, establishing a two-way communication flow can be fairly easy, or very difficult. Since the family needs to be connected before a communication flow can begin, it is important to determine if any psychological or physical barriers are separating the family from the school. Once the targeted family population is connected, then best practices to build the communication flow can be implemented right away. If the family is not "connected" with the school, however, connecting best practices will need to be used to "bridge the gaps." Chapter 6 presents programs, activities, and events that can be implemented to connect with the families.

The families will vary in how much they feel connected with the school. Some parents will be very comfortable with the school, while others are only connected in a marginal way. As indicated in the previous chapter, the Connecting Strategy is intended to overcome barriers and begin to establish a communication flow between the families and the school. The Communicating Strategy interacts with the Connecting Strategy and strengthens the relationship between the parents and the school, while developing effective communication. Therefore, the kind and magnitude of communicating best practices that the school decides to implement will depend on the degree to which the targeted family population is connected. Consequently, some programs and activities are focused, while others are very broad. The process used to select appropriate best practices is described in the Strategic Partnership Planning System (Chapter 10).

Because the connecting process blends into the communicating process, some best practices overlap. Some are similar in format, but differ in intent and emphasis. For example, best practices for making the school more user-friendly are good "connectors" with the families, but the programs and activities are ongoing since a welcoming school is an asset in building partnerships.

In the following sections, best practices are presented that can be used to implement the Communicating Strategy. To help the reader locate and select appropriate best practices; the programs, activities, and events are grouped by the following categories: Communicating in Writing, Telephone and Electronic Communicating, Face-to-Face Communicating, Group Communicating, and Mass Communicating.

Several best practices (e.g., welcoming telephone calls and letters, parent-teacher conferences, and open houses) are presented in special sections because of their importance. Some of them are traditional parent involvement activities, hence the discussions center on how they can be modified to strengthen the collaborative nature of the partnerships between the school and the families. For example, sometimes a parent-teacher conference ends up being an event where the teacher dominates and tells the parent about their child, rather than being an opportunity for all parties to share information and build the partnership. The Parent-Teacher Conference Section presents ways to plan and conduct the meetings so the conferences reflect the partnership philosophy.

Communicating in Writing

Analyzing Current Best Practices

Before deciding on what new best practices to use, it is a good idea to review the written communications currently in use. Gather copies of letters, notices, newsletters, bulletins, and other written materials that have gone out to the families and communities during the past year. Spread the documents out on a table and examine them carefully to ascertain the nature, quantity and quality of the communications. Look not only at what is written, but also for how the message is stated—the tone and clarity. Written messages to the families need to be as positive as possible, communicating respect, trust, and caring.

All too often correspondence from the school talks down to the families and students, or is sterile and impersonal. The school should want the parents to be partners; therefore, the communications should express this desire. Ask yourself, "Are current written communications helpful, informative and respectful," and "Will families know that the school wants to work with them to educate their children?"

The correspondences should be void of educational jargon and be written as simply as possible. This is a good general writing rule, but it is especially important in this case because some parents may have difficulty reading. If English is the second language for a segment of your population, write a version of the materials using the families' native language. This is a major issue for some schools. I visited a school district in Los Angeles where newsletters were written in 17 different languages.

The process of analyzing the written communications that have been sent out to the families should be repeated each year to make sure that the messages are appropriate and effective.

Welcoming Letters

Before school starts, or early in the school year, have the teachers and principal send letters to the students and families. The purpose of these letters is to welcome the students and families to this year's learning community and to establish or build the two-way communication flows. While providing some information, this practice is primarily intended to continue building trust and mutual respect. The letters show the families that the faculty and staff feel they are important and that the school cares. As mentioned, for those families that do not feel connected with the school, the letters may not be very effective. For these hard-to-reach parents, more intensive one-on-one best practices such as connecting telephone calls or home visits may be required to make a connection (see Chapter 6 for a discussion of these best practices).

The following are some guidelines for composing welcoming letters:

- Keep the letters short and to the point.
- State how much you are looking forward to working with the families and their child.
- Let the families know they are welcome at school and how to arrange for a visit.
- Encourage the family to ask if they need information or have questions. Let them know when and how to contact you.

Sending out these welcoming letters can set a positive tone for the whole year. They are very helpful as you reach out to create partnerships with the families.

Welcome Cards

Instead of letters, "welcome back" cards can be used. These cards have positive and inviting messages printed on them, and principals and/or the teachers sign them before they are sent to the students and families. While not as personalized as the letters, they are efficient, especially when you have large numbers of students.

Positive Notes

During the year, make it a regular practice to send the family positive personalized notes about their children's progress, behavior, and activities. Sending positive notes should be a continuous activity, not a "one-shot deal" Reach an agreement among teachers, principals, and counselors, by consensus if possible, on how many positive notes will be sent per week, or per month. I believe a parent should receive a positive note about their child at least once a month.

Obviously, because of the large number of students that each middle- and high-school teacher works with, it is easier to send more notes in the elementary schools. However, when a parent receives a positive note from a teacher about their high-school or middle-school student, it is a wonderful surprise. To make it easier for each teacher, the faculty can rotate which class or group of students they will be responsible for at different times during the year. Some schools use parent volunteers to help organize and mail the notes; however, the teachers still write the notes.

Happygrams or Success Cards

"Success Cards" or "Happygrams" are stamped postcards that the teachers use to write the positive notes. The cards have the school name, mascot, or the partnership theme printed on them with a space for a brief message. To help the teachers, the cards are placed in a container in the school office and the staff mails them. While the cards are less personal than the handwritten notes, the convenience is a plus for the teachers. The important thing is that a positive note goes home to all families.

"Refrigerator Door Culture"

By looking at the refrigerator door you can usually learn a lot about the culture of the family. The refrigerator door is a common spot for displaying photographs of family members, friends, and relatives; schedules of special events like concerts, recitals, and sporting events; awards; and other keepsakes. All too often, there is nothing positive from the school related to the child's learning activities such as positive notes from teachers and examples of school work and children's art. Wouldn't it be nice if the school's mission or philosophy was posted on the door as well? Bulletin boards can be used when the refrigerator door is covered. Having too many positive things to display would be a great problem.

Partnership Magnetic Note Holders

Magnetic note holders can be used to help build the "refrigerator door culture." Each family receives a special partnership note holder to post messages, student papers and pictures, invitations, and announcements from school. The note holders are shaped like chalkboards or apples and are inscribed with upbeat messages such as:

- What's Happening in School!
- Good News from School!
- Look What I Did at School This Week!

The note holders are sent home with a positive note or given out at school meetings, conferences, and home visits. The families are told to expect that positive things will follow.

Use of Logos and Mascots

Most families and students identify with the school's logo or mascot. By placing the logo or picture of the mascot on all positive and upbeat communications, the parents recognize that the letter or note is from school and look forward to the correspondence. A logo representing the family/school/community partnership (e.g., hands joining together, an apple, etc.) can be created and used on the communications. These symbols are especially important when attempting to develop a positive communication system.

Vision Statements

When a collective vision for a family/school/community partnership is decided upon, place it on all school correspondence (e.g., Caring and Sharing, Education Is a Family Affair, etc.). Display the vision on sweatshirts, banners, coffee mugs, glasses, and posters. It is important to promote the partnership between the families, school, and community.

Friday Folders

In elementary and middle schools, a good practice for keeping the family informed about the child's progress is to send home a "Friday Folder" containing the child's work for the week. Student papers, projects, and artwork are great communication links. Provide each child with a heavy-duty file folder or large clasp envelope that can be used as the Friday Folder. Get the children involved by having them label and decorate their folders.

Each week, include a comment or suggestion sheet with a place for the parent to sign. Ask the parent to sign the sheet and send it back with the child on Monday.

Remember, children are not always the most reliable carriers of information. If the use of Friday Folders is a regular practice, ask the parents to call the school if a folder does not arrive home with the child.

Signal Stamps

Provide the teachers with rubber stamps to use on papers that they send home. Messages like "Parents Make It Happen" or "Working Together" are stamped on the students' papers to signal the parents that they should look at it carefully. The stamps are used both to indicate outstanding work and to signal papers that need some parent attention for other reasons.

Teachergrams

Use Teachergrams to maintain regular two-way communications with the family about the child's progress, activities, and special events. The Teachergrams are produced in a "half and half " format. The teachers use the top half for their message, whereas the bottom half is used for the parents' responses, comments, suggestions, and questions.

The Teachergrams can be printed as a two-page form using carbonless copy paper for the top page. When the teacher writes the message to the family on the top sheet, the message is copied on the bottom page. The teacher sends the original and keeps the copy for his or her files.

Interactive Homework

Homework is a fundamental aspect of a student's academic development. Research results have repeatedly shown a direct positive correlation between homework and achievement scores, especially if teachers consistently grade and comment on the assignments. In addition to improving academic performance, parents, teachers, and principals view homework as a tool for developing self-discipline, responsibility, and study habits. Homework should be an interactive activity that provides opportunities for continuous two-way communication   between the families and school.

Homework should have a definite and valid purpose and assignments must be clear. The assignments can create or reinforce positive or negative feelings about school and teachers, so the work must be meaningful.

It is important to let parents know how and when to help the child with homework. Encourage the family to establish a good home learning environment with regular times for doing homework. Homework should be a part of the family's lifestyle.

Separate homework from home-learning activities. The two activities are related, but each has slightly different purposes. Homework is designed to strengthen and increase the skills and knowledge presented in the classroom. Home learning activities enhance, reinforce, and expand the school's curriculum. The family should always be looking for "teachable moments"—situations and events that will help the child. For example, putting groceries and supplies away provides a time when parent and child can interact by reading labels, discussing sources of food, and investigating weights and measurements. The parents should work with the teacher to coordinate the child's classroom work and homework with the home learning activities.

It is a good idea for the teachers, especially middle-school and high-school teachers, to send families information about their course curricula, policies, and expectations about homework, how they can be contacted and ways they can help the students.

TIPS

Dr. Joyce Epstein of Johns Hopkins University has developed a program called Teachers Involved Parents in Schoolwork (TIPS). The program is designed to involve parents in the children's homework and learning activities. The interactive and hands-on activities are correlated with the school's curriculum and focus on specific skills in language arts, science, and math. The idea is for the families, school, and children to work together and to make homework meaningful and an enjoyable aspect of family life.

Weekly Assignment Sheets

Some schools send home assignment sheets that list the students' assignments for the week. In a self-contained class, the assignments can be listed by subject on one sheet. In secondary schools, where the students change classes, a separate sheet can be produced for each subject, or each teacher can record his or her assignments on one calendar.

This practice is helpful, but time consuming. It may be necessary to be selective and prepare sheets only for those students who are having difficulties getting their assignments completed. It is important to coordinate the assignments among several teachers.

Progress Reports

Student progress reports are sent to the families on a regular basis. All students receive all reports, not just those who are having difficulty. This is a good way to let the families know how their child is doing in school and it sends a positive message about the students who are doing well.

The reports are sent at a set time (e.g., first three weeks of a semester). When this practice is built into the school's schedule, the family will know when to expect the reports can notify the school if they do not receive one.

Red Flags
If a student is having severe difficulties with a class or subject and is in danger of failing, it is important to call the parent immediately, rather than wait for progress report time. The parents are partners with the school and need to be informed right away about any problems their child is having. Failing to let the families know about any major difficulties the student is having with schoolwork, behavior, or attendance is a cardinal sin.

Home Study Prescriptions

A family resource center in Wichita, Kansas, uses a clever format to inform parents of areas where the child needs help. Forms that resemble medical prescription sheets are used to indicate specific skills to be worked on at home (e.g., reading, math, basic skills, etc.). The teachers determine the skills that are lacking in the classrooms, or in some cases, the needed skills are identified in a math or reading lab. Copies are given to everyone involved.

Figure 7.1 is an example of an Rx home study prescription.

```
                        MATH LAB REPORT


TO THE PARENTS/GUARDIANS OF:_____

GRADE:   K   1   2   3   4   5   6      DATE_____


Your child's teacher has identified the following skills for Math Lab
instruction:
    ___1. Comparisons_____   ___8. Ordinals_____
          (small, large; tall, short)        (First, Second, etc.)

    ___2. Positional                    ___9. Place Value_____
          Relationships_____
          (beside, under, on, etc.)    ___10. Addition_____

    ___3. Patterning_____   ___11. Subtraction_____
          ( △○□ △○□ )
                                        ___12. Multiplication_____
    ___4. Basic Shapes( △○□◁ )/Geometry
                                        ___13. Division_____
          _____
                                        ___14. Fractions_____
    ___5. Sets_____
          (::)                          ___15. Time_____

    ___6. Numerals_____      ___16. Money_____
          (1, 2, 3, etc.)
                                        ___17. Story Problems_____
    ___7. Counting_____
          (by 1's, 2's, 5's, etc.)     ___18. Other_____

Additional practice at home would help your child.  For free activities
you can use at home contact the Parent Involvement Worker at your school
or visit the
                           CHAPTER 1
                     PARENT RESOURCE CENTER
                       1847 N. Chautauqua
                           833-2315


    _____      _____
         Chapter 1 School                School Telephone Number



                              _____
                              Math Instructional Paraprofessional
```

Figure 7.1 MATH-O-GRAM/Rx Prescription for Home Study.

Report Cards

When sending out report cards, include a sheet of instructions on how to read and interpret the card. Explain the grading system and define any symbols and codes used. Also indicate how the families can receive more information and ask questions.

Noncustodial Parents

Many children live with a single parent, or in a blended family, and have a noncustodial parent living elsewhere. It is important to keep the noncustodial parent involved. If there is not a legal restraint, noncustodial parents' names and addresses are placed on the school's mailing lists so they receive progress reports, report cards, newsletters, positive notes, and announcements.

Parent Policy Handbook

Publish a parent handbook that includes such items as:
- school rules and policies
- visiting and volunteer opportunities
- telephone numbers of teachers, guidance counselors, and principals
- a description of the curriculum
- grade-level learning goals and objectives
- instructions on how to read report cards, standardized test descriptions, and schedules
- a summary of extracurricular activities

Newsletters

Send a weekly or monthly newsletter to the families and community groups, with copies to local newspaper editors and radio station managers. A variety of information can be contained, such as what the children are doing in school, ideas for special projects, reports of joint or individual accomplishments, student artwork, announcements, and invitations to come to school for lunch. Before grades are posted, also include an explanation on how to read a report card, and who and where to call if the family has questions or needs more information.

Include such things as a parent education section and a student column that features fun home learning activities, games, jokes, and so on. List resources such as books, pamphlets, videos, cassettes, and software that are available in the school library or family room.

A mini-survey may be enclosed in each newsletter asking for information, suggestions, comments, and concerns. Data on special topics such as discipline, drug and alcohol abuse, teenage pregnancy, homework, the arts, and adult education are gathered. The survey has a tear-off response sheet with a return mailing stamp.

With the advent of desktop publishing, the newsletter can be enhanced with graphics and photographs. Students can be invited to contribute, or a class can be asked to produce the whole issue as a special project. In many schools, several versions of the newsletters are needed so that they are available in the language used at home.

Yearly Calendars

A calendar is a good means of keeping the families and community appraised of the school's program and activities. The calendars can also serve as "thank-you" gifts. Two popular formats are the wall calendar and the pocket appointment book. Each year, the school publishes the calendars and mails or gives them to parents and community members at meetings and home visits.

The school's collective vision or mission statement is displayed on the cover or top of the calendar. The calendar also lists school personnel and telephone numbers. The calendar outlines the school year and shows when special activities and events are scheduled. Besides holidays, teacher workdays, and vacation times, the calendar shows the times and dates for parent-teacher conferences, PTA/PTO meetings, social and cultural events, marking periods, progress reports, report cards, and similar events. Also included are schedules for athletics, drama and music events, science fairs, and other school activities. As a special touch, the students' birthdays may be noted. Suggestions for helping children at home with homework or learning activities, and other ways to be involved can also be inserted throughout the calendar.

Weekly Event Flyers

One-page flyers updating families and the community on events and activities scheduled for the upcoming week, new happenings, special programs and sports results are published each week. The event and activity sheets are sent home with the students, mailed to the families, and distributed at grocery stores, churches, service clubs, and so forth.

Monthly Calendars

Another variation is to produce a calendar for each month, which is then mailed to the families at the end of the current month. The monthly calendars are up to date on meetings and programs, and they are opportunities to remind the families about special events. With the widespread availability of desktop publishing, this approach is both practical and economical.

Parent Partnership Cards

Develop and publish a series of Parent Partnership Cards that provide information and data on education, the school and family/school/community partnerships. The cards address such issues and practices as positive parent-teacher conferences, parent involvement as a measure of quality schools, and the role of community in building family/school partnerships. The cards are handy resources for the families as well as for school and project personnel, parent groups and community/agency/business leaders.

Teacher Parent Bookmarks

A simple way to help motivate parents to play their partner roles is to give them especially made bookmarks as gifts. The bookmarks can be made by hand and decorated or produced with a computer. Examples of messages that can be placed on the bookmarks include:

- Parents Are the Child's First and Most Important Teacher
- Parents Share with Their Children What They Have Learned . . . and the Children's Lives Become Richer Because of It
- Education Is a Family Affair

The bookmarks are made out of tagboard or heavy paper and are laminated so they will last.

How Are We Doing Surveys?

After the first few weeks of each semester, the principal and/or the teachers send a letter to the families asking two important questions:

- How is your child doing in our school?
- Is there anything we can do to make it better?

A self-addressed stamped envelope is enclosed for convenience and to get a greater response. While this adds to the cost, the stamped envelope conveys the importance you place on the families' comments, suggestions, and opinions.

Annual School Reports

Each year, publish an annual report that describes student outcomes, school achievements, and partnership activities. Included in the report are such items as overall achievement scores, attendance figures, honors and awards earned by students, faculty, parents, and community members, and special programs and activities. The annual report is an opportunity to celebrate the past year's successes.

Thank-You and Appreciation Notes

At every opportunity, send thank-you and appreciation notes to parents, community members, faculty and staff who contribute to the family/school/community partnership's mission and the learning community. For example, appreciation notes are sent to parents for volunteering and supporting the school, working with children at home, going on a field trip with their child's class, participating in a reading program, providing enrichment experiences for their child, and so forth.

Regular thank-you note cards can be used, or cards can be printed specifically for this purpose. Below are two examples of appreciation cards:

```
┌─────────────────────────────────────────────┐
│              YOU ARE A WINNER!                │
│                 I appreciate                  │
│  For: _____│
│                                               │
│       _____│
│  Signed: _____ │
└─────────────────────────────────────────────┘
```

```
┌─────────────────────────────────────────────┐
│                 WAY TO GO!                    │
│              I'm impressed with               │
│  Because: _____ │
│                                               │
│         _____ │
│  Signed: _____ │
└─────────────────────────────────────────────┘
```

The notes are about 5″ by 4″ in size, produced in a pad. The school or project's name and logo are printed across the top of the notes and on the envelopes. The collective vision or mission statement can also be displayed.

Remember. You probably cannot overdo this best practice. People want and need to be appreciated and recognized.

Partnership Request and Message Bulletin Boards

Bulletin boards are placed outside the classrooms and/or family room for teachers and parents to leave messages, make requests and share items of interest. Teachers can make requests for inexpensive items needed for the classroom such as tin cans, paper bags, egg cartons, paper rolls, string, newspapers, magazines, soil, boxes, and so on. The family uses the board to announce meetings, share parenting ideas, list items for sale, and seek babysitting and day care. Remember to write the messages in various languages if needed.

Telephone and Electronic Communicating

In the past few years, telephones, computers, Internet, and other electronic devices have revolutionized how we communicate personally and in the business world. The schools are now beginning to take advantage of this technology. There are a variety of options for reaching out and communicating with the families. These best practices are described and discussed in this section.

The telephone, of course, is not a new innovation, but the use of the phone to build partnerships is not a common practice. The "welcoming" telephone call is an excellent means of strengthening the connections between the school and the families and to establish collaborative relationship. Guidelines for planning and making welcoming telephone calls are presented in the following special section.

Telephone Availability (A Comment)

Wouldn't it be wonderful if all teachers had telephones in their classrooms? How many professionals, other than teachers, don't have phones at their work stations? With the advent of beeper services, fax machines, and e-mail, it is amazing that many schools do not even have a private phone available to teachers somewhere in the school throughout the day. I know of some teachers who bring their own cellular phones to school. It seems like the school districts need to "bite the bullet" and network the classrooms for voice and data communication.

The Welcoming Telephone Call

The purpose of the "welcoming telephone call" is to establish or strengthen a two-way communication flow and to build the collaborative relationship between the family and the school. The difference between a connecting and a welcoming and communicating telephone call is more a matter of emphasis of content than process.

The intent of the "connecting" calls is to overcome any barriers that might exist between the families and the school, whereas, the "welcoming" telephone calls focus on building relationships with families that are already connected. Besides welcoming the parents and students to the learning community, the calls provide information and respond to questions.

Both the "connecting" and the "communicating" calls should be positive and upbeat, with the overall intent being to build partnerships between the families and the school. The types and amount of information provided and the kinds of questions asked during the calls will depend upon the nature of the connection with each family.

When preparing to make Welcoming Calls, it is a good idea to review the guidelines for making Connecting Telephone Calls that are provided in Chapter 6. Many of the connecting suggestions can be incorporated into the communication process.

Telephoning When There Are Problems and Concerns

Of course, all calls to the family cannot be positive. Sometimes, the parents need to be informed about difficulties or problems that their children are facing. When problems or concerns arise, contact the family immediately. These early calls will save a lot of grief later on. The parents are partners, and they need to know what is going on.

It is usually best that the teachers make the calls; however, if there are many students to be called, guidance counselors, assistant principals, or parent volunteers may need to help. If parent volunteers are used, they need to be trained in helping and problem-solving skills.

Sometimes, it is more embarrassing for a family to receive the call from another parent rather than from a teacher, but in other cases it could be the other way around. A family member might be able to identify with another parent. This is why it is important to know the parents.

Either way, a problem-solving approach needs to be used. If the issue cannot be resolved over the telephone, a conference should be scheduled with the parent. Suggestions for planning and conducting problem-solving parent-teacher conferences are presented in the "Face-to-Face" section later in this chapter.

Telephone Technology

As stated before, combining telephone technology with other electronic programs has revolutionized the communication process. Through the use of technology, many options such as voice and e-mail, faxes, answering machines, and other computer programs are used to improve the communication flows between the school and families. Examples of telephone technology best practices include:

- teacher voice mail—The school establishes a voice mail system for the teachers and other staff members. Parents and students can call and leave a message. Teachers can place informational messages on the system for the families.
- attendance hotline—The student absences for the day are placed on the telephone and e-mail system each day so the parents can call and check on their child. A computer program can be installed that automatically calls to the student's home when the child is absent. A difficulty with the computer program is that with so many parents working outside the home, the students may get home and erase the message before the parents can hear it. The opportunity for the parent to call in and get the absentee list helps to alleviate this problem.
- homework hotline—This program operates in the late afternoons and evenings. The hotline is operated by teachers, aides, students, parents or community members. Students call to ask questions and get help with homework.
- parent hotline—This program is similar to the Homework Hotline, except it is a service for family members. They can call in for advice on parenting issues, education concerns, and so on.
- assignment hotline—This is a voice mail system where parents and students can get homework assignments. The teachers place their assignments on the system at the end of the day or for the week. The assignments can also be placed on the school's e-mail system. The system can be set up for the families to leave messages for the teachers.
- 24-hour school announcement line—Parents and students are able to get recorded school announcements such as event schedules and school closings. The callers are able to choose from a selection of messages about parenting and educational issues.

The Transparent Model

Dr. Jerold Bauch of Vanderbilt University has been a leader in the use of computer technology to communicate with families. The Transparent School Model, introduced in 1987, was a forerunner. The first system employed answering machines and an automatic dialing system to deliver the messages. Bauch's new Generation 3 systems are integrated voice-messaging computers that manage all the communication functions.

Telephone Trees

Establish a telephone network so families can be contacted without placing the burden on any one parent. One parent calls five parents and each of those five call five more, and so on. Make sure the callers are capable of conversing in the language spoken in the homes they are assigned to call.

The telephone tree allows families to be notified quickly in case of changes in meeting times, early dismissals and closings due to weather, advance announcements of special events and programs, and similar news. The network can be used to ask parents if they would be able to help with field trips and other activities, provide materials for special projects, and assist new families in adjusting to the community.

Parent Attendance Telephone Committee

Parent volunteers are organized to make calls to the homes of students who are absent. Telephone calls are also made to families of students who have been tardy several times. The parent volunteers are from different attendance areas so that they are familiar with the family cultures and languages in the neighborhood.

TV Parent Hour

Some school districts produce a regularly scheduled TV program that deals with issues of interest to parents. Some cities have their own public channel. The "Parent Hour" program can consist of interviews, call-in sessions, student presentations, and training sessions on parenting issues. Shows are staffed by teachers, administrators, counselors, students, and volunteers.

School Video Loan Libraries

Videotape student performances such as athletic contests, plays, band and chorus concerts, dance recitals; classroom and holiday activities; parent meeting and training sessions; and other events and activities. Copies of the tapes are lent to the families to view or copy at home. The parents are notified what tapes are available.

Face-to-Face Communicating

Telephoning, e-mailing, video teleconferencing, and other technologies are great, but meeting face-to-face is the most effective means of communicating. When attempting to form collaborative relationships, teachers, principals, and other school personnel must find ways to interact personally with the parents. The best practices in this section present different ways the school can reach out to communicate with the families. The parent-teacher conference is one of the most common face-to-face communicating activities in the school. However, many times this practice does not foster partnerships with the families. Guidelines are presented for planning and conducting parent-teacher conferences so that they improve communications and build collaborative relationships between the school and the families.

Meetings with Teachers

Establish and publish times when parents can come by and meet with different teachers. Sometimes, certain planning period times may work, or at other times, monthly or bimonthly evening times may need to be established.

Family Corners

A corner in the classrooms can be set up for family members to visit and observe the lessons and activities in the classroom. The area should have a comfortable adult-sized chair or rocking chair and a table to write on. Observing the classroom helps the parents to understand what the children are learning and how they are being taught. Information related to the school day and the curriculum can also be available in the "corner." Visits such as these increase communications and help the family members become better partners. The family corners are also good places for a parent of a disruptive child to come to school for a couple of days to observe the student.

Interaction Contact Points

Establish a routine of being available to greet and talk with parents at typical school contact locations, such as bus stops, student drop-off and pickup locations, and school campus entrances. Soon, families will get used to having a short conversation when dropping off or picking up a child. These informal encounters are opportunities to share successes and concerns, and ask for information. The interactions lay a foundation for other partnership activities.

Significant Person

Make sure that each child is known well by at least one person in the school and let the parent know who that person is and how to contact him or her. With this connection, the student always has someone who can help if he or she is having a problem or concern.

Neighborhood Walks

Walk through the neighborhoods on a Saturday once a month to meet and chat with the parents. These walks will give you a "feel" for how the

---

Clowning Around

In an effort to reach out and communicate with some hard-to-reach families, the faculty at a school in Nashville dressed up as clowns and rode through a housing project in the back of decorated pickup trucks. They held up signs and gave out pamphlets about the preschool and parent involvement program that was being started. As they drove through the neighborhood, they gave the children and family members candy, balloons and other goodies.

The school contacted the families' favorite radio station and asked if they would parade with the teachers in their marketing van. Music and messages about the new program were broadcast over the van's loudspeakers. Hearing the music, the family came out to the street to see the clowns.

Most radio stations are willing to participate with their van in other events, such as family picnics, school festivals and school registrations. This provides a service to the school and gives the station exposure.

families live. The frequency of the walks will depend how well the school and the families are communicating.

Saturday Question and Answer Sessions

Set up information tables at specific locations in the community where people gather (e.g., grocery stores, recreation centers, department stores, union halls, churches, parks, etc.). Encourage the parents to sit for a moment and ask questions about the school. Ask the families about their children.

Clergy Power

Contact members of the clergy and inquire if you may speak to the congregations about how they can get involved with the education of the children. Keep clergy informed by sending them copies of newsletters, announcements, policy handbooks, resource and service directories, and so on.

Community Leaders and Other Powerbrokers

Locate community leaders, politicians, athletics, and others, and ask them to help you by communicating with the families and encouraging them to be involved with the schools. The community leaders can form a neighborhood connection network to talk about programs, activities, concerns, suggestions, and needs.

Working with Immigrant Populations

Families that use English as a second language may need special help integrating into the learning community. Some schools hire outreach staff members who speak the families' language to make home visits to build relationships and talk about the importance of involvement and listen to family concerns. The staff also speaks to groups in the neighborhood at church, temple, and other community meetings.

Parent-Teacher Conferences

As mentioned above, conferences between the parent and teacher, and sometimes the parent, teacher and student, are one of the most common and important communicating events used by the school. Face-to-face interaction is potentially a very effective form of communication, especially for problem solving. However, to reach their potential, conferences must be planned and conducted in a manner consistent with the partnership philosophy. The following guidelines can be used to build and enhance the two-way communication flows between the family and the school.

Noncustodial Parents

Many children live with a single parent or in a blended family and have a noncustodial parent living elsewhere. It is important to keep the noncustodial parent involved. If there is not a legal restraint and if the legal guardian agrees, the noncustodial parent can be invited to participate in the conferences, or a separate meeting can be held.

The Nature and Function of the Conferences

Historically, most parent/teacher conferences occur in the elementary grades. The frequency and number of conferences taper off in the middle grades, and then again in the upper grades. This is not surprising since parent involvement activities in middle school and high schools have traditionally been less extensive. Naturally, I believe the norms need to change so there are strong family/school/community partnership programs operating in all schools.

There are two general types of parent-teacher conferences, which have different, but interrelated functions. The purpose of one type is to discuss the child's progress and activity at school and at home and to explore ways to enhance the child's academic and social development. It is routinely scheduled once or twice a year. The purpose of the other type of conference is to deal with a particular issue, problem or concern. Consequently, it is held on demand by the school or the family. Sometimes, of course, conferences can end up serving both functions. Both types of conferences should be seen as opportunities to build the partnership between the school and the family. However, if they are not planned, organized and conducted properly, the meetings, particularly the second type, can have a negative effect on relationships.

Like other best practices, it is crucial that all parties enter into the dialogues with appropriate attitudes and expectations. Both types of

parent-teacher conferences should be characterized by positive constructive two-way sharing of information, assessment, problem-solving, planning, feedback, and suggestions. For the conferences to have these
characteristics, the family and the school need to be connected, and some
sort of collaborative relationship has to exist between the teacher and the
parent. However, if this is not the case, the parent-teacher conference,
especially the first type, should be approached as an event designed to
reach out to the families and build relationships.

Sometimes, it is appropriate to expand the conference to include the
student, especially in middle and high school. The notion of a partnership
is that all parties are involved and their self-interests addressed. Including
the student in the conference sends a message that the child is an active
partner in the educational process who is responsible for his or her
learning.

Guidelines for Effective Parent-Teacher Conferences

The following are guidelines for making parent-teacher conferences
more productive and for increasing family participation. These recommendations reflect the partnership philosophy and assume the meetings
should be a helpful learning experience for all parties. Because the nature
and dynamics of the two types of parent-teacher conferences are somewhat different, they are discussed separately. The reader will find that
the suggestions under each type often differ more in intent than in
structure.

TYPE 1: REGULARLY SCHEDULED CONFERENCE

The purpose of this type of conference is more than a sharing of
information. The event is an opportunity to discuss the child's progress
and activity both at school and at home, and to explore ways to enhance
the child's academic and social development. The family members
should look forward to the meeting as a time for active participation. It
is not an occasion when the teacher simply reports to the parents. It is a
dialogue between partners.

Even with the regularly scheduled conferences, the parents and teacher
may be nervous and defensive if the purpose, procedures, and expectations are unclear. Many of these anxieties can be avoided, however, if

the nature and function of the conference are understood and agreed upon by the teacher and parent.

Preplanning the Conference

- It is important to take care of any logistical barriers that might prevent the parents from participating and to create a welcoming environment for the family.
- When deciding on the days, times, and locations for the conferences, recognize barriers such as family schedules, factory shifts, church meetings, distance, and so on, that can limit participation. For maximum attendance, schedule meetings when parents will be most available such as early in the morning, late in the afternoons, and evenings. Some schools hold conferences on Saturdays. Teachers should be compensated for the evening or Saturday work with a scheduled day off during the week or extended vacation time.
- Be sensitive to language and cultural differences. Make contact in the home language, and have interpreters available at the conference if the family does not speak fluent English. Asking a parent volunteer from the neighborhood to serve as a translator can make the family more comfortable with the process.
- Have the students write and send letters to their parents inviting them to attend the conference.
- If the conferences are scheduled to be held on the same days school-wide or district-wide, rent a regular billboard to announce the dates and encourage the parents to attend. Some schools own or rent portable electric marquees and place them in the front of the building.
- Collaborate with other staff members to design and print special conference invitations for everyone's use.
- Have childcare available, especially for single parents.
- Make plans to provide transportation to and from the conference, if no other way is available.
- Hold some conferences in the neighborhoods. This is an especially good idea if the families are not well connected with the school. This way, the parents and teachers can meet on the families' "home" territory.

- If the conferences are being held in the classroom, arrange a seating area outside the room where the parents can wait. Hold the meetings away from the door so you and the parent can have some privacy. Have adult-size chairs available for the conference and in the waiting area. Avoid having a desk or table separating you and the parent. Having coffee, tea, and light refreshments available can help set a positive tone for the conference.

Planning the Conference

- When scheduling the conference, inform the parent and child of your expectations and perceptions concerning the purpose of the conference. Recognize that some parents (and the children) may be apprehensive about the meeting. Assure them that you want the conference to be a positive experience for everyone.
- If you think it is appropriate, ask the parents if they would like the child to attend the meeting. Whether the child attends or not, both the teacher and parent should discuss the purpose of the conference with the child before the meeting. After the meeting, encourage the family member to talk with the child about what happened at the conference. You should discuss the meeting with the child as well.
- Suggest to the parents that they prepare questions to be asked at the conference. Provide parents with sample questions such as:
  —How is my child progressing with his or her schoolwork?
  —What are my child's strengths and weaknesses?
  —How does my child interact with classmates?
  —Does my child take part in group projects and discussions?
  —How often will my child have homework?
  —What kind of homework will he or she have?
  —How can I help with homework?
  —Are there regularly scheduled tests?
  —How can I help my child prepare for them?
  —What textbooks is my child using?
  —Are there any supplies or materials that I need to have available?
- Send a list of potential topics for discussion. School-directed topics include:

—curriculum and course content
—services and programs offered by school
—grading procedures
—standardized test programs
—extracurricular activities
—discipline policies
- Child-directed topics might include:
—special health needs or problems
—outside interests and hobbies
—feelings about school
—relationships with brothers and sisters
- Ask the parent to prepare a list of the child's strengths and weaknesses based on their observations.
- Ask the parent to bring any relevant medical information such as allergies, vision, speech or hearing problems, and so on.
- Organize a folder with examples of the student's work, test results, and any notes or questions from the parent.
- Prepare an agenda for the conference. Decide what strengths and weaknesses to share and what information you need from the parent. Identify potential areas to be included in a collaborative action plan between the family and school.
- Identify and inform the family of any concerns or issues you may have before the conference so they can be prepared.

Conducting the Conference

- Before beginning the dialogue, review with the parent (or parent and student) the purpose of the conference and let them know, again, that you wish the meeting to be a positive experience for everyone.
- Inform the family that you consider the conference to be a meeting between equal partners. Always be careful not to patronize, demean, or lecture the parent or child.
- The conference should be conducted with mutual respect and caring for all parties. Concerns, opinions, and suggestions should be shared openly and honestly.
- Be aware that you are a significant person in the life of the child and the family. Choose your words carefully because what you say will have an impact, positively or negatively, on the family.

- Avoid using education jargon. Let the parents know it is appropriate to ask you to explain any terms or concepts that they do not understand.
- Describe the school's expectations of the parents, and explain what the parents can expect from you. Ask for comments and suggestions.
- Be clear about the time available for the conference. Let the parent know that another meeting can be scheduled if more time is needed.
- Share your agenda and ask the parent for additions. Encourage the parent to take notes.
- Discuss the student's progress in your class, focusing on what has been learned since school started. Talk about areas of growth. Ask the parents how they feel the child has progressed and if they have any concerns.
- Describe the child's strengths and weaknesses, beginning with the strengths. Ask the parents to share their list of the child's strength and weaknesses based on their observations.
- Discuss areas of strength as well as areas that need improvement. Ask the parent for comments, suggestions, or concerns.
- Discuss how you and the family will work together to reinforce the strengths and address the areas needing improvement. Describe any additional programs, services, and resources that are available to the child and parent.
- With the parent, develop a collaborative action plan and reach a consensus on any steps that need to be taken to enhance the child's academic and social development both at home and at school.
- Identify how you and the parent will implement the plan.
- Suggest ways the parent can help at home. Prepare a parent worksheet that describes activities that the parent and child can do.
- Suggest to the parents that they maintain a file of their child's schoolwork, outside projects, and activities.
- If appropriate, initiate a learning contract between the child, parent, and teacher that outlines responsibilities and goals for all parties.
- End the conference by summarizing the child's strengths, areas

for growth, and the action plan. Describe and discuss any follow-up procedures that are appropriate.

Follow-up to the Conference

- Make a follow-up phone call or send a note or letter to let the parents know how much you appreciate their involvement and how important it is to the child. Ask if they have any questions or concerns.
- Provide a feedback form that parents can use when they have questions or concerns.
- If appropriate, send a summary of the collaborative action plan. Telephone the parent two to four weeks later to check on the progress and plan the next step.
- Whether the child attended the conference or not, both the teacher and parent should review with the child the outcome of the conference and the action plan.
- Share the outcomes of the conference with other school personnel if needed.

Communicating When Things Are Not Going So Good

In his book, *The Road Less Traveled,* M. Scott Peck argues that once we accept one of the greatest truths, which is that "life is difficult," then things become easier. I believe he means that because there will be problems, we need to learn to be good problem solvers. Our lives will be less difficult if we are good problem solvers. Teachers, principals, counselors, and parents have the responsibility to be good at solving problems for themselves, but also for the children. It is a function of the school and the family to respond to children when they are having difficulties and to help them learn to be good problem solvers. Therefore, the school and families need to be able to communicate effectively when problems arise.

If it is observed that a child is experiencing difficulties or has shown a dramatic change in behavior, it is essential that someone close to the student contacts the family immediately. The school must use a collaborative approach when communicating with the family. By working together, the school and family will have a better chance of solving the problem. It is important that the child knows that the family and school are partners as otherwise he or she might try to work the parent against the school and vice versa. Many times the family wants help but is afraid or embarrassed to ask. In other cases, parents are not aware of a problem.

- Follow through on your part of the action plan.
- Have the students write notes to the parents thanking them for participating in the conferences.
- Recognize the parents' participation in the conferences in the school newsletter and/or over the school intercom.
- Hold end-of-the-year parent recognition ceremonies with awards, door prizes and refreshments.

TYPE 2: THE PROBLEM-SOLVING CONFERENCE

Creating and maintaining a positive atmosphere can be difficult with this type of conference. When a meeting is scheduled by the parents or the school because the child is having difficulties, it is possible that the family, and maybe the teacher, will arrive at the meeting upset and angry. The parents may blame the school for the problem, and the teacher may be ready to blame the parents. Even in the most difficult encounters, the intent should still be to move the issue from a "win-lose" to a "win-win" decision-making approach. By using a problem-solving approach, the conference will more likely have positive outcomes for everyone.

Because of the problem-solving focus of the Type 2 conference, the dynamics of the meeting are apt to be quite different from that of the Type 1 conference. These differences influence the way the meetings are planned and conducted. For example, when conducting the conference, it is very important that those involved (e.g., teachers, principals, and guidance counselors, etc.) have skills and expertise in establishing help-ing relationships, resolving conflicts, solving problems, and mediating issues. Staff development programs in these areas should be provided for the faculty and staff.

The school should also offer similar workshops and classes for the families so they can enhance their skills. These parent education best practices are described in the Coaching Strategy (Chapter 10).

Preplanning the Conference

As for the Type 1 conference, it is important to arrange the meeting so that it is as easy as possible for the families to participate in the best possible atmosphere. Some of the following suggestions are similar to those listed under the Type 1 conference; however, they have been modified to respond in a helping way specifically to distressed families.

- If you are scheduling the meeting, depending on how urgent the issue or problem is, be flexible on the time and date. To help establish a positive atmosphere, be accommodating and hold the meeting when the parents are most available, such as early in the morning, late in the afternoons, and evenings.
- Be sensitive to language and cultural differences. Make contact in home language and have interpreters available at the conference if the family members do not speak fluent English. If the issue isn't too sensitive, and if the parent agrees, ask a parent volunteer from the neighborhood to act as a translator. This can make the family more comfortable.
- If the family is initiating the meeting, try to gather enough information to ascertain the nature of the issue, problem, or concern so you can be prepared to respond.
- Ask the parents if they will need child care.
- Provide transportation to and from the conference, if no other way is available.
- Consider holding the conference somewhere in the family's neighborhood, usually a community center, an apartment clubhouse, social agency conference room, or similar location. You will have to assess the situation to determine if it would be in the family and the school's best interests to hold the meeting in the home. Having the meeting away from the school is an especially good idea if the family is not well connected and/or is alienated from the school. Meeting in the family's home territory can reduce anxieties and signals to the parents that you want to work with them.
- Hold the meeting in a conference room or office so there will be some privacy. Have chairs available for all family members and staff who may be present. It is awkward to have to excuse yourself to locate more chairs after the family has arrived. Offering the parent coffee, tea, or a soft drink can help set a positive tone, and reduce negative feelings.

Planning the Conference

- If the school is scheduling the conference, inform the family of the problem, issue or concern so they can be prepared. Let them know the purpose of the meeting is to solve problems and that you want the conference to be a "win-win" experience for everyone.

- Consult with all appropriate faculty, staff, and resource personnel to get their perspectives on the problem, issue, or concern. Advise them of the upcoming conference and, if necessary, have them attend the meeting, or be "on-call."

- If you think it appropriate, or if conditions warrant, invite or ask the parent to bring the student to the meeting. Whether the child attends or not, both the teacher and parent should discuss the purpose of the conference with him or her before the meeting occurs.

- Before the meeting, if possible, provide the parent with documents and materials related to the issue to be discussed. This includes such things as policies dealing with discipline, grading, the curriculum, and athletic requirements; and copies of student work, exams and projects, referral sheets, absence notes, and progress reports.

- When the parent asks for a conference on short notice, or if the family shows up unannounced at the school with a concern, you may not have time to get the pertinent materials to the parent prior to the meeting. In this case, gather as many of the documents as possible, and have them available at the meeting. It is important to anticipate meetings of this sort, and to have policy materials handy. The need to document inappropriate student behavior and unsatisfactory progress is obvious.

- If you have time, suggest to the parents that they prepare questions and gather information related to the issue or concern.

- Organize a folder with examples of the student's work and test results and any notes or questions from the parent.

- Prepare an agenda for the conference. Organize the information that is related to the problem, issue, or concern. Determine what information you need from the parent.

- Prior to the meeting, discuss and review possible solutions, alternatives, and contingencies with other relevant individuals. Determine what is acceptable and what is not. You will have to have this baseline information before you can make decisions and negotiate effectively.

- Identify potential areas to be included in a collaborative action plan to be agreed upon by the family and school.

- Ask the parent to bring any relevant medical information such as allergies, vision, speech or hearing problems, and so forth.

Conducting the Conference

- If you have called the meeting, describe the problem, issue, or concern with the parents. Let them know, again, that you want the meeting to be a "win-win" experience for everyone. Encourage the parent to take notes.
- If appropriate, review the child's strengths and weaknesses, beginning with the strengths. Ask the parents to share their perception of the child's strength and weaknesses based on their observations.
- Assure the parents that their knowledge of their child is an important part of assessing the problem. A more complete picture of the child's needs and strengths can be obtained by combining their information with the information that you have gathered or observed yourself.
- Review with the parent what you have tried so far and share the results. Describe how what you are seeing in the child's behavior and attitude represents progress. For example, describe how the child is missing out on learning opportunities. Do not dwell on how you, or the other children, are affected. Ask the parents if they have any questions, comments or suggestions.
- If the parents requested the conference, ask them to describe the problem, issue, or concern. Listen carefully and ask the parent if you can take notes. After the parent has finished with the description, ask questions for clarification or additional information.
- Using good helping relationship skills, empathize with the family and inform them that you want to be helpful. Acknowledge that the family's feelings are real and normal.
- Inform the family that you consider the conference to be a meeting between equal partners. Be very sensitive not to patronize or demean the parent or child.
- The conference should be conducted in a respectful and caring way. Concerns, opinions, and suggestions should be shared openly and honestly.
- Choose your words carefully because what you say will have

either a positive or a negative impact on the problem-solving dynamics of the conference.

- Don't talk education jargon. Let the parents know it is appropriate to ask you to explain any terms or concepts that they do not understand.
- When the conference is called to make an assessment or develop a program for a child with special needs, you need to be prepared to:
  —Share anecdotal records used to collect developmental information about the child;
  —Explain to parents why and how early identification and intervention are beneficial their child;
  —Have referral information that describes the law and process and gives names and telephone numbers;
  —Offer to be part of the process to whatever degree they want you to be involved. Remind them that they are in charge. They have the final say about what is right for their child.
- Attempt to identify solutions or alternatives to resolve the issue, problem, or concern. If appropriate, develop a plan of action and reach a consensus on any steps that need to be taken to enhance the child's academic and social development both at home and at school.
- Identify ways you and the parent will work together to implement the plan.
- If appropriate, initiate a learning contract between the child, parent, and teacher that outlines responsibilities and goals for all parties.
- End the conference by summarizing the child's strengths, areas for growth, and the action plan. Discuss follow-up procedures.

Follow-up to the Conference

- Follow through on your part of any collaborative action plan agreed upon in the conference.
- Send a letter describing the outcome of the meeting and the action taken. Emphasize to the parents how important it is to you and the child to have the family working with the school. Ask if they have any questions or need more information.
- If a problem-solving action plan has been initiated between the school and the family, follow-up with a phone call in two to

four weeks. Inform the family about progress on your end, and check on their progress. If necessary, plan the next step.

- Whether the child attended the conference or not, both the teacher and parent should review with the child the outcome of the conference.
- Share outcomes of the meeting with other school personnel if needed.
- Evaluate the conference and action plan to determine if the issue, problem, or concern was resolved in a satisfactory way.

Group Communicating: Meetings, Events, and Activities

Collaboration is the common thread running throughout all of the best practices. Development of the partnerships should be a goal when organizing, scheduling, and hosting meetings, events, and activities for the families. Guidelines for reaching out to the parents and increasing and maintaining participation at open houses, PTA meetings, parent education sessions, social events, and other activities are:

- flexible meeting dates and times—Be flexible when organizing meetings, events, and activities. Try to adjust the dates and times to fit the schedules of the families. Be aware of church or club regular meeting times, work shifts, and so forth, when scheduling meetings.

User-Friendly Room Location

If parents are not familiar with the school, have the meetings in a room located close to the parking lot and the entrance to the building. Have lots of lights on in the room and halls. Not only will this help the families find the room, but arriving parents will be more comfortable when they can see other parents and teachers in the room from the parking lot.

- transportation and child care—Provide free transportation and childcare. Some schools use their activity bus to transport the parents to and from school. Parents, teachers, and students are usually willing to volunteer to supervise activity centers for the children or take care of babies. This can be a project for the high school's early childhood class. Have fun learning activities available to entertain the children during the meeting.
- translators—Conduct bilingual PTA/PTO meetings, if

appropriate. Send notices in parents' native language. Have translators and sign language interpreters available for non-English speaking and hearing impaired family members when appropriate. Enlist school representatives or recruit community volunteers who are fluent in the language of ethnic groups.

- mixing business with pleasure—At family/school "business" meetings, such as PTA and School Improvement Council meetings, and open house, include also some social activities. Serve a meal at the initial meeting, hold a raffle for door prizes, and have some students perform or present a part of the program.
- upbeat startups—Always begin the meetings on a positive note. This will set the tone for the rest of the activity.
- listen to the parents—Draw out parents' ideas. The families need to feel that they are heard. The school should act as an incubator of ideas and be a place where change and innovations are supported.
- an icebreaker—To get parents acquainted at a PTA/PTO meeting, ask them to break into groups that correspond to their children's grade level. The parents tell the other members of the group about their children and themselves.
- invitations—Have the students write letters to their parents inviting them to attend the events. Use a parent telephone tree to invite the families to attend the activities.
- meeting reminders—Stamp a picture of the school's mascot or a smiling face on the child's hand to remind the family of an evening meeting, or make a string necklace with a picture of an animal and a meeting notice. These gentle reminders are helpful.
- one-on-one—PTA/PTO members call and invite family members to attend and arrange for transportation if necessary. They meet and host the parents at the meeting and introduce the parents to other members.
- recognition—Recognize participation with thank-you notes, special tags and ribbons, and similar gestures. "Gold Stars" can be placed on family members' name tags as an award for attendance, service, and so on. Awards and recognition are very special to all parents, and the stars are very important to them.
- photographs—Throughout the year, take pictures of important

and interesting events where students and/or family members are involved. When developing the films, have double prints made and send pictures to the families.

- videotaping events and programs—Events where students and/or families are involved can be videotaped. The tapes are shown at PTA and other family meetings, open houses, and so on. Some schools have created a "tape library" so the families can borrow tapes.

Classroom Orientations

Schedule a convenient time for the families to come to an orientation meeting to learn about the organization of the children's classrooms and the teacher's philosophy, rules, and procedures. The format should be an open discussion between the parents and teachers. It is a good idea for the teachers to post their philosophy outside their classroom door for all to see.

Muffins with Moms and Doughnuts with Dads

Schedule early-morning or late-afternoon informal meeting times with parents. Organize the meetings around light refreshments. No appointments or reservations are necessary and there is no agenda. The time is used for getting acquainted, asking questions, obtaining information, and discussing issues. Catchy titles add to the informal nature of the meetings.

Lunching with Your Child

Invite the parents to come and have lunch or breakfast with their child. Ask the parents to let you know in advance so arrangements can be made. For the parents to come to school and eat with their children demonstrates that they are in partnership with the teachers.

Informal Group Luncheons

Invite the families to school to have lunch or breakfast in the school cafeteria. The luncheons provide an opportunity for parents, grandparents, and other family members to interact with each other and with different members of the school faculty and staff.

These luncheons work well for parents of middle- and high-school students. Usually, these students are not comfortable having their families coming to school to eat lunch with them, but they like to see their parents in school. It is an event that shows the students that the parents are involved.

Grandparents' Day

Grandparents are invited to school to eat lunch or breakfast with their grandchildren and to visit the classroom. Before or after the meal, grandparents can tell stories about their childhood, culture, family life, and vocation to the whole class.

Communitywide Family Events

Organize communitywide family events like reading celebrations, science fairs, student art shows, and so on. Involve churches, synagogues, businesses, service groups, and similar organizations.

The Open House

THE NATURE AND FUNCTION OF OPEN HOUSES

The "open house" is a common group communicating activity. Traditionally, the event has multiple purposes that include bringing the families into the school and providing them with the opportunity to learn about the school program, increasing PTA/PTO membership, and acquainting families with the faculty and staff. Most schools have open houses and the event is a mainstay of many parent involvement programs. Often open houses are well attended, especially in the elementary schools, and usually families are satisfied with the activity.

However, even with the more successful open houses there usually is a segment of the family population that is missing. And, sometimes those parents who do show up do not feel they got what they came for. Therefore, it is important to evaluate our open house procedures to see if they are doing all that we would like them to do. At times, we continue with a program in a certain way because it is the way it has always been done, and no one has questioned if it is meeting the objectives. It is quite possible the event could be improved with some refinements and adjustments.

Traditional Formats

Let us consider what the typical open house looks like. We have all experienced them. Open houses are usually scheduled early in the school year and are held on a weeknight. The event begins with the first business meeting of the PTA/PTO in the school's cafeteria. The benefits of the organization are hyped, the various fundraising activities are described, officers are introduced, and membership is sought. Then the principal talks to the families about the school's programs, activities, discipline, and other policies. He or she emphasizes the importance of the parents being involvement and expresses the hope that they will be available to act as volunteers.

This is the preamble to the actual open house. The families sit politely and patiently, trying to keep their kids quiet and waiting for the real show to start. Finally, someone tells the parents how the open house will be run. Usually, they already know. The rules and procedures are described in detail, and it is announced that at the end of the open house the families are invited back to the cafeteria for refreshments.

In elementary schools, the parents are directed to the child's classroom to meet with the teacher. The teacher talks with the families as a group and informs them about the curriculum, classroom management, rules and procedures and his or her availability to meet with the parents. During the discussion, the teacher may ask the family members to serve as volunteers, chaperones, and classroom "moms and/or dads."

In middle schools and high schools, the parents are instructed to follow an abbreviated form of their child's class schedule. Because there is such a limited time allotted for each class "period," the parents are asked not to ask the teacher questions or try to get information about their child. The families then go to the first period class to meet with the teacher for a brief meeting. The teacher quickly informs the family about the nature of the course and how he or she will manage the class. After a few minutes, the bell rings again and the family moves on to the next class. This process is repeated until the family has moved through their child's entire schedule. After the last period, the parents return to the cafeteria for cookies and punch.

Doesn't this sound familiar? I've been to many open houses as a parent, teacher, and principal. At the high school my kids attended, there was usually a good turnout of parents. Now as I think about it, those who attended were mostly the "middle-class core" that also attended the band concerts, football games, and other activities.

However, I also recall that when I was a principal at a high school in a middle to lower class rural school district there were more teachers present at the open houses than parents. The elementary school was located on the same campus and parents generally turned out for their open houses and not ours. At the time the low attendance did not trouble me too much. I thought it was just the way it was. Now, I realize that we should have made an effort to reach the missing parents.

ADJUSTMENTS AND REFINEMENTS

I do not want to leave the impression that I think the traditional way open houses are conducted is all bad. However, I do believe adjustments and refinements can be made to make them better and to reach more parents.

Self-Interests

As we consider making changes, it is important to identify the typical self-interests of the different parties. The school is interested in informing the parents about the curriculum and programs and would like to have the support of the families. The PTA/PTO would also like the support of the families and increase their membership.

Within this context, the parents' primary self-interest is their child. They would like to know about the curriculum, programs and activities and their child's teacher. The families will want to find out how they can help their child have a successful year. In many cases, the parents are frustrated if they do not have the opportunity to discuss their child's needs with the teacher.

Consequently, it is usually hard to meet the self-interests of the various parties at one open house. If building partnerships with the families is going to be a major focus, rather than opening the year with the usual open house and PTO/PTA business meeting, host a family picnic instead. The families bring part of the meal and the school supplies the rest. When the family population is not very connected, the school can provide the food (see the "family picnic" best practice in the Connecting chapter).

The picnic is an opportunity to welcome the families to the learning community and for people to get acquainted. Students, acting as best buddies or school ambassadors, give the parents and new student tours of the school. The school band and chorus can perform. Transportation is provided to parents if needed. The school and the PTA can set up places where the families can get information and ask questions.

To meet other self-interests, a more typical open house can be scheduled after school opens. The teachers can meet with parents as a group and the PTA can have a business meeting. At the open house, the teachers can let the parents know when they are available to meet with them individually to discuss their child. The school can schedule certain evenings and even weekend days for the parents to meet with the teachers. (The faculty needs to be compensated for the weekend times.) By organizing and scheduling events and activities to meet the self-interests of the different shareholders, partnerships can be formed and strengthened.

Mass Communicating

Sometimes, mass communication best practices are very effective in informing the families and community about the school and partnership activities. Different best practices can be used to display the family and school's commitment to quality education and the importance of working together. The following are some mass communicating best practices.

Letter Campaigns

Letters and flyers from the clergy, civic clubs, chamber of commerce, company publications, hospitals, banks, grocery stores, and so on, can be sent to the students' homes. The letters urge the families to get involved at home and school, attend meetings and workshops, and support the school and its programs.

Bumper Stickers

Provide bumper stickers for parents and community members that send positive messages about the child and the school. Examples of child-directed stickers include:

- I Have a Super Kid at Fort Mill Middle School
- My Child Has Read 100 Books
- I Am a Parent of a Terrific Student at Central High
- I Have Great Kids

A school-directed bumper sticker is also a way to communicate the school's collective vision and positive slogan. This is an inexpensive way to spread the word throughout the school and neighborhoods and to build commitment. Some examples of messages on stickers are:

- On the Move with Morris High
- Catch the Olympic Pride
- Excellence at Eastover Elementary
- Caring and Sharing at Berryhill

Reactionary Stickers

There is one bumper sticker that I have mixed feelings about. It is the one that states, "I have an honor student at . . . School."

I want excellence, but I also covet equity. Excellence without equity is limited. Only a few students are recognized as honor students. These stickers do recognize the child, but do little to build the learning community. There are many kids who are successful, and hard-working, but are not selected as "honor" students. These children and families need to be recognized as well.

This elitism is vented in a reactionary sticker that I have seen that says, "My Kid Just Beat up Your Honor Student." Even though it can be argued that the sticker is supposed to be funny, it sends a serious message. The "honor student" sticker isolates some families from the school.

T-Shirts

Have colorful T-shirts made with a picture of the school mascot or logo and an involvement slogan such as: We Are Good, But We Can Be Better, Education Is a Family Affair, Working Together for Excellence, and so on. Some schools print their mission statements on the shirts.

The T-shirts are sold by the PTA/PTO, School Improvement Council, and other organizations, and are excellent appreciation and recognition gifts.

Billboards

Rent billboards to promote such events as parent-teacher conferences, open houses, career fairs, test administration dates, and school awards.

The Rockingham Schools in North Carolina rent a billboard along the main road on a regular basis, and I always look for it when I drive across the state. The companies that rent the billboards are usually willing to give the schools a reduced price. Also, organizations such as the PTA/PTO, service clubs, and business can be approached to help defer the cost.

Theater Marquees

Contact local theater managers to see if you can post special messages to the families along with the movie titles. Only ask to use them for important meetings and events (e.g., open house, parent-teacher conferences, standardized test dates, graduation, etc.).

Electric School Marquees

Many schools have electric marquees that advertise and promote school and partnership activities and events. Raising money to purchase a marquee is a good PTA, parent group, or class project.

Student Exhibits

A rotating display of projects in many disciplines such as art, science, social studies, industrial arts, and human ecology is a positive educational message to families and other visitors. Besides the school, airports, hospitals, government buildings, education centers, and performance halls are excellent sites for such displays. The exhibits are a chance to show the many talents of the students and are great for public relations.

Omaha's Creative Billboards

The Omaha Public Schools have a wonderful Youth Art Month program where student art is displayed on over fifty outdoor billboards throughout the city. In March, with the cooperation of local businesses and agencies and the Imperial Sign Company, student artwork is chosen to be reproduced by the sign company's artists and displayed on billboards. On each billboard, the name of the student's sponsor and the school's name are listed along with the student's work. The original pieces of art are displayed at a reception for the student artist, parents, principals, teachers, and sponsors.

I was told of one case where the student and her mother did not have transportation so the school took them to the site where her work was on a billboard. The mother and daughter couldn't believe what they saw and they stood spellbound for several minutes. It was an experience that they will never forget.

Notify the parents when and where their child's work is being exhibited and invite them to see the display. Take photographs of the parents and their student next to the display. Include the photographs as part of the exhibit. Give copies of the pictures to the family and also send them to local newspapers.

Door-to-Door Flyers

When organizing such things as partnership and school improvement programs, new family services, building programs, and so forth, parents, students, and community members volunteer to distribute publicity and informational flyers through the neighborhoods. The material is left in newspaper and mail boxes, on door knobs, and in other convenient locations.

Drive-In Windows

Notices about meetings, workshops, parent-teacher conferences and standardized test dates can be displayed and distributed at bank and fast-food drive-in windows.

Newspapers

Publicize partnership and school programs through the daily newspapers. In addition to sending them materials, notify the papers in advance so they can send a reporter to cover the events and activities. Many papers have a family section and a neighborhood news insert. Don't forget the local weekly newspapers. These publications are eager for local school and neighborhood news and they will use photographs.

Local Businesses, Companies, and Industries

Identify businesses and industries where many of the parents work, and ask employers if they are willing to help. Information materials, announcements and invitations can be placed in their newsletters, on bulletin boards, in paycheck envelopes, and so forth. Businesses are usually willing to place posters and bulletins in their store windows as well.

Many organizations are willing to host parent meetings and other activities. Some companies are even willing to establish family rooms with parenting materials in their facilities.

Utility Bills

Natural gas, electric, telephone, TV cable service companies, and similar organizations are often willing to include educational and partnership information, announcements and invitations in their regular billing envelopes. Messages can be printed on the envelopes themselves.

Shopping Bags

Information about the importance of parent involvement and being partners with the school is printed on grocery and department store plastic and paper bags.

Church Bulletins

Contact the clergy in the families' neighborhoods and ask if information about partnerships events and activities can be placed in their newsletter to members.

Poster Contests

Conduct poster contests to publicize open houses, family picnics, and other events. Place the posters in stores and shops around the community. Don't make the contest a big competition thing, but a "win-win" activity: Everyone is a winner and there are lots of small prizes.

COORDINATING: BUILDING ON THE CONNECTING AND COMMUNICATING STRATEGIES

The next chapter presents best practices that can be used to coordinate service and resources to needy families. Programs and activities for supporting the school are also included in this chapter.

CHAPTER 8

Coordinating: Getting It Together

CONNECTING	COMMUNICATING	COORDINATING	COACHING

As stated in Chapter 3, the underlying notion of the family/school/community partnership concept is that everyone is a stakeholder in the education of children. It is essential that social agencies, businesses, industries, colleges and universities, churches, temples and synagogues, hospitals, service clubs, and community members work with the families and schools to enhance the academic and social development of the children. However, as mentioned before, this kind of collaboration is not the norm. For a variety of reasons, many families are not receiving services and resources from the community and school that would help improve their lives and involve them in the education of their children. Besides the families, the schools are not getting the necessary support from the families and communities that they need. Therefore, the Coordinating Collaboration Strategy is designed to:

- increase family awareness of availability of school and community services and resources
- ensure that school and community services and resources are accessible to all families in need
- facilitate the creation of new services and resources
- organize family and community resources to help support the school's curriculum and programs

135

The Coordinating Strategy is a higher order component of the "energy-out" dimension within the Self-Renewing Partnership Model. It is an intervention strategy whereby the school and community implement best practices to make sure resources and services impact on the families in need so they can solve some of the problems they are facing. The assumption is that by improving the conditions at home and taking care of immediate family needs, the parents will have a greater capacity to be involved with their children and with the school. This strategy builds on the foundation formed by the Connecting and Communicating Strategies.

Within this strategy, the school also uses best practices to reach out to the families and community with the intent of increasing their ability and willingness to be involved with the school. Programs and activities such as volunteer programs and school/business partnerships are developed by the school to help build community and family support for its curriculum and programs.

Frankly, I was a little unsure where to present the "families and communities supporting the school" best practices. I decided to place them in this chapter because to get the support they need, schools use the "energy-out" dimension to reach out to the families and community to stimulate their "energy-in" activities. This is an aspect of the "self-renewing" characteristic of the partnership model presented in Chapter 5.

Both goals, "to increase school and community support to families in need" and "to increase family and community support for the school," are included in the Self-Renewing Partnership Model. When the school and community coordinate services and resources so they reach the families, the parents are better able to be involved with the children and the school. As the family and community support for the school increases, the school has a greater capacity to reach out to more families in need.

The next section presents programs and activities where the school and community, especially the social agencies, work together to coordinate and provide services and resources to overburdened families. Many innovative best practices have emerged from this kind of collaboration and these will also be described.

Best practices designed to facilitate family and community support for the school are presented later in the chapter, including programs and activities for reaching out to the families and community to organize and coordinate volunteer and school/business partnerships.

These traditional practices are important, but the aspect of coordinating services and programs so they reach the families in need is a crucial step in solving "the case of the missing families," which is the major focus of this book. The following section presents best practices to coordinate the services and resources.

COORDINATING SERVICES AND RESOURCES

As stated above, all too often, resources and services are not reaching the families that need them. Using the Coordinating Strategy, the school and community combine and "broker" their efforts so the services and resources reach the needy families. Best practices often need to be implemented to overcome barriers that are preventing the parents from being involved with the child and the school. With the hard-to-reach families, the children's educational and social development needs are often pushed into the background as the parents attempt to deal with major problems and concerns such as lack of food, clothing, transportation, housing and health care, unemployment, a child with special needs, drug and alcohol abuse, and teenage pregnancy. The Coordinating Strategy is intended to help resolve some of these issues by intervening with programs and activities.

There are at least four major reasons why services and resources are not reaching families in need. First, the services and resources are not available in the community. Second, families are not aware of existing services and resources. Third, they do not know how to go about obtaining the services and resources. And fourth, social and governmental agencies are very complex and fragmented, and interagency cooperation is not common. With the wide array of provider organizations and the amount of paperwork that is often required to qualify for services, it is understandable why problems exist. What exacerbates the problem is that resources are scarce, and they are spread too thin.

The Coordinating Strategy requires that all parties move beyond their organizational "walls" to work for the common good of children. Coordinating services and resources can be tricky because it involves combining the educational, business, and social service models. However, as Levy and Copple (1989, p. 1) point out, it makes sense for education and human service agencies, in particular, to collaborate because they face common challenges. In many cases, they are trying to help the same people and respond to the same problems. Recently, other authors have called for greater cooperation and collaboration between the school and social agencies; for example, Dryfoos (1994) and Coltoff (1996). In her book, *Full-Service Schools,* Dryfoos discusses the concept of school-based social services, arguing that the time has come for greater cooperation between the schools and agencies. Writing in the National Center for Social Work and Education Collaboration's newsletter, she contends that:

> The concept of full-service schools represents a fusion of several significant movements: improvement of adolescent health, especially addressing the new morbidities of drugs, sex, violence and depression; school reform with its relevant goals of readiness for school, safe learning environments, adult literacy, and parental participation; and service integration for children and families. . . . Connecting these movements together—the need to respond to the new morbidities, the drive to improve educational outcomes, and the thrust toward more comprehensive service delivery systems—provides the argument for full-service schools. (1996, p. 1)

By combining forces, some of the governmental fragmentation can be eliminated. The bottom line is that often several organizations are targeting the same populations with intervention strategies designed to reach similar goals. Dryfoos maintains, and I agree, that the objectives she alludes to above are unlikely to be reached without greatly expanding the scope of services offered in and around the schools.

While it makes sense, collaboration between agencies, institutions, and other organizations does not happen easily. Often, it is difficult to break down the "turf" barriers, especially where resources are limited, which is usually the case. This difficulty is alluded to by the Committee for Economic Development (1994). While supporting the idea of placing social services in the schools, the committee raises the important issue of funding: Who will pay for the additional programs and services? According to the Committee for Economic Development, neither the schools nor the agencies can be expected to fund the programs and services solely out of their budgets.

These kinds of issues are difficult to resolve, but the school and community must do so. Many communities have moved to another level and are now coordinating their resources, services, and expertise though the schools. Various agencies are working together to make sure that families have access to health and social agencies, food, housing, and employment services. Usually, to form these new alliances, additional staff need to be hired.

Whether the services and resources are provided on campus or whether the school acts as a broker to link the services and resources to the families, both the school and the collaborating organizations must assume new roles and responsibilities in these "restructured" relationships. As a result, school districts and social agencies have to provide training for faculty and staff to teach them how to work in concert with each other.

Coltoff (1996) argues that: "A significant professional crossover is needed in preparing educators and social workers, so that there is no longer an insular view that one is over here, and one is over there" (p. 4). He adds: "We still have difficulty when we get into territorial issues and professional competencies. Shared training is needed, and partnerships are needed. The goals we want to achieve in public schools, not only ought not be done by one institution, but probably cannot be done by one institution" (p. 4).

The Park and the School

In one middle school that I visited in a poor district in California, a county park adjoins the school property. The school had a very limited area for outside activities and asked the County's Parks and Recreation Department if they could use the park for some of its student and family programs. The department initially turned down the request. However, after several meetings between school and government officials, parents, and community leaders, the county agreed to let the school use the park for its activities. In return, the school agreed to help with the maintenance and improvement of the park. Now, the Parks and Recreation Department and the school are working together to provide even more joint programs and activities. Having the park used more fully helps everyone. It turned out to be a win-win situation.

Reaching out to help the parents with some of their problems can go a long way toward strengthening connections and building collaborative relationships by alleviating feelings of alienation and disenfranchisement from the school and society in general. By containing some of these basic problems, the families will be in a much better position to be partners with the school and be involved with the education of their children.

Best Practices

The following programs, events, and activities are organized so that the least labor-intensive appear first, followed by those that are more comprehensive and, therefore, require more effort to implement. For example, some best practices for helping the families are as simple as

publishing directories listing and describing available services and resources. Other programs are quite complex. For instance, a comprehensive intra-agency school-based center is described where a variety of
services are rendered to the families at one location in the neighborhood.

It is crucial that various stakeholders (parents, teachers, principals,
community leaders) know what services and resources are available and
how to access them. For services and resources to reach the appropriate
families, everyone involved with the families needs to know what is
available and how to get it. Developing this understanding reaps large
dividends and does not require a great deal of money or personnel to
accomplish. The following are some best practices to accomplish this.

Services and Resources Directory

Develop and publish a directory of social and community service
agencies that includes a description of programs, addresses, telephone
numbers, and names of representatives to be contacted. The directory
lists social service agencies, crisis centers, health clinics, service clubs,
and school resource centers. In addition, it includes such facilities as food
pantries, clothing centers, reading and language centers, museums, nature centers, and libraries.

Distribute the directories to teachers, principals, counselors, and social
service representatives so they can work with the parents and help
"broker" the services when needs are identified. Ideally, the directory
should be made available to the families so that they know what is
available. Businesses and service clubs can be approached to help with
the cost of publication. Often these organizations are willing to use their
expertise to organize and publish the directory.

Services and Resources Yellow Pages

A variation of the directory booklet is to publish "Yellow Pages,"
which lists various community programs and organizations. This format
is economical, eyecatching and easy to use. Holes are punched in yellow
pages so they can be stored in a notebook.

Electronic Directories

Place the directory of services and resources on-line so that it is easily accessible to school and community personnel. List e-mail addresses, telephone, and fax numbers so school and community personnel can network with each other. An electronic newsletter can be sent out to keep users informed about changes, new programs, and ideas.

Family Forums

Schedule informational family meetings on such topics as Social Security benefits, Aid for Dependent Children (AFDC), food stamps, how to get electric power service restored, available health services, and how to obtain domestic violence help and counseling. At the meetings, family members meet school and social service representatives, and are able to ask questions about programs and procedures.

If the parents are not very connected with the school, or if the school is located a distance from the families, it is a good idea to hold the forums in the neighborhoods; for example, in churches, community centers, or business or hospital conference rooms. Housing authorities are usually also willing to host the meetings and help in notifying the families. Information about the forums can be sent home from school in newsletters, be posted in grocery and drug stores, and given to parents when home visits are made.

Service and Resource Referral Committee

A group of parent and community volunteers are organized to be an informational and referral service for families who need childcare, after-school and weekend recreation programs, cultural events, transportation to the library, and other social services.

School/Community Coordinating Committee

A committee made up of teachers, administrators, guidance counselor, social workers, and parents is established to help coordinate services and resources to needy families. If the school is fortunate enough to have a family/school/community coordinator, that person can chair the committee. The committee is notified when a teacher, principal, counselor, parent, or coordinator discovers a family facing a problem that is preventing them from effectively playing their parenting roles.

After discussing and investigating the family problem, the committee designs a collaborative action plan and identifies best practices to help the parents solve the problem. The committee members are well informed about the nature of the services and resources and the procedures for making them available to the families.

The Mother with a Big Stick

At one school, a teacher looked out of the window and saw a mother beating her two young children with a stick. The teacher got the principal, and they stopped the woman and took the stick away. It was obvious that the mother was "spaced out" on drugs. They took the woman and the child to the office and telephoned the school's social worker. The family/school coordinator was called to the office and an impromptu community/school coordinating committee meeting was held when the social worker arrived. Because they were prepared, the Department of Social Services was able to care for the woman's two children, and the mother was taken to the hospital. The next day, the mother was admitted to a drug rehabilitation program and the children placed in foster care. The mother had been participating in a parent education program at school. When she was released from the rehabilitation center, she continued coming to the "parent club" meetings, even after the children were taken from her.

This is a real success story, because eventually the mother overcame her drug addiction, and the children were returned to her. Her involvement with the school expanded. In fact, eventually she was hired to be one of the teachers for the parent club's literacy program. Without the swift action by the school/community coordinating committee, both the children and the mother would probably have been lost.

Types of Family Centers

A wide variety of "family or parent centers" are being established in the schools and in the neighborhoods to reach out to the families. These exciting new settings for working with and helping families have been spawned by the recent interest in building partnerships between the families, school, and community. Establishing a family or parent center sends the families the message that they are valued and the school, and community want them as partners.

An array of facilities could be categorized as "family centers." These are places where family members can go for information, training, support, resources, services, and even, food, clothing and shelter. The centers have such titles as family rooms, family resource centers, family service centers, and family food pantries, and clothing centers.

As discussed in Chapter 1, because of the variety of family structures and responsibilities, I favor using the word "family" over "parent" when categorizing things to acknowledge the total family's involvement. Using the all-encompassing term "family" extends a welcome to parents, surrogate parents, grandparents, aunts, uncles, siblings, and other relatives to the facility. On the other hand, if you believe the families, school, and community are more comfortable with the term "parent," and it is still understood that the programs and activities are for the whole family, I would probably use that term. The idea is to communicate, not confuse.

Usually, the centers are located in or near the school, but sometimes they are housed in the neighborhoods or at a central location away from the school. These locations may be more convenient to get to and can help make connections with the families. This is particularly important for those family populations who are not comfortable in a school setting. Located away from the school and in the neighborhood, the center is perceived as inviting and accessible.

The "Family" Chair

Some states (e.g., Kentucky) require school districts to have a family center in each school. When visiting different successful centers in Louisville, I was told that at one school, not in Louisville, a chair was placed in the lobby of the school in an effort to comply with the requirement. The chair hardly qualified as a family center. However, the story illustrates the need to enlighten some educators about the importance of family involvement.

As indicated above, family centers come in all sizes and shapes, ranging from a single room in a school or community center, to a separate building. Likewise, the programs and services offered by the centers vary greatly. Some are limited in scope, others are very comprehensive. For example, a center can be a place for the families to socialize, obtain materials, and take parent education and other classes; or it may be a site at the school where the various social and community agencies provide a wide range of family services.

Depending on how they are organized and focused, family centers have the potential of serving as vehicles for carrying out all four School/Community Collaboration Strategies: Making connections with the families, establishing communication flows, coordinating resources, and coaching the parents.

Each of the School/Community Collaboration Strategy chapters includes discussions on how family centers can be used as sites to implement best practices relative to the particular intervention strategy. For example, family rooms located in the schools that are designed to help connect and communicate with the family members are described in the Connecting and Communicating Strategy chapters (Chapters 6 and 7).

A major function of most family centers is to provide parent education classes, workshops, and support groups. As a result, the centers offer programs and activities designed to enhance Parent Partner Role skills and knowledge. Best practices for using family centers as coaching sites are presented in Chapter 9.

The primary function of the school- and neighborhood-based family centers described in this section is to coordinate and provide services and resources to needy families. The type of center, or centers, appropriate for a particular community depends upon many factors and variables such as need, funding, demographics, and family populations. It is important to be adaptable, flexible, and resourceful when attempting to implement any best practice, including those designed to coordinate services. Otherwise, you can become frustrated and discouraged.

Parent or Family Rooms

While the primary function of this kind of center is to connect and communicate with the families, family rooms are excellent settings for providing information and instruction about services and resources. Social agency representatives, doctors, dentists, police officers and domestic violence and drug abuse counselors can come to the school and provide information and support. Programs such as "Question and Answer" sessions with a dentist are very valuable. In some cases, parents have never had the opportunity to talk with a dentist and know little about dental care.

Food Pantries and Clothing Centers

Food pantries and clothing centers are established so families in need can obtain emergency supplies. They are located in the school, neighborhoods, or a central location. In schools, they can be located near the parent room, family resource center, main office, or in a spare room or trailer. In the neighborhoods centers and pantries can be housed in community centers, churches, and so on. Some school districts have one central location (e.g., the staff development center, warehouses, etc.). Obviously, the centers and pantries need to be located where they are easily accessible and where families are comfortable going.

Food pantries can be stocked with canned goods and commodities such as flour, sugar, salt, and spices. However, some pantries are also organized to offer prepared foods. Many times, grocery stores, delicatessens, cafeterias, and similar businesses discard macaroni and cheese, bread, stews, salads, and puddings at the end of the day even though it is perfectly good. These items are thrown away because they cannot be sold the next day.

Some schools and communities have been able to make arrangements for the stores and restaurants to donate the food items to the pantries. There are health and liability issues to be dealt with, but with some effort it can be worked out. In addition, federal legislation was just passed to enable stores to give food away more easily.

Schools, service clubs, PTA/PTOs, and other groups hold clothing drives or go to garage sales to supply the clothing centers. Usually, getting people to donate clothing is not a problem. Organizing the clothing, and making sure it is in good condition, takes a lot of time and effort.

SHARE: A Food Cooperative

A volunteer community development organization called SHARE-Southern California is a cooperative that provides members an opportunity to purchase food packages at discount prices while they participate in a community and individual development program. Each member must volunteer at least two hours of community service each month for each package purchased. A monthly food package valued at $30–35 is offered for two hours of service, and $13. Around the first of the month, the participants pay in advance when they order their packages. At the end of the month, members bring their receipts and proof of community service and pick up their food. The food is available at a reduced price due to volume buying, special contacts with growers and manufacturers, and the purchase of bulk goods which are repackaged at the warehouse. The food packages are different each month and include such items as chicken, turkey, fish sticks, cabbage, broccoli, tomatoes, cantaloupes, apples, pasta, flour, vitamins, and cake mixes.

The cooperative has a network of host organizations, staffed by volunteers, that order the food, collect funds, and distribute the food. The host organizations are churches, schools, and community-based organizations.

In some cases, the SHARE program is an aspect of the school's volunteer program. Family members help in the classrooms and around school for their community service credit. The volunteers assist other parents by picking up their packages when they arrive from the warehouse. Not only does the program provide food at lower prices, it also develops individual partner skills and responsibilities, and supports the school. This is a good program for senior citizens.

While parents and community members can be enlisted to help supervise the centers and pantries, someone, usually paid, has to be in charge. A room full of clothing and shoes that is unorganized and piled in boxes is of little use to anyone.

Similarly, with the pantries, the food must be fresh and the environment clean. Ideally, the clothing centers and pantries should be directed and coordinated by someone working with the families (e.g., a family/school/community coordinator, school social worker, community agency worker) or an individual hired specifically for the task.

Quite often, it is necessary to provide families with transportation and babysitting for them to be able to use the centers and pantries. One coordinator, in an effort to empower the parents, used the trips to the clothing center as "teachable moments." When she provided transportation to the center, she asked the parents to volunteer in the classroom or enroll in a parent education class. In this way, she linked the free service to the development of responsibility and commitment.

School-Based Family Resource Centers

The primary function of this type of center is to link needy families to services and resources in the community. The goal is to enhance the students' abilities to succeed in school by helping children and their families to solve problems and meet their basic needs. The center directors, who are often teachers, work closely with the school faculty to assess needs and to coordinate the services. The director and his or her

---

The Battered Wife

When I was visiting a family resource center in Kentucky, the director related to me how she was able to respond to a family in crisis. One morning when she arrived at the center, which is located in a portable classroom outside an elementary school, she found a mother and her two children sitting in a car. The mother was waiting for her and had come to get help. The night before, her husband had beaten her and threatened to kill her and the children. She was afraid and did not know what to do.

The director contacted a women's center, the police, the domestic violence court, and a social worker. During that day, she was able to place the woman and the children in a shelter, had an injunction order issued against the husband, obtained financial assistance, and arranged for a police escort to protect the woman so she could retrieve some belongings from the house. This coordinated response would never have happened without the network the director had established with the various agencies in the community.

staff members serve as advocates for the families. In this type of center, the social service agencies collaborate with the center staff, but services are not based at the center. The director builds a rich network of agencies that can be called on when needed.

School-Based Limited-Service Family Centers

Some centers have a few agency representatives located at the school site that collaborate with the center director and school faculty and staff. Social workers, Communities-in-Schools counselors, youth agency representatives, and others have offices in the school where they can meet with the students and families. These "outside" people become an integral part of the faculty and staff. They can respond quickly when problems arise and needs are identified.

I visited a family resource center located in a California middle school that had agency representatives assigned to the school. Juvenile court representatives, county attendance officers, Communities-in-Schools, and other social agency representatives were assigned to the school to counsel and advise the students and families. The center director reached out and worked with the families to get them involved, and coordinated the services and resources.

In addition to her other responsibilities, the director supervised the school's in-house suspension program. Most of the students sent to her for disciplinary reasons were prime candidates for the agency representatives. By coordinating their programs, the school and agencies were able to help many of the adolescents before they failed in school, dropped out, or got into real trouble.

The Camping Trip

The week I visited the school program discussed above, the director and agency representatives were taking some of the students on a weekend camping trip. Most of the students had never been camping before. The trip was intended to provide the children with new skills and knowledge, but most important, it was designed to help the students to build trusting and caring relationships. This is an excellent example of how agencies and the school can work together to help the children and prevent problems from occurring.

School-Based Full-Service Family Centers

At this type of center, families can obtain services and resources on site. The families can do "one-stop shopping." An example of a very comprehensive intra-agency school-based center is located in Louisville, Kentucky. This collaborative endeavor, called the Neighborhood Place, was established in conjunction with the school and county to deliver services to the parents and children in a lower socioeconomic community. The center serves as a main access point in the service delivery system by identifying, coordinating, and rendering existing services. If services are not available on site, the center serves as the catalyst for the development of such resources. Core services available at the Neighborhood Place include:

- health services that include school physical examinations, immunizations, health education, and other services
- childcare that includes infant and toddler care, part-time before and after school care, summertime care, and a Parents' Day Out program, which is coordinated with the local churches
- a "Families in Training" program that includes parent support groups, nutrition education, family empowerment sessions, behavioral problem programs, and literacy classes for parents
- mental health, and drug and alcohol abuse counseling that includes assessment and evaluation, individual therapy, group sessions, recovery groups, and access to specialized child and family services, such as acute psychiatric and domestic violence care
- family financial assistance programs that include food stamps, aid to financially dependent children, subsidized daycare, and emergency financial assistance
- employment services that offer counseling, job training, mentoring, pre-employment skill development, and part-time employment

The Neighborhood Place is funded by the county government and the school system. This type of center is very effective and cost efficient. An example of how well this interagency approach works is illustrated by the way the center deals with immunization.

Before any child can attend school, the parent must provide evidence that the child has been immunized for different diseases. If the parent fails to do so, the matter is turned over to the courts, because the child is not attending school. As you can imagine, the time and money involved in all the referrals and court costs is enormous. At the Neighborhood

Place, the child can be examined and immunized at school before enrolling. The child and families are screened for other problems, and if any are identified, social service and school representatives are available at the center to provide counseling and resources. Because of the Neighborhood Place, the problem of children arriving at school without their shots has virtually been eliminated in this community.

The Door—A Center of Alternatives

The Door, a center for young people, aged 12–20, located in lower Manhattan, provides health, human, educational services and creative and physical arts in a stimulating environment. The Door was founded in 1972 by a group of volunteers who "believed in cutting through the bureaucracy surrounding youth services, and treating adolescents as whole individuals with a variety of needs and hopes." The program operates in a building that was formerly a department store, and a professional staff and over 100 volunteers come together to provide a range of training, services, and counseling for young people.

A wide range of services is offered at the Door, including medical, legal, counseling, social, health education, sexual/health/family planning, nutrition and prenatal, GED preparation, tutoring, computer training, career counseling, college preparation, leadership training, music, drama, dance, weightlifting, and basketball. The Door has been cited as an exemplary model for serving at-risk youth.

When I visited the Door several years ago, I was struck by the excitement and caring attitudes of the volunteers and staff. They are able to reach out to a very fragile at-risk population and provide much-needed services and opportunities. The Door's address is 555 Broome Street, New York, NY (212) 941-9090.

COORDINATING FAMILY AND COMMUNITY SUPPORT

While many families are not getting the services and resources they need, many schools are not receiving the support they need from the families and communities. As discussed in Chapter 2, typically, only a small percentage of the families, and very few community members, are involved with the school.

As I argue for reaching out the parents to get them involved at home, I do not want to appear to diminish the importance of family and community support for the school. Support for the school's curriculum, programs, and activities is essential. Therefore, the schools must intervene and reach out to stimulate family and community support.

Many times parents, community members, businesses, service clubs, and other organizations are willing to help out, but no one asks them to. Or they lose interest when they try to be involved if the support is not coordinated in an appropriate manner. Part of the problem is that the schools, community members, and parents are not sure about what can be done and how to do it. Since community and family support for the school is an important aspect of a family/school/community partnership, all stakeholders have to understand of the "what, why, and how" of being involved.

Best Practices

This section describes programs, events, and activities the school can use to increase family and community support. As with most best practices, the positive outcomes from the interventions can be far reaching and overlapping. For instance, developing a volunteer program can help the school perform its duties, while also supporting the families in their parenting roles. That is, through assisting in the school, the parent volunteers will learn and improve their skills and knowledge. The outreach best practices have self-renewing qualities that affect the families, school, and community in positive ways.

Volunteers

Volunteering is one of the most common "energy-in" dimension activities. Historically, the idea of parents coming to school to help in the classrooms and around the school is almost synonymous with the notion of parent involvement. When people are asked to give examples of parent involvement, volunteering to assist in the classroom, on field trips, at ball games, and around the school is always near the top of the list. The traditional roles of "homeroom moms" in the elementary schools or "parent chaperones" at the middle-school dance are part of the American lore. As a result, calls for more parental involvement are often centered on getting more family members to work in the schools. (A more detailed discussion of the traditional parent involvement approach can be found in Chapter 1.)

In a family/school/community partnership, the parents need to be deeply involved in the curriculum, instruction, and school life. Therefore, volunteering is an important activity. This section presents best practices that focus on engaging family and community members as tutors, mentors, teacher aides, storytellers, career advisors, and curriculum resource people. Guidelines for designing and implementing a volunteer program are also presented.

Volunteer Roles and Activities

There are a variety of ways that volunteers can be helpful. For instance, volunteers can:

- assist classroom and resource teachers in reaching classroom and individual student goals
- share a special talent or expertise with the school, a classroom, or an individual child
- help with the operation of the library, media center, computer labs, and so forth
- relieve or assist teachers with many of the noninstructional duties and responsibilities
- assist the staff with the daily operation of the school and offices
- assist the schools by refurbishing the playground, building playhouses, painting murals, fixing furniture, and so on
- tutor and mentor students
- provide assistance to a child with special needs
- work with students on cooperative learning projects
- supervise children in the computer lab
- prepare bulletin boards and displays
- produce a family/school/community partnership newsletter
- check attendance and call parents about absent or tardy students
- organize fundraisers
- act as chaperones for field trips, dances, and other events
- teach a class session or lead a support group
- answer the office telephone, send faxes, and copy materials

The following is a discussion of some volunteer roles and best practices.

TUTORS

Many family members, retired persons, university and college students, church members, business and industry employees, and service club members are willing to engage in one-to-one and small-group tutoring activities. For example, they read to the children and have the children read to them; help with math, science, writing, spelling, grammar; or show students how to use the computer and accompanying software.

It is important to offer appropriate training to the tutors before they begin working with students. Workshops for volunteers cover such topics as curriculum, learning styles, human development, self-concept, reading, math, and language development. Individual training sessions deal with how to work with particular age children (e.g., middle grade students); helping children with learning difficulties; verbal and nonverbal communication; being yourself; and attending to the needs of the children. The teachers provide the volunteers with their strategies for teaching reading, developing math skills, and so on.

Math Superstars

The Florida Department of Education has developed a program to provide math enrichment for grades 1–6. Math Superstars volunteers provide the motivation, implementation, and total support for the program. Designed to enhance problem-solving abilities and higher order thinking skills, the program is strongly endorsed by teachers. The Department reports that students who were weak in these areas showed improvement after participating in the Math Superstars program.

MENTORS

Volunteers can act as "significant persons" and "big buddies" for the students. Mentors advise, counsel, encourage, and support the students in their endeavors. If necessary and appropriate, they can also serve as a liaison between the parents and school. The mentors visit regularly with their students.

The Woman in the Power Suit

The NationsBank in Nashville is in partnership with an inner-city school. One of the partnership activities is a "Santa Tree" party for kindergarten and preschool students, all from very poor families. Each of the bank employees volunteers to be a big buddy. They are given the name and age of a student and purchase a gift for the child. Just before school lets out for Christmas vacation, the bank's shuttle bus picks up the students and teachers at school and transports them to the downtown bank.

The volunteers find "their" children, have refreshments and get acquainted. The presents that are placed under the Santa Tree are given out. The children and the volunteer open the presents and enjoy the gifts together. It is a very emotional and happy experience for the volunteers and the children.

One year, after the gifts had been opened, I noticed a woman on the floor playing with a child. She was on her knees, helping the child with his red truck. Fully decked out in her "power blue" suit, and without shoes, she was totally absorbed and entranced with the child. Gone was the corporate image. It was obvious that something special was happening between an adult and a little child.

SATELLITE TUTORING CENTERS

Typically, volunteers come to school to tutor, but the schools and communities can reach out to the families and set up tutoring centers in the neighborhood at community centers, businesses, or churches. The students and volunteers meet at the sites after school, in the evenings or on the weekends. Some programs also operate during the summer months. The tutors are parents, community members, high school and college students, and others.

While some children may voluntarily choose to go to the tutoring sites, others are recommended by the teachers. The family and the school decide together to place the student for tutoring and coordinate the effort. The tutors work closely with the classroom teachers, who diagnose weaknesses, give assignments, make suggestions, and review progress.

An Inter-Church Effort

An elementary school in Charlotte, North Carolina, located in a lower socio-economic community, set up a satellite tutoring program with a nearby church and a partner church from a more affluent part of the city. The tutors are members of both churches. They work with the children two days per week, for two hours in the afternoon after school. After school is dismissed, the students are transported by bus to the church. Snacks and drinks are provided for the students.

Students who need extra help are identified by the teachers, and the parents are contacted to tell them about the program. Agreements are made between the parent, student, and teacher that attending the tutoring sessions is a good idea. The students or parents can also initiate the tutoring. The tutors work closely with the teachers, so the students will always have homework or other assignments when they arrive. This cooperative effort has proved to be a rewarding experience for all.

FRIENDLY LISTENERS

This is a reassurance telephone call program. Volunteers are matched with elementary and middle-grade students who are either "latchkey" children or anyone who wants contact with an adult. The children call their volunteers if they have a problem or if they want to talk when they return home from school. Not only do the children "check in" with the volunteer, the phone calls provide an opportunity for both to share the happenings of the day.

Meetings are set up by the school for the volunteers, students, and parents to get together and become acquainted. These meetings are also an opportunity to begin to develop a relationship. Screening and training is provided for the volunteers, who are tied into the network of school service personnel if needed. This is a good activity for any volunteer, but particularly so for senior citizens, especially for those who are home a lot.

Hug Center

An elementary school in New York City has a "Hug Center" in their family room. Any time that a student is feeling down, having problems, or gets a little bump on the playground, with permission from the teacher, the child can come to the family room and get a "hug" from one of the parent volunteers. Usually, after some tender, loving care, the student returns to class, lunch, the playground, or other activity. If the problem seems to be more serious or is chronic, the volunteer will send a message to the school counselor or the student service team. The children know there is always someone who cares at the hug center.

AIDES

Volunteers assist teachers in the classroom with clerical duties, discipline, food service, and cleanup; ride school buses; help supervise halls and playgrounds; and work in the office copying, collating, answering telephones, and greeting visitors. It is important to match the aides to the kind of jobs that they are good at and want to do. Aides should not feel that they are being "used" by being assigned to just menial jobs.

STORYTELLERS

Parents, grandparents, aunts, and uncles tell students stories about their childhood, family histories, cultures, and vocations. The stories provide links between the home and school, between cultures, and between generations. The storytelling can be part of Grandparents' Day. Grandparents are invited to school to eat lunch with their grandchildren and before or after lunch they can tell stories to the whole class.

FAMILY "SONGSTERS" AND DANCERS

Parents, grandparents, aunts, and uncles can also be invited to come to school to sing, dance, and/or play instruments from their childhood, family life, culture, and other experiences. They can teach the children the songs and dances and show them the instruments. The volunteers talk with the students about the meanings of the dances and songs, and the origins and history of the instruments.

VOLUNTEER CHEFS

Family and community members come to school and tell the children about foods and special dishes from their childhood, families, and culture. If facilities are available, the parents, grandparents, aunts, and uncles cook different foods for the children to taste or prepare a whole meal for the students to try.

SENIOR CITIZENS

Senior citizens are a great volunteer source that is often untapped. This population is a storehouse of rich experiences and knowledge that needs to be shared with the children and parents. Not only do senior citizens usually have time that they are willing to share, but working in this capacity is a meaningful experience for them. Volunteering gives them an added sense of purpose: By being involved with the students and teachers, senior citizens are less likely to feel isolated and along.

Senior citizens make ideal storytellers, mentors, tutors, and general helpers. Some school districts have organized intergenerational programs designed to share skills, knowledge, and experiences between old and young. Senior citizens can tell the students about their childhood, culture, way of life, and view of the world. They can share interesting hobbies and talk about their professional careers. This sharing can break down any stereotypes and barriers that may exist between generations when there is only limited contact. By working together, the generations can learn to cooperate rather than compete.

An example of an intergenerational program is an organization called SCOPE (Students, Community, Older People, Parents, and Educators), located in Madison, Wisconsin. Volunteers act as room grandparents, tutors, arts and crafts teachers, and pen pals, and give seminars on history and aging.

The volunteers, in turn, receive health screening, transportation, and meals. Also, senior citizens, living alone, receive daily telephone calls from middle school students. The students also provide snow shoveling and spring cleanup services to SCOPE participants.

Grandma and Grandpa Staugner

Several years ago the grandparents of a student in my significant other's kindergarten class started coming to school each week to have lunch with their grandson. The lunches quickly expanded to longer visits to the classroom. Grandpa and Grandma Staugner read to the children, listened to the children's stories, and at times comforted the students if they were having problems.

The next year, when their grandson moved on to the first grade, Grandma and Grandpa Staugner continued to volunteer in the kindergarten class. During the second year, Grandma Staugner unexpectedly became ill and passed away. After a brief mourning period, Grandpa returned alone to help in the classroom. The children wanted to know where Grandma was. Grandpa talked with them about the loss of his wife, which helped the students understand about death and helped him to deal with his grief. This was an experiential lesson in grief and death.

Grandpa said that the students provided him with "an anchor" and an opportunity to continue with his life. He continued to be a volunteer in the school even after we moved to another city.

FAMILY/COMMUNITY TALENT TANK

Within the families and community there is a vast array of talent just waiting to be used. To tap this resource, family and community members are asked to enroll in a program that provides them opportunity to share their expertise, talents, interests, and careers with the students. These programs go by names such as family/community talent tanks, speakers' bureau, and community resource program. The families and community members are surveyed to find volunteers who are willing to serve the schools by sharing their experiences and knowledge. A resource file is developed that lists the volunteers' names, specific skills and knowledge, and days and times when they are available. The community resource program acts as a clearinghouse for all teacher requests and as a liaison between the volunteer and teacher.

The resource volunteers are used to augment the curriculum, introduce special topics, and expose students to various careers. Talent tank members come to school to provide enrichment and supplementary activities. They work in the classrooms, with small groups, and make special presentations to large groups of students and the whole school.

These programs can be offered during and after the school day and on the weekends.

There is probably no limit to the potential topics that could be included in the talent tank resource directory. Common topics include use of the Internet, personal communication skills, arts and crafts, music, dance, computer technology, family living and health, career fields, and topics related to science, math, economics, social studies, geography, history, and much more.

For a talent tank or community resource program to work, there has to be a coordinated system. The system should be simple and flexible. The idea is to fill teacher requests and to "broker" the volunteers in an efficient and effective manner.

A Visit with President Lincoln

When attending a presentation on volunteers at a national conference, I had the pleasure of visiting with a very special person. The session leader announced that we were going to have a guest speaker. The door opened and in walked Abe Lincoln. The President was dressed in his usual black suit, white shirt, black tie, and top hat. He greeted the group and told us how happy he was to be with us and explained why he had come. Since we "had been studying the Civil War and his career," he felt that he could personally fill us in on some important details.

The President indicated that things had not always been smooth during his political career. He described his defeats as well as his victories. When discussing the war, Mr. Lincoln read a letter that he sent to a mother in Boston who had lost her five sons. After answering some questions, he thanked us for allowing him to visit and left.

"Honest Abe" in reality was a volunteer who was a student of the life and career of Abe Lincoln and had transformed his interest in Lincoln to a dramatic learning strategy. He traveled to different schools to visit and make presentations. He had prepared lessons that were geared to different grade levels and on various topics. Our visit was designed for secondary students.

Having Abe Lincoln tell us about his life "in person" made the topic meaningful and exciting. A community can find similar individuals who would be willing to assume the roles of famous figures in history and visit the schools. What a wonderful resource this would be for the schools.

SCHOOL-BUSINESS PARTNERSHIPS

In most communities there are organizations that are willing to be involved with the school by providing resources and services. The Adopt-a-School program is a good example of a best practice to get organizations to work in partnership with schools. A coordinating Adopt-a-School agency finds business and service clubs that are willing to be partners and then brings the organizations and schools together. The partner organizations can provide financial support to get equipment and supplies, volunteers, and share other expertise. For example, one bank sent an information management specialist to set up an accounting system for a school.

The volunteers help in the school as tutors and trainers, act as school-to-work counselors, and assist in other ways such as hosting celebrations or transporting parents to feeder schools for orientation sessions.

Many partner organizations are also involved in student internships. These experiences allow high-school students to explore various careers. Businesses, professionals, and government agencies work in partnership with the school to offer internship placements. The internships can be of different lengths, depending upon the situation. In some cases, the

---

General Dollar Learning Center

The Sam Levy Learning Center located in Nashville, Tennessee, was created by a unique school-business partnership. A "Skills for Success" program is offered to low-income residents living in and around the Sam Levy Public Housing Complex through a partnership between the YWCA, Dollar General Corporation, Tennessee Department of Human Services, and Metro Social Services. The partnership works closely with the staff of the family resource center in the nearby Caldwell Elementary School.

What is unusual about this program is that the classes are taught in a training center located in the back of a Dollar General Store built for this specific purpose. Before the Dollar General opened, there was only a small convenience store operating in the neighborhood. The new Dollar General Store not only provides the residents with a place to shop, but also a place to work and learn.

The trainees in the first phase of the training program learn computer, communication, and employment skills. In addition, they participate in work-shops dealing with such topics as assertiveness, personal health, nutrition, money management, child management, and legal rights. An opportunity to prepare for the GED is also available.

During the second phase, the participants receive on-the-job training in the Dollar General Store, where they learn basic retail skills and teamwork. The trainees also receive career counseling and help in enrolling in college or vocational school.

The evolution of this coordinating best practice is an excellent example of cooperation between the school and many facets of the community. For the Dollar General Store Corporation to make this kind of commitment is the essence of a family/school/community partnership.

students are paid a small wage for their involvement. The long-term benefit for the "employers" is that more students may choose their areas for careers. For the short term, the school should recognize publicly the contributions made by the different organizations and individuals. For example, articles and photographs can be published in newspapers and school and organization newsletters, as well as displayed in school, offices and business lobbies. Also, award banquets, and symbols may be used. Thank-you notes from the children and teachers are important. Very rewarding forms of recognition are exhibits, demonstrations, and performances by students who have worked with the volunteers.

GUIDELINES FOR DESIGNING AND IMPLEMENTING VOLUNTEER PROGRAMS

A good volunteer program does not just happen. It evolves from a coordinated plan of action and strong leadership. Like most aspects of a family/school/community partnership program, it is a "top down–bottom-up" operation. That is, the program must be supported by the administration, faculty, and staff. Usually it is wise to start small. After a foundation is built, the program can be expanded based on the early successes. The Strategic Partnership Planning System presented in Chapter 10 can be used to plan for a volunteer program.

Leadership

The impetus to develop a volunteer program can come from anyone, a teacher, librarian, secretary, parent, or a community member, but it is usually the principal of a school that leads the charge. With the support of the central office and the superintendent, the principal can work with the faculty and staff to reach a consensus about the benefits of parents and community members being involved in the school.

It is great to have lots of volunteers but they and the school have to be prepared for the relationship. If the volunteer program is well organized, teachers, students, and volunteers will all benefit. Kussrow (1988) says teachers find they devote more time to the professional aspects of teaching and learn more about individual children when there are volunteers in their classrooms. In addition, they discover that a number of parents have good ideas for instructional strategies, are good teachers, and are eager to learn. Also, parent volunteers often extend their school activities to home learning for their children.

Teacher Concerns

As you plan a volunteer program, you may discover some teacher concerns that need to be addressed. For example, some teachers may feel:

- It takes too much time to plan for volunteers.
- They are uncomfortable with volunteers in their classrooms.
- They will be subject to criticism by the volunteers.
- Involving volunteers may lower classroom and school standards.
- Having volunteers may reduce the number of aides and teachers who are hired.
- Volunteers may try to be a dominant force in the classrooms.
- The volunteers will not follow their instructions.
- Volunteers will be disruptive.
- Volunteers may not be confidential about what they see, hear, and read.
- Volunteers are not dependable.
- Volunteers may not have the skills and knowledge to work with children and young adults.

The school needs to be sensitive to these concerns and work with the teachers to help alleviate their fears. The concerns are there because the teachers have experienced or heard of negative things that have happened in a volunteer program. This is why the programs need to be carefully planned and administered.

The principal can work with the School Improvement Council, PTA/PTO, local businesses and service clubs, and other organizations to publicize the program and to seek volunteers. As the program develops and grows, it is important to hire a coordinator to direct the volunteer program because it is a time-consuming job. If this isn't possible, it may be possible to find a parent or community member who would be willing to assume this role on a voluntary basis. The principal should still monitor the program and be available to assist with the coordination.

Self-Interests

In working with volunteers, remember that they are volunteering. This may be stating the obvious and sound silly, but unless the volunteers have some of their self-interests met in some way, they probably will not remain as partners (see Chapter 3 for a discussion of self-interests and partnerships).

The volunteers have to feel wanted, valued, and effective. Therefore, it is important to determine what the prospective volunteers are interested in doing and what they are good at. By matching the volunteers' self-interests and skills with the needs in the school and classrooms, the likelihood of success is greatly increased for everyone. For example, a parent may be very interested in working with children on an individual basis in the classroom or computer lab. On the other hand, some volunteers may be interested in being around many people and want to be in the center of things. As a result, they may want to help out in the office, greeting visitors, answering telephones, and delivering messages. Other volunteers may want to be less visible and prefer to work at home putting together a newsletter or helping with a telephone tree. Finally, there will be volunteers who could be considered to be "generalists." These individuals are ready to perform a variety of duties. And, there will be "specialists," who are willing to volunteer for specific tasks, such as working with children with learning difficulties, sharing an expertise with a group of students, or tutoring a student on the use of a computer.

Some volunteers will be available on a regular basis and be in the school for a specific and defined time each week. Others may be on the roster to be called to school for special occasions and events.

A volunteer program needs to accommodate a variety of self-interests, skills, knowledge, and schedules to fully utilize the available volunteers.

Some schools use a structured system to recruit volunteers. Each parent is expected to contribute some of their time, expertise, or resources during the school year. A list of volunteer programs and activities is sent to each family in the fall so they can choose how they would like to be involved.

I believe that one should be cautious if this approach is considered. If the idea is for the parents to be in a partnership, and one "equal" partner feels pressured by the other "equal" partner, it can be a "turnoff." The school needs to be sensitive to the differences in family resources, culture, needs, and capacities, and the opportunities for volunteering should be broad and flexible.

Interviewing Volunteers

Conducting an interview with prospective volunteers is probably the best way to gain knowledge about interests, skills, and availability. If this is not possible, telephone or written surveys may be used. Group interviews can also be used in certain situations. Suggestions for interviewing prospective volunteers include:

- Begin to build a collaborative relationship with the parent or community member.
- Let the volunteers know that they are considered equal partners in the learning community. They have something to offer the children and the school.
- Tell them about the volunteer program and how it is organized. Explain how the volunteer program fits into the family/school/community partnership program.
- Outline the various types of volunteer duties, responsibilities, and activities.
- Discuss the issues of confidentiality and communication.
- Ask about the kinds of things that they would like to be involved in, and what skills and knowledge they bring to the school.
- Find out how often they would be willing to volunteer and if they can be on a regular schedule.
- Describe any benefits or "perks" given to volunteers.
- Provide an opportunity for questions.

Special Training

As indicated before, volunteers will probably need special training if they are going to be involved with such things as tutoring, especially when working with children with special needs; assisting in the computer labs; working in the guidance and administrative offices; and communicating with families. The training and information needs to be practical and specific and should reflect the basic assumptions underlying a family/school/community partnership, that is, everyone is a stakeholder in the education of the children; everyone is treated with warmth, caring, and respect.

Keeping Volunteers

As discussed earlier, volunteers need to have some of their self-interests met by the program. In addition, it is very important to thank and recognize them for their work. Let the volunteers know how beneficial their services are to the children, the school, the teachers, the other families, and the entire community.

It is crucial that the school and community acknowledge publicly the efforts of the volunteers. While a major motivator for the volunteers may be altruism, they need to feel they are valued members of the learning community.

There are many best practices that can be used to "thank" volunteers. The following are some examples of activities and events for recognizing, appreciating and rewarding volunteers.

Saluting the Volunteers

Depending upon the availability and schedules of the volunteers, faculty and staff, an appreciation dinner, banquet, afternoon tea party, or breakfast can be held for the volunteers. These are important ceremonies that praise the contributions of the volunteers. The school band and chorus can perform and the cheerleaders can lead a cheer for the volunteers.

Certificates of Merit

Certificates of merit are awarded to the volunteers to recognize their contributions. These certificates are signed by the principal, volunteer coordinator, teacher, or others, and given out at the dinner, banquet, or breakfast.

Letters of Appreciation

Volunteers receive a letter of appreciation thanking them for their efforts. Emphasize how valued they are, and how they have helped the school.

Name Tags

Provide volunteers with permanent name tags with the school's logo, a picture of the mascot, or the mission statement printed on them. Stars or some other symbols can be added to recognize years of service, special achievement, and so forth.

Partnership Lapel Pins

Special lapel pins are created for volunteers to show the public that they are partners with the school.

Photographs

Pictures of the volunteers in "action" and at the social gathering can be taken and displayed in the school lobby, parent room, and elsewhere. Copies of the pictures are sent to the local newspaper, along with a short story. The volunteers should also receive a copy of their photograph.

Newspaper Articles and Newsletters

Articles about the activities of the volunteers can be written and sent to the local papers. Volunteer information should also be included in the school's newsletter. This public recognition is very important to many volunteers.

Other Incentives

To get parents involved and to help with empowerment, you can provide incentives. For example, parents who work a certain number of hours receive family tickets for a pizza, party, movie, theme park, and other fun activity. More examples of best practices for showing your appreciation can be found in the Communicating chapter (Chapter 7).

COACHING: BUILDING ON THE OTHER SCHOOL/ COMMUNITY COLLABORATION STRATEGIES

The Coaching Strategy is found in the next chapter. This intervention builds on the other School/Community Collaboration Strategies. While the first three strategies are primarily concerned with overcoming barriers, establishing communication flows, and coordinating services, the Coaching Strategy is designed to enhance the families' ability to play their parenting roles. By using the Connecting, Communicating, and

Coordinating Strategies to build collaborative relationships with the families, the school is in the position to help the parents learn how to get involved in the social and academic development of their children. The Coaching Strategy used in conjunction with the other interventions will solve "The Case of the Missing Families."

CHAPTER 9

Coaching: Building a Team

CONNECTING	COMMUNICATING	COORDINATING	COACHING

A good friend of mine, Suzanne Brown, told me a wonderful story that captures the spirit of the Coaching Strategy. Suzanne is a family/school/community coordinator and director of a parent involvement program at an inner-city elementary school in Nashville. One day when she was out in the neighborhood visiting families, one of her parents approached on the other side of the street. Suzanne waved to the woman as she drew closer. The woman waved back and shouted across the street, "You gotta reach the parents to reach the kids."

This remark was insightful and profound. Paraphrasing the mother's statement, the function of the Coaching Strategy is to "reach and empower the parents so they can reach their kids." Specifically, one of the purposes of the intervention strategy is to enhance the family member's ability and capacity to play the eight Parent Partner Roles.

The Coaching Strategy addresses a barrier that is created when the families are not able to effectively play their parenting roles. The fact that this barrier exists for some families is not surprising, since most of us have not had training on how to be an effective parent, especially how to be involved in our child's education. Since babies do not arrive with instruction manuals, we usually have to learn the parenting skills and knowledge on a trial-and-error basis, using our family experiences as a frame of reference.

167

As I was growing up, and even now, I feel my parents have been, and are, excellent role models. Yet, even with this background, I still found parenting to be a mysterious adventure at best. So, I can relate to the family members who are struggling with parenthood. It isn't easy!

What makes being involved even more complicated is that you have to be able to work closely with the school. Schools are complex organizations and many families have limited knowledge about procedures and policies, styles, cultures, and expectations. For example, parents are often unclear about the curriculum, their rights and their children's rights, programs and activities, and how the school operates. They do not know who to go to for information, and how to ask questions in the right way. Sometimes parents are so unsure about working with the school that they worry that if they try to get involved they might "rock the boat" and hurt their children.

COACHING AND ENHANCING

Because parenting is often an overwhelming task, particularly for families who do not have the appropriate skills and knowledge, the Coaching Strategy is used to help the parents to enhance their capacities to play the Parent Partner Roles. The notion of "enhancing" family members' capacity to play their Parent Partner Roles is a subtle, but crucial way of thinking about the process.

The concept of enhancement conjures up words like "strengthen," "reinforce," "augment," "magnify," and "embellish." To "enhance the parents' skills and knowledge," is a "softer," more gentle approach than "to develop or train the parents." Granted, these approaches are very similar, but what makes them different is the attitude on which the notion of "coaching" is based. Certainly, the intent of the strategy is for the parents to acquire new skills and knowledge, but coaching is an act of mentoring to achieve the goals. It has been said that "a coach guides from the side, rather than being a sage on the stage." The coach does not give you the answers, but leads you toward the solution.

Therefore, as with all of the intervention strategies, when working with the families, the coaching needs to focus on strengths, not weaknesses. This is important since the relationships with the parents, especially with the hard-to-reach families, are usually rather fragile. The intent of coaching should be to strengthen the partnerships. Family members should not have the feeling that we believe they are bad parents and that we are trying to "fix" them. As stated before, even the families living in the most distressed conditions have strengths and some sense of pride. Most of the parents are doing the best they can. Therefore, as we work with them, we need to be very careful not to be demeaning and patronizing.

Because the Coaching Strategy involves working with adults in a collaborative manner, the individuals responsible for the coaching need to understand the functions and nature of family/school/community partnerships and the Self-Renewing Partnership Model. The families should perceive the coaches as helpers, learners, teachers, and facilitators.

The Coaching Strategy is intended to empower the parents, not to make them co-dependent. The idea is for the family members to feel competent, with a sense of self-determination and responsibility. Urie Brofenbrenner states: "Not only do parents become more effective as parents, but they become more effective as people. It's a matter of higher self-esteem. Once they saw they could do something about their child's education, they saw they could do something about their housing, their community and their jobs" (Amundson, 1988, p. 4).

If they are responsible and independent, parents are more likely to be fully involved active, confident partners. Therefore, the Coaching Strategy is designed to:

- enhance the parents' ability and capacity to effectively play the Parent Partner Roles
- enhance the parents' general sense of well-being, knowledge and skill level

COACHING FROM A COLLABORATIVE FOUNDATION

As discussed in Chapter 5, the School/Community Collaboration Strategies are progressive and hierarchical. The implementation of the strategies is sequenced, with one building upon the other. Coaching, the highest order intervention strategy, is used after a collaborative foundation is formed by the Connecting, Communicating and Coordinating Strategies.

Before you can effectively coach parents, you need to be connected and communicating. And if needed, outside resources and services are coordinated to resolve some of the problems facing the families so they are able to focus on their parenting skills and knowledge.

Coaching Settings

Coaching is planned, or it can be spontaneous. It happens in a variety of settings: workshops and classes, parent/teacher conferences, school hallways, family social events, and in the home. While the informal coaching that occurs during "teachable moments" is important and significant, most coaching best practices are carried out in a planned and coordinated way. The parent education activities and programs are targeted at certain family populations and offered in settings that are conducive to learning.

Two settings are particularly good vehicles for implementing the Coaching Strategy and the other School/Community Collaboration Strategies. One setting is a family, or parent, center; the other is the home. I refer to them as "vehicles" because they can be fertile environments for reaching and working with the parents. For example, programs and activities can be implemented at the centers and in the home to connect with the parents, to establish two-way communications, and to coordinate services and resources. How the centers and the homes can be used for coaching is discussed in the following sections.

Family Centers

Family, or parent centers, are beginning to spring up in the schools and neighborhoods. These exciting facilities for working with and helping families have been spawned by the recent interest in partnerships between the families, school, and community. The centers are places where family members go for information, instruction, support, resources, services, and even shelter.

There are several types of centers, which provide different kinds of services and resources. For example, the Coordinating Strategy chapter (Chapter 8) describes school-based family resource centers and family service centers that serve needy families by coordinating or providing school and community resources and services. The Connecting Strategy chapter (Chapter 6) presents ways that family centers are used to overcome barriers and make connections with hard-to-reach parents. The current section describes how the centers can be used for parent education classes and workshops, support groups, computer labs, educational toy and game loan libraries, and so on.

As indicated in Chapter 1, because of the variety of family structures and responsibilities, I prefer to use the word "family" over "parent" when referring to many of the best practices, roles, and relationships. I feel the broader term acknowledges the involvement of different family members as care givers and surrogate parents. Thus, with the centers, using "family" in the title extends a welcome to parents, surrogate parents, grandparents, aunts, uncles, siblings, and other relatives.

Usually the centers are located in or near the school, but they may also be housed in the neighborhoods or at a central location away from the school. These locations may be more convenient and, therefore, more conducive for making connections. This is particularly important for those family members who are not yet comfortable in a school setting. However, if the center is located in the school, the parents will get used to being with the children in the learning community. As they become partners, they will be able to be involved at school and in the home. Establishing a family center in the school or community sends the family members the message that they are important partners.

CENTER CHARACTERISTICS

Family centers vary in size, ranging from parent corners in classrooms and rooms in the schools or community centers, to separate buildings. Likewise, the programs and services offered by the family centers vary; some are limited in scope, while others are very comprehensive. Many centers start small and then expand as resources and expertise become available. As the family/school/community partnerships grow stronger, the centers, in turn, usually are able to reach more families.

Family centers can be used as sites to coach all of the Parent Partner Roles. Best practices include providing information and materials on parenting, drug abuse, nutrition, school curriculum and policies, and other relevant subjects; forming and facilitating support groups; and offering classes, workshops and other parent education sessions. The "ideal" family center will have books, audio- and videotapes, games, puzzles, telephones, computers, copying machines, software, and so forth, available for the coaching. Adequate space will also be available for classes, workshops, support groups and childcare. Some centers even have kitchens, laundry rooms, and sewing machines to help coach the families in a variety of skills. In brief, the facilities should reflect the needs of the targeted families. Schools can seek foundation grants and approach businesses, industry and service groups for donations to buy equipment, supplies, software, and other needed items.

INVITING ENVIRONMENTS

Family centers should be user-friendly and look, feel, and smell like a welcoming home environment. This is especially important for those families that do not live in comfortable conditions. For example, have fresh flowers in the center, and if facilities are available, occasionally have cookies baking or other foods cooking to create a nice ambience. The centers should be places that the parents look forward to visiting.

ORGANIZED GRAFFITI

To build family "ownership" of the center and the school, a practice called "Organized Graffiti" is used. Sheets of paper are taped to the walls of the center, and parents are asked to draw pictures that represent their families and how they are involved in the education of their children. The symbolic images of the families "decorate" the center and illustrate the parents' partnership with the school.

A Cooperative Learning Center

In Buffalo, New York, the school district, in cooperation with the Urban League, operates a family center in the downtown area. Housed in a marvelous building that formerly served as a bank, the center includes an Even Start program with preschool and nursery facilities. School buses are used to transport the parents to the center and for field trips. Parents enroll in a variety of classes and workshops dealing with life skills, parenting, foreign languages, GED preparation, and general education. There is also a computer lab with an extensive network of software. The center is a fine example of cooperation between the city schools and the private sector. Seeing the preschool children and teachers working together in the room that contains the large bank vault is a reminder of the collaborative relationship between the schools and the private sector.

The results from a recent study of 28 family centers indicate that three-fourths of the centers offered programs designed to get family members involved in the governance of the schools and many coordinated volunteer and parent tutoring programs (Johnson, 1993). While it is terrific that these centers are offering such programs, it appears that the programs are still based on the "families supporting the school" approach. That is, they seem to be focusing primarily on the Supporter and Collaborator Roles, both of which are school-directed.

An underlying assumption of the Self-Renewing Partnership Model is that the parents' involvement in the homes is a prerequisite for their involvement at school (see discussion in Chapter 1 of the "Case of the Missing Families"). Because the Parent Partner Roles are progressive and hierarchical, the centers must make sure that the family members have the capacity to play the lower order roles before coaching the higher order roles.

Cycling out Parent Supervisors

In Omaha, Nebraska, the school district hires parents to supervise the family rooms in the schools. The parents are paid at the minimum wage rate and the district provides them with free inservice job training when they are not on duty. The goal of the training is for the parents to be able to break out of the poverty cycle and get better higher paying jobs in the school or community. When the family room supervisors "cycle out " to different jobs, new parents are hired and the process is repeated.

THE COACHING HOME VISIT

While home visits are great ways to make connections and establish communication flows with parents, they also offer excellent opportunities for coaching. Programs such as Even Start, Title 1, and Head Start require home visits to coach the parents. Once a family is "connected" with the school and a relationship is established, the coaching best practices can be implemented during home visits. (Ways to use the home visit as a Connecting best practice are discussed in Chapter 6.)

The need for coaching varies greatly among families. As the families become more comfortable interacting with the school, their self-interests can be identified and appropriate activities introduced. Most families want help to enhance their parenting and teaching skills. For example, the home visitors work with the parents to enhance their Parent Partner Role skills and knowledge by modeling behavior and demonstrating home learning activities with their children. The parents are provided with materials (e.g., books, toys, games, paper, crayons, paints, etc.).

Hawaii Healthy Start Program

Hawaii's Healthy Start Program is built on the premise that certain families, because of single parenthood, poverty, lack of education or support, need help to build positive parenting skills and promote healthy development of their children. In 1995, the Hawaii legislature appropriated six million dollars for the program.

Healthy Start workers screen the records of half of the 18,000 babies born in Hawaii each year. The screenings look for risk factors such as domestic violence, lack of prenatal care, attempted abortions, and signs of substance abuse. The parents are contacted and weekly home visits are made by para-professionals who are high-school graduates from the same communities as the parents.

The home visitors work with the parents to enhance their Nurturing and Teacher Roles. The parents and children's development is closely monitored. Similarly, North Carolina is piloting a Healthy Start program that focuses on families for whom child abuse has been a problem.

The programs and activities need to build on the present family conditions. In other words, the best practices have to relate to the family members' self-interests. This is why it is important to do your "homework" and find out as much as possible about the cultures and needs of the families you are targeting. Conducting need assessments with the parents helps to identify strengths, desires, concerns, problems, and other issues. The results of the needs assessment will help to determine what sort of coaching is appropriate for a particular family or group of families.

Sometimes the level on which the families are functioning can be determined during the connecting home visits. The home visitor can become aware of situations such as poverty, unemployment, drug abuse, poor living conditions during the visits. Coordinating best practices, in turn, can be used to get resources and services to the needy families.

COACHING BEST PRACTICES

The following sections present best practices that can be used to enhance the family members' Parent Partner Role skills and knowledge. Programs and activities to enhance each of the Parent Partner Roles are described. The discussions begin with an overview of workshops and classes, and support groups. This is followed by best practices to increase and maintain participation and support conducive to coaching environments.

Workshops and Classes

Offering parent education workshops and classes is a popular and efficient way to enhance family members' ability and capacity to assume the eight Parent Partner Roles and to enhance their general knowledge. Which workshop or class is appropriate for a parent will depend upon a family's state of readiness to be involved in the social and educational development of their children. By assessing the families, appropriate classes and workshops can be offered to meet their needs.

Sometimes you may have to follow a circuitous route to arrive at a point where you can enhance a particular role. For example, for those parents who have difficulty reading, the logical thing is for them to take literacy classes, and many of them will. However, some family members are embarrassed to admit that they cannot read, so they will be reluctant to enroll in a reading class. Consequently, it may be necessary to begin by getting them to take classes on self-esteem or assertive training before they are ready to participate in a reading class. Coaches need to be flexible and creative in their approaches.

Some of the workshops and classes focus directly on educational, social, and parenting issues, while others have a broader focus, designed to enhance the family's overall condition and general sense of well-being. The more general high-interest sessions are helpful in reaching those families that are not very connected. Offering classes and workshops on such topics as craft-making, cooking, hobbies, car repair, and so on, will attract parents to the school. After the parents are involved, they can be encouraged to take other classes that deal directly with the Parent Partner Roles.

The workshops that focus on ways to improve quality of life have a broad appeal not only to families, but to some faculty and staff as well. An added benefit is that when parents and teachers participate together in the sessions, collaborative relationships are built and connections between the families and the school are strengthened.

Why Angels Can Fly

A Scottish proverb says, "The reason angels can fly is that they take themselves so lightly." While education is serious business, it should be enjoyable as well. The workshops and classes should be as positive and upbeat as possible. Always try to include activities that are fun. Suggestions for making the parent education programs fun and enjoyable are included in this chapter.

Workshop and Class Topics

Potential topics for workshops and classes are presented in two places to make it easier for the readers to plan interventions that fit their particular situations and the needs of the families they are working with. Topics related to each of the Parent Partner Roles are presented at the beginning of the section devoted to that particular role. At the back of this chapter, a summary of the potential workshop and class topics is presented. The topics are listed under headings such as Life Skills, Self-Help, Educational and Social Issues, Quality of Life, and Question and Answer Sessions.

When developing a Coaching intervention plan, first identify the Parent Partner Role(s) to be enhanced. Look at the suggested workshop and class topics listed under the role. If the focus of the workshop or class has been determined (e.g., educational issues, quality of living, etc.), then peruse the topics listed under the appropriate heading in the summary at the end of the chapter.

Support Groups

Many times parents feel isolated and alone when they are having difficulties with their children or are facing problems in their personal lives. They may believe they are "bad" parents. By being brought together and participating in support groups, the family members will find that others are dealing with similar issues and that they are not alone.

During the sessions, a facilitator helps the parents to support each other while they work to help themselves. Support groups can be organized

---

Parent Abuse

A middle-school principal in San Jose, California, said that one of the things she found parents of young adolescents having trouble dealing with is that their children often become physically or psychologically abusive to them. This remark seemed rather harsh, but it is probably true. As children reach this age, they are fighting for their independence and may push the parents away in the process.

I heard someone remark, when describing middle-school children, that they could understand why alligators eat their young. I'm certainly not suggesting anything that harsh, but middle-grade students are a different breed. However, organizing support groups for the parents can help them get through this difficult phase in their child's life.

around most any issue that is of concern to a group of parents. Some of the more common include single parenthood, living with middle-grade students, effects of divorce on children, grandparents raising grandchildren, drug and alcohol abuse, and dealing with unmotivated students.

LOGISTICAL BEST PRACTICES

While it is essential to offer workshops, classes, support groups, and so forth, that are appropriate to meet the parents' self-interests and needs, it is equally important to organize and schedule the best practices in such a way that the targeted families want to attend and participate. The following are some suggestions on ways to increase and maintain parent participation and attendance.

Flexible Locations

At times, the programs should be offered in locations other than the school. Often the families' neighborhoods are located some distance from the school, especially in school districts that have large busing programs. Meetings, classes, workshops, and other events can be held at neighborhood churches, community centers, hospitals, or businesses. Holding the sessions on the families' "home turf" is particularly important if the family members are not comfortable coming into the school. The neighborhood locations will be less threatening and the parents will recognize that the school is reaching out to them. Once the parents are connected and feeling good about working with the faculty and staff, you can suggest that some of the meetings be held at the school.

Flexible Meeting Times

Be aware of the limitations placed on the families' time (e.g., both parents working, factory shifts, traffic, distances, etc.). Schedule the workshops and classes at the most convenient times. Hold multiple sessions if one meeting time won't work for a lot of families.

Child Care

Some families may not be able to attend because they lack child care. Recruit older students (especially those in child care–related classes), family members, and community volunteers to supervise the children. Child care is also a good opportunity for academic and social enrichment. Equip the area with educational toys, books, videos, and games.

Transportation

Arrange transportation for families that have no means to get the sessions. Public transportation or school buses can be used to get the family to and from the meetings. Be cautious about using faculty or volunteers to transport parents because of liability considerations.

Language

If you anticipate that some of the people you want to participate do not speak English, present the sessions in their language or provide translators.

Student Invitations

Having the children write personal invitations asking the parents to attend classes, workshops, or support group sessions is often the "little push" that gets some family members to attend.

Parent Recognition

Hopefully, the parents are attending because they are interested and feel that their participation will help them and their children. But even if this is true, people like to be recognized for their efforts. Little forms of recognition can sustain attendance and participation. There are many ways to recognize the parents' participation. For example:

- The names of family members attending classes and sessions are published in the school newsletter or read as part of the morning announcements.
- Group pictures are taken and submitted to the local newspaper for publication. Copies are also given to participants.
- Family members are given name tags at the opening meeting and are awarded a gold star for their tag when they attend subsequent sessions.

- Small, inexpensive door prizes are given at the end of the sessions. The schools may purchase the items, but often the prizes are donated by local business and agencies. Teachers and community members may be good sources. Most people have great "prizes" stored away in closets and drawers.
- Have an awards ceremony for the family members at the end of the year. Make sure that everyone gets an award of some kind.
- At the first session, conduct nonthreatening "icebreaker" activities designed to help people get acquainted.

ENHANCING THE PARENT PARTNER ROLES

The Progressive Nature of the Parent Partner Roles

Like, the School/Community Collaboration Strategies, the Parent Partner Roles are hierarchical and progressive; that is, they build upon one another as the involvement and support increase and develop. The roles progress from the more basic and fundamental (Nurturer, Communicator, Teacher and Supporter) to the more specialized (Advisor, Advocator, and Collaborator). All of the roles are essential, with the "lower" order roles forming a foundation for the "higher" order roles.

Consequently, roles such as, Advisor, Advocator, and Collaborator cannot be played unless the parents are able to play the lower level roles effectively. For example, for parents to be good advisors, they have to know what is going on in the child's life in school (Communicator Role) and a learning environment has to be established in the home (Nurturer Role). The family members are expected to play the lower order roles all the time, whereas some of the high-level roles, such as Advocator and Advisor, are played only when the need arises. Although the higher level roles are played less frequently, the parents must be prepared to assume them at the appropriate times. Therefore, they must be skilled in such specialized areas as mediation, problem-solving, advising, and conflict resolution.

When implementing a best practice to help the parents play a particular role, make sure that the family members are already able to play the roles leading up to that role. For example, when enhancing the Advocator Role by offering a workshop on student and family rights, the assumption is that the participants are already communicating with the school and know and understand how the school works. This is a big assumption. Therefore, before implementing best practices to enhance a certain Parent Partner Role, determine if the parents have already had the opportunity to enhance their lower order roles. If not, provide them with programs and activities to build the foundation before attempting to enhance a higher order role.

In the following sections best practices to enhance each of the Parent Partner Roles are described and discussed. Because the roles are hierarchical, the programs and activities to enhance the higher order roles are more specialized. Consequently, there are more best practices presented for the lower order roles, and these may need to be implemented in order to enhance the higher order roles. For example, when working with parents on their Advocator Role, workshops on negotiating and problem-solving will enhance their skills and knowledge in that area. However, it may first be necessary to provide them with parent handbooks and having question and answer sessions with principals, counselors, and teachers to enhance their Communicator Role. Again, empowerment is a developmental process, and as you work with the parents to enhance their parenting roles, implement best practices that move them up through the various levels.

Coaching the Nurturer Parent Partner Role

The goal of the Nurturer Parent Partner Role is to provide an appropriate environment where the child will flourish physically, psychologically, and emotionally. This role is concerned with the child's overall health, shelter, and safety. The role encompasses the responsibility of maintaining positive learning conditions and environments at home. It is the most basic and fundamental role in the Parent Partner Role hierarchy.

When playing the Nurturer Role, it is expected that fully involved parents will:

- offer love, praise, and encouragement
- support the child's education by providing appropriate learning environment
- provide day-to-day necessities, school supplies and equipment, medical examinations, vaccinations, and so on

- regulate TV use, schedule daily homework times, and establish family learning and living routines
- respond to the school's request for registration forms, schedules, report card signatures, permission slips, and other information
- monitor the child's in-school attendance and behavior and out-of-school activities
- enroll the child in enrichment programs such as dance, music and art lessons, after-school sports, and community recreational programs
- encourage the child to participate in religious services and youth groups

Workshops and Class Topics Related to the Nurturer Role

A variety of workshops and classes can be offered to enhance parents' Nurturer Role skills and knowledge. Such sessions focus on ways the family members can help themselves and the children while improving the living and learning conditions in the home. For example, a "How to Survive Morning" workshop can provide the parents with strategies to prepare for the early morning rush. The strategies include things the family and child can do the night before to help the morning go smoother, such as choosing and laying out clothes, packing lunches, placing book bags by the door, setting the table for breakfast, and so on. The following are other examples of workshops and classes to enhance the Nurturer Role. The examples are presented as "How To" or "Question and Answer" sessions.

"HOW TO" WORKSHOPS AND CLASSES

Many parents need to enhance their skills and knowledge in dealing with the crises and pressures of family life. The "How To" sessions offer strategies and information in this area. Some examples are:

- how to build relationships between siblings and other family members
- how to improve your child's feelings and attitudes toward school
- how to discipline your child
- how to find and get a job
- how to find and work with support agencies in the community (e.g., department of social services)

- how to apply for food stamps, social security, and so on
- how to locate and select a day-care program
- how to get your electricity, gas, or telephone service restored
- how to make birthing arrangements
- how to sustain hope in the face of long-term adversity
- how to increase control over your life
- how to be a good role model
- how to overcome social isolation
- how to relax and reduce stress
- how to eat healthy and control your weight
- how to deal with grief and loss
- how to build self-esteem and social skills
- how to make funeral arrangements
- how to maintain your car
- how to fix simple things around your home

The Lady in the Red Shoes

At a parent education class on how to find and get employment, the group was working on their interview skills. One of the parents arrived for the role-playing session wearing bright red high heel shoes and a miniskirt. The other parents shared with her that maybe she should dress a little more conservatively for a job interview, and definitely not wear red shoes. Everyone laughed, and she accepted the suggestion with good humor.

"QUESTION AND ANSWER" MEETINGS

Many parents have never had the opportunity to talk informally with professionals and government officials about health care, social services, rules and regulations, health and safety, and other issues. A dentist or a social service agency representative may be invited to meet with the families for a "Question and Answer" session. The parents ask questions and receive information about services, resources, and prevention programs. In some cases, the parents may not know what questions to ask, so the guest tells them about his or her specialty. Question and Answer meetings can feature sessions with a:

- dentist
- pediatrician
- lawyer
- public health nurse

- poison control center representative
- nutritionist
- fireman
- police officer
- drug abuse counselor
- mayor

The Birthing Experience

Often, when working with the families you discover that parents are not prepared to deal with the most fundamental issues. One time when I was observing a parent education meeting at a family center in Nashville, an event occurred that illustrates this point.

The family/school/community coordinator was talking with a woman who was very pregnant. It was the woman's first baby and they were discussing the upcoming birth. During the conversation, the young woman revealed that she had never been in a hospital before. She did not know what was going to happen and was scared and apprehensive.

Her remark was especially poignant because it contrasted so much with another discussion I had experienced earlier in the day. At another school, I had overheard a pregnant teacher telling a colleague that she and her husband were trying to decide which type of birthing room to use. She was expecting her third child and was discussing the pros and cons of each alternative. It struck me that two women were preparing for a similar event, yet each had vastly different agendas.

I shared this with the coordinator who arranged for the two pregnant women to get together and talk. My teacher friend shared with the young mother-to-be what to expect when she went into labor and gave birth. The coordinator took the young woman to the hospital to visit the maternity ward. Because of these interventions, although still anxious, the new parent-to-be was much better prepared for the blessed event. This scenario illustrates how families may need help in the most basic areas. Many parents do not have skills and knowledge, nor experiences that are typically taken for granted.

Other Nurturer Role Coaching Best Practices

PROVIDING LOVE, AFFECTION AND ATTENTION

When working with the family at school or in the home, encourage the parents to give each child abundant love, affection, and attention. Some of the outward demonstrations of love may change as the child grows older, but it is important to maintain a constant level of affection. Even in situations where there is limited family time (e.g., a single parent, both parents working, many children in a family, etc.), each child still needs some quality time with the parent. Help the families to plan their routines so each child gets the love, affection, and attention he or she needs.

PROVIDING PRAISE AND APPROVAL

As with love, affection, and attention, it is crucial that each child is praised and shown approval. Even when the child's behavior does not live up to the family's expectations, the feedback needs to be given in a positive constructive manner. Show the parents how to avoid delivering their messages in a punitive or derogatory way. Making these adjustments in parent and child behavior often requires changes in the family culture. This is a developmental process and it takes time and effort.

PROVIDING RECOGNITION AND SUPPORT

The children must get the message from the parent that education is important and that what they do in school is valued. To help with this process, suggest to the family members that they:

- discuss with the children what they did each day in school and review papers, projects, and other materials that come home
- have a place in the home where the child's schoolwork is displayed in a prominent place like on a bulletin board or on the refrigerator door
- share examples of the child's work, stories, poems, artwork, and so forth, with relatives and friends. Not only does this help the child, but grandparents, aunts and uncles love to receive these "goodies" in the mail.

PARENTS' AND KIDS' SPORTS NIGHT

Professional and college athletes are invited to come to talk with the parents and students about the importance of education. The evening can include videos of the athlete's highlights, prizes, and autographs.

FOOD PANTRIES AND CLOTHING CENTERS

Establish food pantries and clothing centers where families in need can obtain emergency supplies. The clothing centers and food pantries can be located in a variety of settings. If at the schools, they can be housed near the family center in a spare room or trailer. If at a central location, they can be placed in housing offices, community or staff development centers, churches, and similar locations. Obviously, the clothing centers and food pantries must be easily accessible and located at sites where families are comfortable going. A more detailed discussion of the use and development of food pantries and clothing centers can be found in the Coordinating chapter (Chapter 8).

MONITORING TELEVISION AND COMPUTER GAMES

Several studies suggest that too much television is detrimental to the child's social and academic development. Studies also indicate that children who watch educational programs rather than general programs have higher reading scores. Therefore, the school should work with the parents to help them regulate how much time the children spend watching television and playing computer games, and what program they watch. The school can suggest which programs would be most helpful to the children. A list of programs may be included in a newsletter and placed on the school's voice mail. Or, the amount of TV time per day or week can be part of a learning contract.

CONTRACTS, COVENANTS, AND COMPACTS

The use of written agreements between the families and the school to help form partnerships and foster support in the home and at school is proposed by many educators, policymakers, and community leaders. The agreements are referred to as "contracts," "covenants," or "compacts." I believe the names are synonymous.

The Improving America's Schools Act of 1994 requires that schools receiving federal funds offer School-Parent Compacts that are developed jointly with the families. The school and families are seen as equal partners in the education of the child. The compacts outline how families, faculty, staff, and students will share the responsibility for improved student achievement and the means by which a partnership between the families and the school will be built. The focus of the contracts is on student learning and support. They are voluntary agreements between the family and the school and define goals, expectations and shared responsibilities. The joint contracts (see Figure 9.1) are developed and signed annually by the parent, teacher, and child.

On the surface, having the families and the school sign a contract which pledges cooperation, and outlines the responsibilities of each partner, seems like a good idea. And it is, under the right conditions. You cannot legislate commitment. It has to be developed and nurtured. For a family that is feeling "disconnected" with the school, getting the family to sign an agreement will be extremely difficult, if not impossible. Under those conditions, even if the family were to sign a contract, it would probably be meaningless, even though the terms compact, contract, and convenient sound very official. For example, the definition of covenant is a formal binding written agreement of promise between two or more parties. The "contracts" are "handshake" agreements which are based on trust.

On the other hand, if the family is "connected" with the school and you are attempting to build support and strengthen the partnership, signing a covenant could be very useful. When everyone understands their roles in the partnership, the collaborative relationship can be more effective. The written agreement provides clarity and has great symbolic value. For those family members, faculty and staff who may not be fully committed, signing a contract may at least achieve compliance on their part. While it is difficult to get 100% commitment, having compliant "partners" is a major step toward helping the children.

As you would think, compacts, contracts, or covenants, although similar, have different formats and content. The compacts prescribed in the Improving America's Schools Act are comprehensive policy statements. The act states that they shall:

(1) describe the school's responsibility to provide high-quality curriculum and instruction in a supportive and effective learning environment that enables the children served under this part to meet the State's student performance standards, and the ways in which each parent will be responsible for supporting their children's learning, such as monitoring attendance, homework completion, and television watching, volunteering in their child's classroom; and participating, as appropriate, in decisions relating to the education of their children and positive use of extracurricular time; and (2) address the importance of communication between the teachers and parents on an ongoing basis through, at a minimum (a) parent-teacher conferences in elementary schools, at least annually, during which the compact shall be discussed as the compact relates to the

Parent/Family Member Agreement

(Any person who is interested in helping this student may sign in lieu of the parent.) I want my child to achieve. Therefore, I will encourage him/her by doing the following:

See that my child is punctual and attends school regularly.
Support the school in its efforts to maintain proper discipline.
Establish a time for homework and review it regularly.
Provide a quiet well-lighted place for study.
Encourage my child's efforts and be available for questions.
Be aware of what my child is learning.
Provide a library card for my child.
Read with my child and let my child see me read.
Respond to request for information from the school.
Initiate home learning activities.
Continue to learn how to play my parenting role.

Signature _____

Student Agreement

It is important that I work to the best of my ability. Therefore, I shall strive to do the following:

Attend school regularly.
Come to school each day with pens, pencils, paper, and other necessary tools for learning.
Complete and return homework assignments.
Observe regular study hours.
Conform to rules of student conduct.
Be involved in home learning activities.

Signature _____

Teacher Agreement

It is important that students achieve. Therefore, I shall strive to do the following:

Provide regular homework assignments for students.
Provide necessary assistance to parents so that they can help with assignments and initiate home learning activities.
Encourage students and parents by providing information about student progress.
Use special activities in the classroom to make learning enjoyable and meaningful.

Signature _____

Principal Agreement

I support this form of parent involvement. Therefore, I shall strive to do the following:

Work to establish positive two-way communication flows between the teacher, parent, and student.
Build collaborative relationships with the families.
Encourage teachers to regularly provide homework assignments and home learning activities that will reinforce classroom instruction.
Implement strategies to help parents with their parenting skills and knowledge.

Signature _____

Figure 9.1 Student/Teacher/Parent Contract.

individual child's achievement; (b) frequent reports to parents on their children's progress; and (c) reasonable access to staff, opportunities to volunteer and participate in their child's class, and observation of classroom activities.

Coaching the Communicator Parent Partner Role

The goal of the Communicator Parent Partner Role is to communicate effectively with the child and the school. Usually, when the child is doing well at home and in school, there is a good communication flow between the family members and the child, and the parents and the school. On the other hand, when problems arise in the family or with the school, usually there is a breakdown in communications. This section focuses on ways to enhance a family member's ability to play the Communicator Parent Partner Role.

The Communicating Strategy chapter (Chapter 7) presents best practices the school can use to establish two-way communication flows with the families. Since the process is reciprocal, some of the program and activities included in the Communicating chapter can also help to enhance the parents' communication skills and knowledge.

When playing the Communicator Role, it is expected that fully involved parents will:

- communicate with the child about successes in school and home, problems and concerns and how they will support him or her in programs and activities
- communicate a strong sense of ethics and standards, high expectations, positive values, and character traits, such as respect, responsibility, hard work and integrity
- know what is going on in the school life of the child
- maintain continuous communication with the school, especially about ways to support the child's learning
- monitor homework, projects, and other assignments
- dialogue with the school about the child's progress, strengths and weaknesses
- participate in productive parent/teacher conferences
- respond promptly and effectively to letters and phone calls from school
- make timely and appropriate requests for information, assistance, and advice

- visit the school regularly and talk with teachers, counselors, and principals

Workshop and Class Topics Related to the Communicator Role

The workshops and classes are designed to enhance the family member's ability to communicate more effectively with their children and the school. For example, the parents need to know how to obtain information from their child's teacher and other members of the school staff. They need to be able to find out how they can reinforce in the home what is happening in school, and what services, such as tutoring centers, homework hotlines, and community agencies, are available.

The examples of potential workshop and class topics to enhance the Communicator roles are organized as "How To" and "Question and Answer" sessions, and under a general heading.

"HOW TO" WORKSHOPS AND CLASSES

Examples of potential topics include:
- how to find out what is going on in your child's school life
- how to help your child be successful in school
- how to help prepare your child to take a test
- how to read report cards and student records
- how to monitor homework assignments
- how to give and receive constructive feedback
- how to understand the daily school schedule

"QUESTION AND ANSWER" SESSIONS

Meetings can be scheduled with faculty and staff so family members can ask questions and become familiar with programs and services. The sessions can be held at school or in the neighborhoods depending upon the situation. Examples of Question and Answer sessions are meetings with the:
- principal
- guidance counselor
- school nurse

- speech therapist
- communities-in-schools representative
- reading recovery teacher

OTHER COMMUNICATOR ROLE WORKSHOP AND CLASS TOPICS

The following is a list of other potential workshop and class topics that can be used to enhance the Communicator Role:

- communicating with your child
- interpersonal facilitation skills
- parent-student-teacher conferences—skills for families
- homework without tears
- homework and homework skills
- interactive homework
- standardized testing and other benchmark programs
- extracurricular activities and policies
- grading policies
- discipline policies
- availability of school support services
- pre-kindergarten and kindergarten parent orientation
- transitioning from elementary to middle school
- transitioning from middle to high school

Other Communicator Role Coaching Best Practices

FAMILY DISCUSSIONS (DINNER TABLE TALK)

Many children, especially middle- and high-school students, report that they do not feel they communicate often enough with their parents. Encourage and help the families to schedule a time each day to discuss the happening of the day with the children (e.g., what occurred in school, activities after school, etc.). Find a time when the whole family is together, like at the dinner table or other meal times. Family discussion times are great opportunities to tell stories, recount experiences, and share problem-solving strategies.

Parents may need help in conducting discussions with the children. For example, being a good listener is very important. Family members can be shown how to listen to their child's opinions as well as giving their own.

PARENT HANDBOOKS

Provide the families with a handbook that includes information on topics that they need to know such as:

- school board policies
- the school's mission and goals
- school regulations
- curriculum
- grade-level learning goals and objectives
- procedures for monitoring student progress
- grading and exam policy
- homework policy
- discipline policy
- attendance and tardy policy
- standardized testing program
- student and parent rights
- schedule for school events and programs
- visiting and volunteer opportunities

Include a directory and organizational plan that designates the persons responsible for the day-to-day operation of the school and school district. List the names of the faculty and staff and telephone numbers where they can be contacted at school.

Since the Communicator Role is a lower order role, these best practices can be used to form a foundation for the higher order roles. For example, the parents will need to know and understand the information in the parent handbook in order to mediate and negotiate for the child (Advocator Role).

Coaching the Teacher Parent Partner Role

The goal of the Teacher Partner Role is to assist with the child's moral, intellectual, emotional, and social development. The parent, or surrogate, is the child's first teacher and possibly the child's most important teacher. The effect the family has on the child, especially in the early years, is significant and dramatic.

The Nurturer and Communicator Parent Partner Roles provide the foundation for the teaching function. The Teacher Parent Partner Role builds on this foundation by working with the child to provide him or her with the basic skills and knowledge. When the "missing" families are not involved in the education of the children, it is the parents' inability to play the Teacher Partner Role that has the most negative impact on the children's development. By enhancing the parents' capacities to assume the Teacher Partner Role, more children will be better prepared for the schooling experience.

When playing the Teacher Role, it is expected that fully involved parents will do the following:

- Initiate learning activities or respond to the child's requests for help.
- Work with the teachers to coordinate the child's classroom work with home-based learning activities.
- Meet with teachers to make home learning materials and learn how to teach particular skills and knowledge (e.g., reading, writing, math).
- Engage the children in family games that relate to schoolwork and home learning.
- Utilize instructional techniques designed to help children with homework and other projects and activities.
- Expose the child to various cultural, career, scientific, and historic sites, events, and programs.
- Select creative and educational television programs that the families watch together, and discuss.
- Depending on the age of the child, read to the child, have the child read to you, read together; and ensure that the child reads alone.
- Praise the child's work.
- Take the child to the library to select books, videos, and CDs.
- Use "make-and-take" educational aides and materials developed at family/school sessions.

Workshop and Class Topics Related to the Teacher Role

To help family members learn how to teach and work with their children at home, offer workshops and classes on various instructional strategies and educational issues. Faculty, curriculum coordinators, and other resource personnel can be enlisted to conduct the sessions. Organize the workshops and classes so that different teaching strategies are demonstrated and modeled. When appropriate, ask the families to bring the children to the sessions so they can practice with their own children.

"HOW TO" WORKSHOPS

Some examples of "How To" workshop and class topics include:

- how to motivate your child
- how children learn
- how to build self-esteem in your child
- how to read a book to a child
- how to have a child read to you
- how to use home-learning activities
- how to improve your child's skills in reading, math, writing, and other subjects
- how to develop a home reading program

OTHER POTENTIAL TEACHER ROLE TOPICS

- study skills
- expected math and literacy skills by grade levels
- creating summer learning opportunities
- songs and finger plays
- teaching math, reading, writing, science, social studies, and so on

Coaching the Use of Home Learning Activities

Helping the parents with the use of home learning activities is probably the most important best practice to enhance the Teacher Roles. Many of the workshop and class topics listed above relate to home learning activities. However, because this area is so important, this section presents an array of suggestions for enhancing the parents' ability to work with their children on home learning activities. Guidelines for helping children to develop literacy and math skills are presented and discussed. These suggestions can be conveyed to the families through a variety of settings such as workshops and classes, parent/teacher conferences, and during home visits.

Opportunities for home learning can occur anywhere and at any time. Learning can happen when you are doing the dishes, driving the car, shopping, putting the children to bed, or sitting watching TV. The interactions the parents have with their children, especially during the younger years, play a major role in literacy and math basic skill development. Urge the families to make the most of the time they have with their children by looking for "teachable moments"and conducting home learning activities.

Encourage parents to do the following:

- Make reading a part of the daily family routine by reading to young children at least 20 minutes a day.
- Have older children read to them each day.
- Make it a practice to have the child read or read to them before going to bed. On weekends, as a special treat, let the child stay up a little later and read in bed.
- Discuss with the child the books they read to them or that the child has read.
- When reading a poem, ask the child to guess what the next rhyming word may be.
- Have them ask the child to think if the content of the book relates to them or experiences they have had.
- Ask the child how he or she might have changed the story, or before finishing a story, ask the child how he or she thinks it will end.
- Tell stories about their childhoods, family life, vocations, hobbies, and dreams.
- Keep good books, magazines and newspapers in the house.
- Serve as a role model by reading at least 30 minutes themselves. They might find this difficult to fit into their busy schedules, but try to convince them that reading can prove therapeutic.
- Always have books available in the car for long road trips and traffic delays and to read in restaurants when waiting for the food.
- Have the child read the map when traveling.
- Vary the daily reading settings (e.g., read under a tree in the yard or at a nearby park).
- Have reciprocal spelling bees where the child gives the parent a word and the child checks, and the parent gives the child a word, and they check it together.
- Teach the older child how to use and read the newspaper. They can show them the different sections and where to find such things as a summary of the headlines, sports scores, the weather report, entertainment schedules, and horoscopes. The parents

can give the child a list of local and national headlines and have them locate where the headlines are printed.

- Look through a catalog and newspaper ads, especially the Sunday inserts, and identify common household items (e.g., sports equipment, clothing, etc.). Have the child practice reading and saying the names of the items. Also, have the parents cut the names of items out of the catalog or newspaper and tape them on the real items around the house. Again, have the child read the names and identify the objects.

- Use a newspaper or magazine to work with the child and find all the "A's," "B's," and so on, or certain words like, "that," "which," "when," "many." Ask older children to find nouns, adverbs, adjectives, and so forth.

- Give the child a ruler, yardstick, and measuring tape and ask him or her to measure things around the house, the size of rooms, chairs, TV set, kitchen table, and so on. Have the child measure the heights of their brothers and sisters, and their height.

- Talk with children about time (e.g., A.M. and P.M., positions on a clock face, hours in a day, etc.). Have them practice telling time and adding and subtracting times of day.

- Have the child read the recipe or the directions on the package when they are cooking and have the child measure out the ingredients. Discuss how the different amounts relate to each other. Talk about how you would double or triple a recipe. Have the child see how many cups of water fit into a quart jar, how many teaspoons of sugar in one tablespoon, and so forth.

- Have the child read the labels and determine the weight and size when putting groceries and other supplies away.

- Talk about the groceries and supplies that you buy at the store. Discuss where certain foods are grown (e.g., bananas, grapes, apples); what some products are made of and why they work the way they do (e.g., detergents, glass cleaners, etc.).

- Help the child to notice things when walking or driving in the neighborhood, at a park, in the city, out in the country, or other places. Discuss where they are, what they are seeing and hearing, and what is happening.

- Show the child what they are buying in the grocery markets and other stores and how to compare prices of similar items. Show the child the "price by unit" labels on the shelves beneath the products, and ask the child to name the items.

- Ask the child to read the signs and posters displayed in stores.
- Limit TV viewing to no more than two hours a day. This should apply to everyone. Ask the parents to set an example.
- Find a television program that everyone enjoys and watch it together. Have the parents lead a discussion about what happened, the meaning of the program, what was funny, sad, boring, unrealistic, and so forth.
- Have the child write as much as possible. This can include such things as telephone messages, letters, diaries, and grocery lists.
- Discuss with the child the nature of tides and tide tables when you are near the ocean. Have the child keep track of the changes in tides during a week.

The following are brief descriptions of two excellent Coaching Strategy best practices that can be implemented to enhance the parents'

Family Math

The Lawrence Hall of Science at the University of California, Berkeley, has developed a program that brings parents and children together to learn about mathematics. The program, funded from a grant by the U.S. Department of Education, gives parents and children (kindergarten through grade 8) opportunities to develop problem-solving skills and to build an understanding of mathematics using hands-on materials. Manipulatives like blocks, beans, pennies, and toothpicks are used to help children to understand mathematical concepts such as numbers and space. Family Math topics include arithmetic, geometry, probability and statistics, computers, and logic. It is not a remedial program. The emphasis is on the families having fun as they learn together and parents get involved in their children's math education.

A typical Family Math course includes six or eight sessions of an hour or two. The classes are usually scheduled in the evening (6:30 P.M–8:30 P.M.) or on weekends. The families are given overviews of the mathematics topics at their children's grade levels and explanations of how these topics relate to each other. To ensure that the reason for studying mathematics is clear, men and women working in math-based occupations come to some of the sessions and talk about how they use math in their jobs. Usually, light refreshments are served, and sometimes schools have door prizes and surprise awards. Families are recognized in some way for their involvement (e.g., certificates, T-shirts, badges, bumper stickers, etc.).

The Family Math model was one of the pilot parent involvement programs introduced and evaluated in Tennessee. The families, generally, turned out for the sessions. It should be noted that before the parents respond to invitations to participate in programs such as these, they must feel comfortable with the school and be connected. For more information about Family Math, contact the Lawrence Hall of Science, University of California, Berkeley, CA 94702; (415) 642-1823.

MegaSkills

Dr. Dorothy Rich, Director and Founder of the Home and School Institute, has been a long-time proponent of family, school, community partnerships. Her publications on home learning activities are internationally known. Her program called "MegaSkills" (1988) is about academic and social development. Dorothy has always been on the "cutting edge," and the MegaSkills program combines her "home recipe" approach with what is now being called "character education." The "MegaSkills" are what she calls, "inner-engines of learning." They are: confidence, motivation, effort, responsibility, initiative, perseverance, caring, teamwork, common sense and problem-solving.

The MegaSkills program is designed to help both students and parents. Rich reports that after participating in the program, children and adults are more proactive and "feel more in charge of their lives, more resilient in the force of adversity, and better able to take advantage of opportunities." The program is an excellent Coaching Strategy best practice. For more information, contact the MegaSkills Education Center of the Home and School Institute, 1500 Massachusetts Ave., NW, Washington, DC 20005; (202) 466-3633.

Teacher Role skills and knowledge, while strengthening the partnerships between the families and the school.

Other Teacher Role Coaching Best Practices

FIELD TRIPS

Many parents have never visited the places where their children

---

A Scavenger Hunt

A family/school coordinator in a rural community near Chattanooga, Tennessee, made a field trip a family learning experience by adding a scavenger hunt to the event. A trip to downtown Chattanooga was planned for the parents and children. Most of the family members had never visited any of the sites and many had not been downtown.

Prior to the trip, the coordinator took photographs of some of the things families and children would be expected to see on the trip. She took pictures of buildings that were the focus of the trip: the museum, library, and aquarium. She also photographed more common objects such as pieces of outdoor sculpture, clocks, unusual signs, a bus stop shelter, and a manhole cover. The coordinator made enough copies of the pictures so that each family would have a set. Before leaving on the trip, she gave the parents and children the pictures along with a check list. They were instructed to check off an item when they found the subject shown in a photograph. During the field trip, the families enjoyed the scavenger hunt and learned a lot in the process.

---

typically go on class field trips such as the library, fire stations, museum, zoo, hospital, and so forth. Encourage the teachers to invite the family members to join their children on these field trips. The school can also organize and conduct trips just for the families. By experiencing the different sites, the parents are better able to help their children use the field trips as learning experiences.

LIBRARIES

Encourage parents to take the children to the library on a regular basis to check out books, videos, and educational software. Make sure the family members have library cards and know how to check out items. If some families are not familiar with the location and use of the library, conduct a tour after school or on a weekend. As noted earlier, if a visit to the library is a classroom field trip, invite the family members to go along.

Suggest to the parents that on the occasions when their child asks them a question they cannot answer, they sometimes take the child to the library to find the answer. It will be an opportunity to find the answer to the question, and at the same time a lesson in the use and value of the library.

FAMILY TOY AND GAME LIBRARIES

Establish programs for lending educational and creative toys, puzzles, books, video and audio tapes, and games to the families for home learning activities. Locate the toy and game libraries in the school or community. The programs are often supervised by parents and community volunteers.

COMPUTER LOAN PROGRAMS

Computers and software are loaned to the families to help them with home learning activities. Training is provided by school staff and volunteers. Programs like this can help reduce the gap between the computer literate "haves" and the "have nots." Monies to buy equipment and software and run the programs often come from grants, private donations, and Title 1 funds.

Computers in the Home

The Buddy System Project in Indiana is attempting to place a computer in the home of every 4–12 grade student. The intent is to extend learning beyond the classroom and to ensure equal access for all children in Indiana to the many resources and advantages afforded in the information age. It is reported that during the 1994–95 school year, the Buddy System Project served over 6,000 students and their families at 51 sites (USDOE, 1994).

"MAKE-AND-TAKE" PARTIES

Hold sessions where parents come to the school to make or produce home learning materials. The teachers show the family members how to make the activity, and how to use it with their child. The learning activities usually relate to the child's schoolwork. The school supplies the paper, crayons, glue, glitter, feathers, and other materials. Sometimes the children join the family members at the workshop.

An example is a "Make a Book Workshop." The parents work together to create a book for each child in the family. The family members make up stories, write them down, make illustrations, and put the pages together in a book. When finished, the books are taken home and read to the children.

Another example is a "Tote Bag" party. The parents make tote bags for a reading project. The school or PTA buys books for the children to check out and they carry the books back and forth in the tote bags.

The "Make-and-Take" parties can be scheduled around holidays such as Halloween, Thanksgiving, or Mother's Day. The families make things that can be used to celebrate and learn about the holiday. Some schools have found funds to pay teachers to conduct "Make-and-Take" parties during the summer as part of their summer "shady tree" enrichment programs.

A nice touch is to take pictures of the families with their creations. One copy of the photograph can be given to the family, another can be displayed in the child's classroom.

"HAVE TOYS, WILL TRAVEL"

Establish programs that take educational materials to the homes. Payed visitors or volunteers bring a toy or games for the week, month, etc. Parents are shown how to use the toy or game and are instructed on how it relates to the child's academic or social development. Each time a home visit is made, a new toy or game is exchanged for the previous one.

FAMILY EDUCATIONAL PLANS

Help the families to develop collaborative educational plans for working with the children at home. Goals and objectives can be established and strategies can be outlined. Teachers can send weekly activities to help coordinate the home learning with the child's schoolwork.

LEARNING CONTRACTS

The parent, teacher, and student sign a learning contract that establishes guidelines for the student's learning and the parents' and teacher's involvement. In the contract, the parents agree that they will provide an appropriate learning environment in the home and monitor the child's progress. Examples of contracts, covenants, and compacts are included in the Enhancing the Nurturer Role section earlier in this chapter.

TV CONTRACTS

All members of a family sign a contract stating that the TV will be unplugged or turned off for a period of time (i.e., a week, month, etc.). The families are given communication strategies and home learning activities, in reading, writing, math, and other subjects. Books and educational toys are made available for the families to check out. With the popularity of computer games, the families agree to use the computer only for educational purposes during the period of time.

FAMILY STUDY NIGHTS

Schedule family study nights two evenings per week at schools, churches and community centers. These two- or three-hour sessions provide a quiet place for students and family members to work together on schoolwork or enrichment tasks. The study nights are a structured way to get away from the TV, computer games, and other distractions. Usually teachers, parents or community volunteers are available to act as resources. Snacks and refreshments are provided to help make the sessions more relaxed and enjoyable.

SATURDAY ENRICHMENT DAY

This activity is a variation of the family study night. Parents and children meet on Saturday morning to work together on a high-interest learning activity. The sessions should be fun and fast-moving to ensure that the families attend.

SATURDAY SCHOOL

Four-year-olds receive home visits and attend a 3-hour session in school on Saturdays. Parents assist the teachers during the sessions. All parents receive a weekly guide to home-based learning activities and other ideas for things the families can do together during the week.

FAMILY TEACHING RESOURCE DIRECTORY

A directory is compiled that describes school and community teaching resources available to families. The directory lists such things as family reading and language centers, museums, nature centers, and libraries. Copies of the directory are distributed to the families and school personnel.

SCHOOL BUS CLASSROOMS AND PARENTING CENTERS

The first time I ran across a program that used converted school buses to reach out to children and parents was in Murfreesboro, Tennessee. The program placed the mobile learning centers in low-income neighborhoods to increase the language and concept development of at-risk three- and four-year-old children and to enhance the parents' commitment to help with their children's education.

The "learning centers" were two school buses that were no longer being used to transport children because of a state total mileage law. Although they could not be used for their original purpose of moving children, the buses could be driven from place to place by adults. The buses were in reasonably good condition and were remodeled for the project—the bench seats were removed, and lights, air conditioning, heating, tables, shelves, chairs, and so forth, were added. Each bus was supplied with preschool equipment and materials. A teacher and an aide were assigned to each mobile classroom and drove the buses around the city to certain sites to offer the program. After plugging into an electrical and water supply, the classrooms were ready for business.

Groups of neighborhood children would come to the buses for instruction. An individual child visited the bus twice a week for about two hours. The sessions included group learning activities, free time to play with educational toys, and other learning activities. Materials were also sent home each week for the child and parent to work on together. Local radio stations, newspapers, and personal contracts were used to make the public aware of the program. Funding sources for the program came from the local school board, civic organizations, church groups, and individual contributions.

The Classroom on Wheels program began in 1968 under the direction of Ruth Bowdoin who was the Director of Instruction in the city school system. By the way, this is the same Ruth Bowdoin who developed and produced a series of parenting booklets called the Bowdoin Method (1976). In 1986, with the help of a state grant, a family/school coordinator was hired to develop parenting skills, increase the communication flow, and provide overall direction to the program. With the addition of the coordinator, monthly parenting seminars were established for the families at a central location. Because the parenting classes were not held in the neighborhood, transportation and childcare were provided. Before each meeting, special notices were sent home with the children encouraging the family members to attend. A Parent Advisory Council was formed to assist in the seminar and program development. Through the Council, such things as a toy and book library, coupon exchange, and volunteer programs were organized.

The coordinator was able to make three to five home visits each day where parents were shown ways to help their children in basic skills and social development. The home visits were an extension of the visits by the mobile classrooms. Each child was given a tote bag to carry newsletters, books, pictures, and learning activities between the bus and the home.

The program was greatly enhanced by the hiring of a family/school coordinator. While the mobile classroom remained the center piece of the project, the supporting home visits, parent seminars and advisory councils brought the family in as partners.

This program was an excellent way to use old equipment in a most productive way. It provided a way to establish an instructional and parenting center in several neighborhoods at the same time. Since visiting the Murfreesboro program, I have found a variety of programs using mobile units to reach families. Besides being used as classrooms, mobile units also house family resource centers, health clinics, and social service centers.

PRESCHOOL SCREENING PROGRAMS

The school and social agencies collaborate to screen young children before they enter pre-kindergarten or kindergarten programs. The purposes of the screening programs are twofold: (a) to identify potential problem areas, and (b) to train parents to work with the children to remediate the identified problem areas. The goal is for the children to arrive at school in the fall ready for their classes.

The school district in Athens, Tennessee, offers a program where the physical screenings are conducted by the county health department. The physical screening includes physical examination, immunization, blood work, urinalysis, weight and height, and vision and hearing tests. The children are also screened in the educational and developmental areas to determine strengths and weaknesses. The screening informs the teachers about deficiencies and problem areas. The children are administered the LAP-D, DIAL-R, *Gessell School Readiness Test, Battelle Developmental Inventory*, or other similar instruments. A profile is developed and the results are used by the kindergarten, or preschool, teachers and parents to plan an educational program to remedy problem areas. The screenings occur in June, with a makeup screening day scheduled in September.

A "Parent Day" is held in the early summer where the parents come to school to learn what they can do to help prepare the children for school through at-home learning activities. When needed, provisions are also made for parents and families to counsel with school and agency personnel, such as the school psychologist and speech therapists.

The media is used to disseminate information about the screening activities and training. After school starts, teachers use newsletters, notes, telephone calls, and letters to continue the intervention.

This program involves the families and builds partnerships before the children enter school. The parents and teachers work together from the beginning to help ensure that the children will have a successful school experience.

Other best practices for coordinating services and resources, such as school-based family resource and service centers, are presented in the Coordinating Strategy chapter (Chapter 8).

Coaching the Supporter Parent Partner Role

The goal of the Supporter Parent Partner Role is to be actively supportive of the child's and the school's activities and programs. While the role is both school- and child-directed, it is played in the school environment. Providing support to the child in the home is one of the functions the Nurturer Parent Partner Role.

This role is a middle-level role, and it is assumed that the family members are already playing their lower level roles. I want to emphasize again that the term "lower order" does not apply to the importance of the role, but rather to the need to be able to master them before the upper level roles can be assumed. In fact, the Nurturer, Communicator, and Teacher Roles are probably the most crucial of all the roles.

The programs and activities that are implemented to enhance the Supporter Role are designed to strengthen the "families supporting the school" aspect of the partnership. However, it is expected the parents are involved with the child's education at home (Nurturer and Teacher Roles) and that they know and understand what is going on in school (Communicator Role).

When playing the Supporter Role, it is expected that fully involved parents will:

- participate in classroom events, open houses, and PTA/PTO programs
- attend school concerts, plays, award assemblies, sport events and other productions
- assist teachers, administrators, and children in the classrooms and in other areas of the school
- participate in booster clubs and other fund-raising activities
- chaperone field trips and dances
- organize and conduct campus cleanups and beautification projects

Workshop and Class Topics Related to the Supporter Role

Since the family members should already know about the school's curriculum, programs and activities at this stage, the workshops and classes concentrate on such activities as volunteering, tutoring, mentoring, and so forth. Some examples of "How To" workshops are:

- how to be a classroom volunteer
- how to tutor in science and math
- how to be a mentor
- how to work with special needs children
- how to organize fund-raising projects
- how to supervise students at social events and on field trips

Other Supporter Role Coaching Best Practices

VOLUNTEER PROGRAMS

Chapter 8 presents a series of guidelines for developing an effective volunteeer program. These suggestions can be used to enhance the parents' ability to play the Supporter Role.

Coaching the Learner Parent Partner Roles

The goal of the Learner Parent Partner Role is to obtain new skills and knowledge that will help directly and indirectly with the child's educational and social development. While ultimately the family members' learning is directed at the child, the obtainment of new skills and knowledge will also help the parents with their own educational and social development.

The assumption is that by enhancement of the parents' general skills and knowledge, they will be better able to support their children and be involved in their education. The new federal Even Start program is based on this notion. The program requires that the parents be enrolled in classes such as GED preparation, literacy, English as second language, parenting, and so forth, when their children are in school or in the program's daycare center. The parents generally eat breakfast and lunch with their children and some time during the day they work with the children on learning activities.

While the Learner Role encompasses all of the program and activities that are implemented to enhance the Parent Partner Roles, the best practices included in this section focus primarily on the parents' growth, which in turn, will help the child. When playing the Learner Role, it is expected that fully involved parents will:

- participate in parent education programs that focus on such things as child development, parenting skills, alcohol and drug abuse, and teenage pregnancy
- obtain and read materials on such topics as school curriculum and activities, school board policies, school rules and regulations, basic skill development, parent and student rights, college preparation, and dropout prevention
- enroll in adult education classes to improve general knowledge and skills in such areas as math, language, geography, education issues, reading, and literature

Workshop and Class Topics Related to the Learner Role

A vast array of workshops and classes could be offered to enhance the family members' skills and knowledge. Some examples of parent education topics are:

- GED preparation program
- reading and basic literacy
- math
- English as second language (ESL)
- foreign language
- human development
- adolescent behavior
- ages and stages in child development
- special health needs of children
- drug and alcohol awareness
- gang influence
- AIDS awareness and prevention
- sex education
- teenage pregnancy

Other Learner Role Coaching Best Practices

This section presents some examples of unusual programs and activities that can be used to enhance the parents' skills and knowledge. The best practices reflect a high expectation that the family members will respond positively to learning opportunities.

SNOW WHITE, A PARENT PLAY

A teacher at an inner-city school in Nashville read in the newspaper that a consultant had been hired by the district to work on a special project with gifted and talented students. The plan was for the consultant to spend a week with the students and have them learn a play. At the end of the week, the class would present the play to the whole school. After reading the article, the teacher had an idea and went to her principal and family/school/community coordinator.

She said to the principal and coordinator, "Let's see if the consultant would come to our school and work with our families." "Most of our family members have not completed high school and I'm sure they have never been in a play, but I think it is a great idea. Let's give it a try," the coordinator replied.

The principal agreed, and went to the district office to see if the consultant could come to the school to help the families put on a play for the children. Permission was granted, and arrangements were made.

The parents and faculty worked feverishly with the consultant for a week and on Friday presented "Snow White and the Seven Dwarfs." The play was presented as a satire. The family members made the scenery and props, including a giant candy kiss made out of aluminum wrap. The play was wonderful and the children loved it. After the performance, the school held a celebration for the families. Refreshments were served, and each family member received a rose and a certificate.

It was a new experience for the families who were very excited and proud. The family members experienced success because the coordinator and teachers had high expectations for them. They thought the family members could do it, and they did. Performing in the play was a life-changing experience for at least one parent. The woman who played Snow White assumed the name "Snow" after the play. Soon after the performance, she enrolled in classes at the community college to finish her hospital aide's training. She said that being in the play inspired her to return to school. After completing the hospital aide program, she got a job and moved out of the housing projects.

The following year, without the aid of the consultant, the parents and the faculty presented "Peter Rabbit." At the celebration party following the successful presentation, the family members gathered around the television to watch a video of their performance. They squealed in delight when they saw themselves on the screen. "What are we going to do next year?" they asked.

Berryhill Family Affair

Berryhill Elementary School in Charlotte, North Carolina, organizes and hosts an event each October, called the Berryhill Family Affair. It is an evening of family workshops combined with food, fun, and fellowship.

The Family Affair begins with a free supper (hot dogs, cole slaw, baked beans, dessert, and drinks) prepared by the cafeteria staff for the whole family. Over the years, organizations such as AT&T, Belk Department Stores, and others have covered the cost of the meal and some of their employees have helped with the serving. Free transportation is provided if needed. Bus transportation and meal reservation forms are sent home with the children. The affair is very popular with the families and the forms make it home and are returned.

During supper, there is usually an inexpensive raffle ($1.00 per ticket) to raise money to support programs for the children and the families. The prizes include such items as two tickets to a Charlotte Hornets' basketball or Charlotte Panthers' football game, entertainment coupon book, sports jackets, and money. In addition to the raffle, door prizes are given out.

After dinner, the family members select a workshop to attend and the children go to the multipurpose room and other classrooms, by age groups, for games and activities such as bean toss, cakewalk, basketball shoot, and go fish. The teachers and assistants organize and conduct the games and activities. The children receive small inexpensive prizes. Babies and younger children are cared for by teachers and volunteers in a separate room.

To bridge the time between supper and the start of the workshops, the school arranges activities such as a police officer showing off his or her "drug-sniffing" dog and a clown making balloon animals for the children. The PTA has a membership and a sale table where parents can join the organization and purchase school T-shirts and sweatshirts. The workshops are fast-moving and last no more than one hour. PTA members and families are asked what sort of session would be helpful and interesting. A committee comprised of the counselor, Communities-in-School representative, principal, assistant principal, PTA president, and teachers decide on the topics and identify individuals to lead the workshops. One year the following workshops were offered:

- Coping with Homelessness—Homelessness is affecting more and more people each year. This workshop discusses services available to assist families in overcoming homelessness and explore community resources.
- Positive Discipline—The workshop coaches parents on how to discipline without using corporal punishment and how to teach children responsibility, cooperation, and problem-solving skills.
- Health Education Curriculum—This session is designed primarily for parents of 5th- and 6th-grade students. The program's parent handbook is used to guide the participants through a discussion of the components of the comprehensive Health Education instructional program (e.g., Family Living, Ethical Behavior and Human Sexuality).
- Berryhill Reading Program—The SRA Direct Instruction reading program is discussed. The parents are shown ways they can help their child be a better reader.
- PETALS (Parents Exploring Teaching and Learning Styles)—PETALS is a system of evaluations and activities that connects the parents with the child's learning processes. The workshop presents information on how children learn and shows the parents how to be a positive influence in their child's life.

The Berryhill parents look forward to the annual event and a high percentage of the total family population participate. The Family Affair did not just happen. It has taken lots of work and has grown and matured over the years.

The Berryhill Family Affair is a comprehensive family/school/community partnership strategy. The event employs *Connecting* best practices to reach out to the families, *Communicating* best practices to communicate effectively, *Coordinating* best practices to combine resources, and *Coaching* best practices to enhance the parents' skills and knowledge. The Berryhill Family Affair is a good example of an activity that demonstrates the commitment the faculty, staff and community have made to establishing and maintaining partnerships between the families, school, and community.

SURVIVAL SKILLS PROGRAM

When I arrived at an inner-city elementary school, the family/school/community coordinator and a group of parents were practicing for a graduation ceremony. The parents were "graduating" from a program called, "Survival Skills for Women." The ten women had been attending this self-help training program developed by Dr. Linda P. Thurston of Survival Skills Education and Development (there is a similar program for men). The program is designed to be presented as a series of ten 3-hour workshops. The topics of the workshops are: Assertiveness, Personal Health, Nutrition, Money Management, Child Management, Self-Advocacy, Legal Rights, Coping with Crisis, Community Resources, and Re-Entry/Employment. The goal of the program is to empower the participants with the confidence and competence to have positive attitudes and beliefs in self, and to take charge of their external world.

The women were all single mothers on welfare who were living in the public housing complex that surrounded the school. The parents were reading at a third-grade level or below. After completing the survival program, they are encouraged to take basic literacy classes and enroll in a GED preparation program.

The graduation ceremony was an important conclusion to the training. The coordinator used the activity to recognize the women's accomplishments and to provide them with the opportunity to affirm their sense of empowerment.

The rehearsal was being held in the school's gym/auditorium. I was the only adult observer (three children rode tricycles across the old, but shiny hardwood floor). The coodinator coached the women on their speeches. One by one, they approached the lectern and read their statements. The women said such things as:

- "Once I was passive, now I am assertive."
- "I learned how to stand up for my rights."
- "I did not expect to learn so much, so fast."
- "I learned to be more assertive, rather than aggressive."

The next day the women, wearing caps and gowns, "graduated" before the entire student body. Each parent received a rose along with her diploma. The graduation speaker congratulated them on their accomplishments and encouraged them to continue with their education. A reception with refreshments followed the ceremony and the women continued to beam and smile as they had throughout the day. This was a big event in their lives.

The impact of self-help workshops can be dramatic. Whether you purchase a program or design your own, rituals and ceremonies are an important aspect of the training. The recognition and praise will help to reinforce the concepts presented in the program.

Coaching the Advisor Parent Partner Role

The goal of the Advisor Parent Partner Role is to wisely counsel and advise the child about personal and educational issues. Playing this role, the parent advises the child, rather than tells the child what to do. Since this is a higher order role, to be effective the family member and child need to be able to communicate (Communicator Role) and to have a trusting relationship (Nurturing Role). Because the Advisor Role builds on the other Parent Partner Roles, the best practices to enhance this role are focused and specific. It is assumed that, if needed, the parents have been coached to play the lower order roles.

When playing the Advisor Role, it is expected that fully involved parents will:

- help with personal concerns and problems
- assist with curriculum and program issues
- advise about potential career paths and opportunities
- be familiar with contents of the student's records
- know and understand school procedures such as the standardized testing process, school-to-work homework activities, and so forth

Workshop and Class Topics Related to the Advisor Role

Some examples of workshop and class topics to enhance the Advisor Role are:

- advising skills
- the helping relationship and counseling
- school-to-work programs
- applying to college

Other Advisor Role Coaching Best Practices

Since this is a higher order role, it is important to assess the families and determine if they have skills and knowledge of such areas as:

- school board policies
- the school's mission and goals
- school regulations
- curriculum
- grade-level learning goals and objectives
- procedures for monitoring student progress
- grading and exam policy

- homework policy
- discipline policy
- attendance and tardy policy
- standardized testing program
- student and parent rights
- college application procedures

Best practices found in the Communicator Parent Role section in this chapter and in the Communicating Strategy chapter (Chapter 7) are implemented if it is determined that some areas need to be enhanced.

CAREER AND COLLEGE NIGHT

Schedule and host a Career and College Night at the school. Invite representatives from local colleges and universities, businesses and industries, government and social agencies and professions to talk with the families and students. Have guidance counselors available to answer questions.

FIELD TRIPS TO LOCAL COLLEGES AND CORPORATIONS

Organize field trips for the parents and students to visit the local colleges and corporations. The families tour the facilities and learn about programs, products, and opportunities. Representatives from the different organizations are available to answer questions.

COLLEGE STUDENT/FAMILY NIGHT

When local college students are home on vacation, invite them to the school for a meeting with interested students and parents. The college students answer questions and talk to the families about what they need to do to prepare for college.

Coaching the Advocator Parent Partner Role

The goal of the Advocator role is to effectively and actively advocate, mediate, and negotiate for the child. Like the supporter role, this is generally played in the school setting. Specific skills and knowledge are needed to play this role. And, as for the other higher order roles, the parents need to be willing and able to play the lower order roles as well.

As indicated in the previous section, the parents will need to know and understand the information contained in parent handbooks, curriculum guides, and other policy materials. While being able to communicate and be supportive, they must also be skilled in mediation and conflict resolution. Most family members will need help to enhance these skills.

When playing the Advocator Role, it is expected that fully involved parents will:

- help to resolve conflicts, concerns, and problems related to curriculum, programs and activities
- reinforce the proper enforcement of family and student rights
- monitor the application of school policies and practices
- know and understand school and school district policies
- advocate for curricular and operational policy and procedural reform

Workshop and Class Topics Related to the Advocator Role

Workshops and classes designed to enhance the Advocator Role build on the parents' existing lower level role skills and knowledge. Some examples of workshop and class subjects are:

- conflict resolution and negotiation
- decision-making skills
- student and parent rights and responsibilities
- school policies and practices
- appealing school actions
- classroom inclusion programs

Other Advocator Role Coaching Best Practices

As with the Advisor Role, the family members need to be assessed to determine if they have skills and knowledge in such areas as

- school board policies
- the school's mission and goals
- school regulations
- curriculum
- grade-level learning goals and objectives

- procedures for monitoring student progress
- grading and exam policy
- homework policy
- discipline policy
- attendance and tardy policy
- standardized testing program

When the parents have the prerequisite foundation built by the lower order roles, best practices like the following can be implemented to enhance the Advocator Role.

PARENT RIGHTS HANDBOOKS

Publish and distribute materials to the families about parent and student rights. For example, parents need to know they have the legal right to:

- look at their child's school records
- a hearing if it is believed that the contents of any record are untrue, inaccurate, or misleading
- insert written explanations with respect to the contents in any record
- expect that the child's records are not released to any individual, agency, or organization without written consent (There are a few exceptions such as to individuals in the same school who have a legitimate interest or another school where the student is transferring.)
- look at all official school policies
- have a special needs child placed in an appropriate program
- be present and represent the child at any hearing regarding suspension
- enroll the child in a particular course if he or she is eligible
- expect the school district to adequately supervise and protect the child while being transported in a school bus and in attendance at all school activities

PARENTS OF CHILDREN WITH SPECIAL NEEDS

Additional handbooks and materials need to be available to parents who have children with special needs (e.g., autistic, academically gifted, hearing impaired, mentally handicapped, specific learning disabled, orthopedically impaired, etc.). The handbook should contain information such as related legislations and regulations, evaluation procedures, types of programs and related services, processes for consent, mediation, appeal, and so forth.

Coaching the Collaborator Parent Partner Role

The goal of the Collaborator Parent Partner Role is to work effectively with the school and community to help with problem solving, decision making, and policy development. The term "Collaborator" is used because it expresses the partnership relationship. The Collaborator Role is the highest level role and it builds on all of the other Parent Partner Roles. Realistically, few parents will act as collaborators.

Yet, as the school and community form partnerships with families, it is very important to have representation from all segments of the family population when establishing committees, councils, and planning groups. Being a collaborator requires specific skills and knowledge in such areas as policy formation, decision making, curriculum development, and so forth. To be involved in the planning and development of family/school/community partnerships, the collaborators need to understand the Self-Renewing Partnership Model.

When playing the Collaborator Role, it is expected that fully involved parents will:

- participate in family/school/community partnership planning groups, school improvement and community councils, special projects, and school committees where parents have equal status with professionals and representatives from the community
- assist in reducing educational barriers
- monitor health, library, and cultural services to make sure they are easily accessible to the school and neighborhood
- attend school board meetings when appropriate
- serve on the school board and city council
- be prepared to influence school policy and appeal local school or school system decisions that are questionable or not understood
- participate on committees that focus on issues such as maintaining a safe environment in and around the campus and

bus safety, upgrading and beautifying the school building and grounds, and establishing and maintaining high standards and expectations, quality programs, and extracurricular options

Workshop and Class Topics Related to the Collaborator Role

Because this is the highest order Parent Partner Role, the potential workshop and class topics cover a wide range of subjects and issues. Some examples of topics are:

- decision making and problem solving
- small group behavior
- school and bus safety
- school violence and discipline
- computer-assisted instruction
- inclusion of physically and mentally challenged children in the classroom
- curriculum development
- policy formation
- school governance
- school budget
- school effectiveness

Other Collaborator Role Coaching Best Practices

FIELD TRIPS

Organize family field trips to regular school board meetings; public hearings on such issues as pupil assignment, violence, curriculum

---

Committee Work

When involving parents in committee work, make sure that meetings are structured and action-oriented. They should be guided by well-planned agendas so they move along swiftly. Do not waste time on trivial matters or issues. The participants need to know and understand the scope and responsibilities of the committee or project. The expected outcome should be clearly stated.

The family members must feel their services are wanted and that their comments, suggestions, and recommendations will be thoroughly considered. If necessary, provide a workshop on group decision making.

change; town council sessions; and district-wide education and parent conferences.

STANDING ADVISORY COMMITTEE

Organize a standing advisory group, or committee, of parents, teachers, and staff to make recommendations to the principal on school improvement, restructuring, enhancement, and the use of discretionary funds. If the school is involved with a university as a partner school or professional development school, it is a good idea to also have a higher education representative on the committee.

The groups meet regularly and are called into session when special needs or projects arise. If space is available, the chairperson of the group is provided an office or desk near the principal. The titles for this type of group include: family/school/community partnership committee, school improvement council, school planning and management team, and similar names.

AD HOC COMMITTEE

If a special issue is facing the school district or school, and if there is a need to develop new policies, a broadly representative parent and community Ad Hoc committee is formed to study the issue and make recommendations. The committee considers such issues as school reorganization, bond proposals, building needs, curriculum changes, smoking, and alcohol and drug abuse, and so forth.

In cooperation with school officials, the group drafts a policy or regulation, which is circulated among the entire student and family bodies for suggestions and comments. After the discussion sessions, the draft is revised and sent to the school board to be considered for adoption.

The Empowering Playground Fence

This chapter began with a story about a remark made to Suzanne Brown, the director of a family/school/community partnership program in Nashville. When Suzanne came to the inner-city school, drug trafficking was so rampant that dealers drove across the school grounds to get into the neighborhood to sell or to run away from the police. One day a car roared through the playground with a police car following closely behind. Fortunately, no children were outside playing. When this happened, a group of parents was meeting with Suzanne. The parents were perplexed and angry. "Those dealers are using the lawn for a racetrack and we do not know what to do," one of the parents exclaimed.

The parents said that there used to be a fence around the playground to protect the children and adults, with gates allowing neighborhood residents access to and from the school grounds. Now the fence was gone and only a few posts remained.

"Over the years the fence was getting torn up and the city did not repair it," said one parent. "The drug dealers pretty much finished it off," added another.

Suzanne had been working with the parents to enhance their Collaborator Role skills. For the past few weeks they had been studying how to be more involved in school governance and community development. Suzanne had an idea and went to the principal to discuss her strategy. The principal made some suggestions and said she would help in any way she could. When the coordinator met with the parents again, she presented her idea.

"Let's get the city to rebuild the fence," she said. "We will never be able to get them to do that," replied a parent, "Nobody listens to us." "Oh yes they will, if we work together," exclaimed Suzanne. "Let's form a plan."

Suzanne helped the parents to compose a letter to the mayor explaining the problem at the school. They took pictures of the playground and the remaining fence posts and enclosed them with the letter.

The parents were first very excited and then disappointed when the reply from the mayor arrived the next week. The letter thanked the parents for letting him know about the problem and said that he had passed the letter and pictures onto the superintendent of schools. In a few days, a letter arrived from the assistant superintendent for building and grounds, indicating he was concerned about their problem, but that there was no money in the budget for a new fence.

"They ain't going to do nothing," said a dejected parent. "We are not through yet," said Suzanne encouragingly. "I think we need to present our request to the school board. Maybe if they heard about our problem they will find the money." "I would be scared to do that," responded a parent. "There is nothing to be afraid about. We just need to do it right," said Suzanne.

She said if the parents worked as a group they would have more power and have a better chance to be heard. They talked about communication, conflict resolution and negotiation. The group decided which parent would call the school board office to see if they could be placed on the next meeting's agenda. When the parent returned, she was very excited. "They said we would be able to speak to the board at their next meeting." "Now we have to get as many parents and teachers to the meeting as possible," commented Suzanne.

The group decided how they would go out into the neighborhood to get people to come to the meeting. The principal agreed to find funds to pay for a school bus to transport the parents to the meeting. The parents met with the school's faculty to see if they would support their effort. Suzanne explained to the parents the importance of keeping the mayor, superintendent, and assistant superintendent on their side and not alienating them. She helped them write a letter explaining why they had decided to meet with the board.

Finally, the day arrived for the meeting. An excited group of parents gathered at the school and loaded onto the buses. So many parents had decided to attend that two buses were needed.

"This is great," exclaimed the principal. "Let's hope this works," thought Suzanne.

The spokesperson for the parent group presented the problem of the playground fence to the school board. The board members asked the parents, principal, coordinator, superintendent, and assistant superintendent many questions and discussed the issue among themselves. The board president said that they would consider their request after they had a chance to get more information from the city. The parents were feeling down as they left the meeting.

"Well, at least we tried," said one of the parents. "We learned a lot even if they decide not to get us a fence," said another.

The parents all agreed that trying to get the fence was a learning experience and they felt good about what they had done. The following week, the principal asked Suzanne to come down to her office.

"I just received a call from the assistant superintendent of building and grounds," she bubbled, "They are going to put up a new fence next week."

The school board members, mayor, superintendent, and assistant superintendent attended the dedication for the new fence. The parents had planned the program themselves. When Suzanne spoke, she praised the parents for their good work and courage.

"You did it," Suzanne exclaimed. "Working together, you helped the children, the community and yourselves." "Now I know what Suzanne means by empowerment," said a parent to the group.

But this great story does not end here. Suzanne worked with the parents and showed them how they had acted as a team, learned to negotiate and to be assertive. The group continued to meet and found other ways to help their community and the school.

A SUMMARY OF WORKSHOP AND CLASS TOPICS

The following is a summary of potential topics for workshops and classes designed to enhance family members' skills and knowledge. The topics are categorized under the headings: Life Skills, Self-Help, Educational and Social Issues, Quality of Life, and Question and Answer Sessions. The topics that relate to a particular Parent Partner Role are also presented in the section that discusses the best practices to enhance the role.

LIFE SKILL TOPICS

- improving job skills and finding employment
- locating and working with social service agencies
- applying for public assistance (e.g., food stamps, social security, etc.)

- obtaining citizenship
- locating and selecting a daycare program
- getting your electricity, gas, or telephone service restored
- making birthing arrangements
- making funeral arrangements
- maintaining your car
- fixing simple things around your home

Self-Help Topics

- GED preparation
- reading and literacy
- basic math skills
- English as second language (ESL)
- foreign languages
- sustaining hope in the face of long-term adversity
- controlling your life
- being a good role model
- communicating with your child
- improving relationships between siblings and other family members
- overcoming social isolation
- relaxation and stress reduction
- exercise and weight lifting
- nutrition
- weight management and control
- time management
- dealing with grief and loss
- self-esteem and social skill enhancement
- interpersonal facilitation skills
- driver education

Educational and Social Issue Topics

- knowing what is going on in your child's school life
- helping your child be successful in school
- helping your child prepare to take a test
- reading a report card
- understanding student records and standardized test scores

- tutoring in the classroom
- appealing school actions
- improving your child's feelings and attitudes toward school
- interactive homework
- extracurricular activities and policies
- understanding the daily school schedule
- grading policies
- discipline policies
- school support services
- parent-teacher conferences—skills for families
- dropout prevention
- violence and school safety
- school bus safety
- computer-assisted instruction
- inclusion of physically and mentally challenged children in the classroom
- pre-kindergarten and kindergarten parent orientation
- transition from elementary to middle school
- transition from middle to high school
- student and parent rights and responsibilities
- school policies and practices
- curriculum and curriculum development
- policy formation
- school governance
- school budget
- school effectiveness
- building self-esteem in your child
- motivating your child
- helping the children at home
- improving your child's skills in reading, math, writing, and other subjects
- developing a reading program
- how children learn
- study skills
- home learning activities
- creating summer learning opportunities
- discipline techniques
- human development
- adolescent behavior

- ages and stages in child development
- special health needs of children
- small group behavior
- drug and alcohol awareness
- gang influence
- teen depression, suicide, and death education
- student eating disorders
- AIDS awareness and prevention
- sex education
- teenage pregnancy
- advising and counseling skills
- mentoring
- conflict resolution and negotiation
- decision-making skills

Quality of Life Topics

- arts and craft-making
- dancing and dance lessons
- group singing
- holiday card and gift making
- halloween costume design
- ethnic cooking
- weight lifting

"Question and Answer" Sessions

Many families have never had the opportunity to talk informally with professionals about health care, social services, agency rules and regulations, and similar issues. Sessions with various experts allow the families to ask questions and be informed about services, resources, and prevention programs. Question and Answer sessions can include meetings with a:

- dentist
- pediatrician
- public health nurse
- poison control center representative
- nutritionist

- fireman
- police officer
- drug abuse counselor
- mayor
- principal
- guidance counselor
- school nurse
- speech therapist
- community-in-schools representative
- reading recovery teacher

As suggested, earlier, when deciding on workshop and class topics, first identify the Parent Partner Role(s) to be enhanced. Look at the suggested topics listed under the role and make a decision. If the focus of the workshop or class has been determined (e.g., educational and social issues, life skills, self-help, etc.), consider the topics listed above.

SUMMARY

The Coaching Strategy is implemented on the foundation built by the other Collaboration Strategies. What best practices are appropriate is determined by the School/Community Collaboration Strategy that is being emphasized, which in turn, is determined by the goals and objectives. The goals and objectives are included in the family/school/community partnership plan. In the next chapter, the Strategic Partnership Planning System is presented. It is a comprehensive method the school and community leaders can use to develop the partnership plan.

CHAPTER 10

The Strategic Partnership Planning System: Readying the Troops

"Would you tell me please, which way I ought to go from here?" asked Alice to the Cheshire Cat.
"That depends a good deal on where you want to get to," said the Cat.
(Carroll, 1946, p. 71)

Like Alice, when planning a family/school/community partnership program, you have to know where you want to get to before you can decide which way to go. Once the destination is determined, you not only want to reach your goal, but you want the best return on your investment of time and other resources. Therefore, for a partnership program to be successful, a well-thought out plan is required. This chapter presents the Strategic Partnership Planning System that the school and community can use to decide "where to go," and "how to get there."

Family/school/community partnerships vary in focus and magnitude. For example, school districts design district-wide programs, individual schools create partnership programs for the school, Title 1 and Headstart centers develop partnerships, and individual teachers take it upon themselves to implement best practices to involve the parents as partners. While different in size, all partnership programs have a similar purpose: Involving the parents in the education of the children in the home and at school.

A "top-down and bottom-up" approach is used to create the partnership programs. At the top, you need leadership and political and financial assistance from a superintendent, principal, center director, or project coordinator to initiate and sanction the planning process. At the same

225

time, you need to have "bottom-up" support and involvement from the teachers, staff, parents, and community members to plan, implement, and sustain the program.

Therefore, in keeping with the family/school/community partnership concept, the planning process should include the perceptions and judgments of the major stakeholders: the faculty and staff, parents, and members of the community. The stakeholders are all partners in the education of the children, and the various partners, at the top and bottom, need to be involved in the development, implementation, and evaluation of the partnership plan.

Consequently, the shared decision-making process is used throughout the planning system. While shared decision making is time-consuming, it is the best way to build commitment. A good decision is effective only when it is accepted and embraced by those affected by the decision. The partnerships are planned collaboratively so teachers, principals, parents, and community members are committed to the program.

Forming partnerships between the families, school, and community is not a "quick-fix" strategy. The partnerships are long-term investments in the children, designed to stimulate lasting social and educational improvements. Therefore, like any organizational change, the development of a family/school/community partnership is an ongoing process, not a single event.

When creating partnerships between the families, school, and community, you are in the business of restructuring the way the different parties are used to interacting and working together. This change involves the development of new roles and relationships, and usually a paradigm shift is required. As stated in Chapter 5, a paradigm is a "scheme for understanding and explaining certain aspects of reality" (Covey, 1992). Covey argues that if we want to make major changes, we need to shift our paradigm and perceive the issue in a totally new way. Therefore, as we plan the reach out to the "missing families" and build partnerships, we need to broaden our view of parental involvement. The partnership concept discussed here is built on the notion that the involvement occurs through collaborative relationships between the families, school, and community.

As you attempt to make significant changes in the family, school, and community cultures, many variables will be continually changing and evolving. The person(s) leading the partnership program has to be able to adjust and adapt to the changing conditions. As the partnerships are being planned and implemented, the schools continue to function, and family and community life are ongoing. It is the proverbial case of "building the airplane as you are flying it."

Consequently, I believe my definition of a leader as, "a person with buttered feet standing in a pool of ball bearings," is apropos. A good partnership plan provides the leader with the "solid flexibility" to deal with the change process.

Based on the results of my studies, I have found that faculty, staff, and administrators who are involved in successful partnerships are committed to the idea of self-determination and responsibility (Lueder, 1989). Their schools have a positive organizational culture and a strong sense of community. Very importantly, they care about the families and each other, and believe they can make a difference in the children's lives. Not surprisingly, these are characteristics found in most successful school programs. Therefore, having this kind of organizational culture is very important. As Rutherford (1995) argues, "The development and implementation of programs are shaped more by the diversity within systems, and perceptions, attitudes and beliefs, than by the organizational patterns of the school" (p. vii).

While the plan, itself, is an essential outcome of the activity, so is the experience of the planning process. Deal and Peterson note that: "Good planning serves as a meaningful ritual that draws people together emotionally and spiritually. Values and hopes are connected to objectives" (1994, p. 101). The act of collaborative planning helps to reaffirm beliefs and attitudes and develops commitment among the various stakeholders.

THE STRATEGIC PARTNERSHIP PLANNING SYSTEM (SPPS)

A comprehensive planning system has been devised to help schools and communities with the difficult and complex task of developing a partnership program for involving families, especially those that are hard to reach, in the education of their children. The Strategic Partnership Planning System (SPPS) is a method for planning, designing, and implementing family/school/community partnerships. Using the system, Partnership Action Plans are produced that identify the targeted population(s), the School/Community Collaboration Strategy(ies) to be emphasized, and the best practices to be implemented.

The Strategic Partnership Planning System is designed primarily for use in individual schools, centers, and classrooms, but aspects of the system can also be employed at the district level. The collaborative relationships between the families and the school are played out in the home and at school. Therefore, the partnership programs are usually developed for these settings.

The conceptual framework for the system is based on the principles of collaborative decision making, organizational renewal, and site-based management. The system is designed to assess needs, develop commitment, identify goals and objectives, select intervention strategies, and evaluate results. The planning process is divided into three phases: Pre-Intervention Planning, Intervention Planning, and Intervention. Figure 10.1 outlines the system's thirteen steps. The system is designed to answer several "happening" questions:

- What is happening now?
- What do we want to happen?
- Why isn't it happening now?
- What do we need to do to make it happen?
- How can we tell if it happens?

Pre-Intervention Planning: Building the Foundation

Step 1. Understanding the nature and functions of family/school/community partnerships and the Self-Renewing Partnership Model.
Step 2. Identifying shared beliefs about parent involvement and partnerships with families.
Step 3. Assessing the levels of parent involvement in the home and at school.
Step 4. Developing a collective vision.
Step 5. Developing a shared mission statement.

Intervention Planning: Setting the Direction

Step 6. Identifying the family population, or populations, to be targeted.
Step 7. Identifying the barriers to overcome.
Step 8. Determining the Partnership Program Goals.
Step 9. Determining the School/Community Collaboration Strategies to be emphasized.
Step 10. Determining objectives.

Intervention: Reaching and Working with Families

Step 11. Selecting and implementing best practices.
Step 12. Evaluating the effects of strategies and best practices.
Step 13. Redefining goals and objectives.

Figure 10.1 The Strategic Partnership Planning System. (Some portions of the Strategic Partnership Planning System are adapted from Senior High School Improvement Model, 1993. Published by National Study of School Evaluation, Falls Church, VA.)

The Strategic Partnership Planning System is intended to be used as a guide to plan and implement partnership programs. At first glance, the system may appear to be somewhat cumbersome. Clearly, going through the thirteen steps is time-consuming. However, I believe the steps need to be followed carefully for the partnerships to effect the social and educational changes for which they are intended.

The necessity of following each step "to the letter" depends upon the particular circumstances of each school, center, or classroom. However, the first step, "Understanding the nature and function of family/school/community partnerships, Parent Partner Roles, and the Self-Renewing Partnership Model," is essential. This step is the basis for determining, "Where you want to go and how to get there."

If the faculty and staff of a school or center, or an individual teacher, are just beginning to develop a partnership program, it is recommended that the planners go through the three phases, and follow each step carefully. It is necessary to understand the underlying partnership concepts and strategies, and to identify a set of beliefs, a collective vision, and a shared mission statement before planning for the interventions. By building the foundation and setting the direction, the intervention strategies can be easily determined and the best practices implemented.

For some schools, the formation of a family/school/community partnership program may be a component of an ongoing school improvement or school restructuring project. If the school has already gone through the process of identifying needs, developing a collective vision, and writing a shared mission statement, the faculty and staff, parent representatives, and members of the community can determine if the present school improvement plan encompasses the needs of the families and the concepts of a partnership program.

If the outcomes of the Pre-Intervention Planning Phase are already in place, the planners move onto the Intervention Planning Phase. In this second phase, family populations to be targeted and the barriers to be overcome are identified, and the School/Community Collaboration Strategies to be emphasized and goals and objectives determined.

In some cases, the faculty and staff at a school or center already know what families need to be targeted. After going through Step 1, then, they can quickly move through the Intervention Planning Phase and be ready for the Intervention Phase. The planners have determined the appropriate Collaboration Strategy to be emphasized and they can select the best practices to be implemented. After implementing the programs, events, and activities to reach the partnership goals, the effects of the best practices can be evaluated.

The following is a description of the thirteen steps in the Strategic Partnership Planning System (SPPS). Using the description, a school district, individual school, or teacher decides where they are in the partnership planning process and where they should "plug" into the system.

PRE-INTERVENTION PLANNING: BUILDING THE FOUNDATION

The purpose of the Pre-Intervention Planning Phase is to provide those involved in the planning process with a conceptual framework for developing and implementing a family/school/community partnership program. Ideally, the planners should agree on the definition of the various terms so everyone starts from the same point. In this phase, the planners assess the current nature and degree of involvement by the parents and agree on a set of beliefs, a collective vision, and a mission statement. The purpose of this phase is to build a foundation for the Intervention Planning Phase.

STEP 1. UNDERSTANDING THE NATURE AND FUNCTIONS OF FAMILY/SCHOOL/COMMUNITY PARTNERSHIPS AND THE SELF-RENEWING PARTNERSHIP MODEL

Explain to the teachers, principals, parent representatives, and community leaders how the children's academic and social development will be enhanced by forming collaborative relationships between the families, school, and community. Discuss the nature and functions of family/school/community partnerships as presented in Chapter 3. The benefits of the partnership for all stakeholders are described. It is important to understand that the collaborative relationships are based on caring, trust, respect and that the partnerships are related to a positive organizational culture.

Present the desired outcomes of parent involvement both in the home and with the school. Describe and discuss the eight Parent Partner Roles (Chapter 2). By understanding what is meant by "parent involvement," and knowing the benefits of partnerships between the families, school, and community, the faculty, staff, and community members will be able to use the Self-Renewing Partnership Model to develop and implement their program.

After introducing the Self-Renewing Partnership Model as a method for creating family/school/community partnerships, describe and discuss the four School/Community Collaboration Strategies. Give examples of best practices that can be used to implement the intervention strategies. Show how the Parent Partner Roles are a component of the model. It is important that the planners understand the progressive and interactive nature of the Parent Partner Roles and the School/Community Collaboration Strategies.

Emphasize and explain how the Self-Renewing Partnership Model differs from the traditional parent involvement approach. Point out that you realize the idea of using school and community resources to reach out to the families is not the norm, and introduce the paradigm shift concept.

Discuss how in the past, top-down bureaucratic school and community models have sometimes proven strongly resistant to collaboration with the family and outside agencies. Explain that even in the best of situations, individuals or groups are still concerned about their "turf" and the possible loss of power when forming partnerships. Stress that this resistance must be overcome, and that the schools and communities need to work with the families to involve them in their children's education at home and at school.

Keep in mind that the leadership must be vigilant in keeping the collective vision in the forefront and working toward the common good of the families and children. By creating a learning community where the parents, community, and school combine forces to educate all of the children, the focus can be on prevention of educational problems, rather than merely the symptoms. Issues such as low achievement, poor attendance, dropouts, misbehavior, teenage pregnancy, and drug abuse are symptoms of deep-rooted social and family issues. These social problems cannot be solved unless the families, schools, and communities work together.

STEP 2. IDENTIFYING SHARED BELIEFS ABOUT PARENTAL INVOLVEMENT AND PARTNERSHIPS WITH FAMILIES

Those who are planning a partnership should have similar beliefs and desires about the program. Leadership, according to Roland Barth (1990) is, "Making happen what you believe in." Your beliefs will be based on your values and assumptions about the roles of families and their relationships with schools. Work with the teachers, principals, and community and family representatives to reach a consensus on a set of beliefs about parent involvement and partnerships with families. Ask the participants to think about their children, society, education, schooling, schools and communities and pose such questions as:

- What and who are schools for?
- What should a learning community look like?
- How should families be involved in the education of their children?
- How do you want families involved?
- How important are partnerships between the families, schools, and communities?
- Should the school and community use resources to reach out to the families?

While it may be difficult to reach a consensus on all beliefs, it is vital that the various stakeholders have some common views about the importance of parent involvement, the need for all children to have an opportunity to succeed, and that some families will need help to get involved.

The planners develop an initial list of potential beliefs using a collaborative decision-making process. The list is then distributed to members of the learning community, faculty, staff, and community leaders for suggestions, comments, additions, or deletions. After receiving feedback, the planning group edits the original list and sends the revised list out for any additional suggestions or comments.

The group then agrees upon the set of shared beliefs and distributes them to all stakeholders, including the families. Some schools and communities ask the members of the learning community (faculty, staff, family representatives and community leaders) to each sign a copy of the shared beliefs indicating their commitment and support. This process helps ensure that the stakeholders "walk the talk."

At one point, I had "identifying shared beliefs . . . " as the first step of the model. However, a principal of a middle school made an excellent observation when I was explaining the system. She said if the teachers identified their beliefs before they were introduced to the nature and functions of a family/school/community partnership and the Self-Renewing Partnership Model, and if their beliefs conflicted with the concepts, the group might feel that they had been "set up." If their stated beliefs differed significantly from those suggested by the model, they might feel that the identification of their beliefs was just an exercise before they received the "right" answer. This suggestion made sense, so I reversed the first two steps. Since trust is a fundamental ingredient in successful partnerships, any possibility of being perceived as deceptive should be avoided.

Even so, when asking a group to identify a set of beliefs, you will have the problem of not knowing if the stated beliefs are really held and shared, or if they are just "politically correct." Also, you can assume that even with a set of "shared" beliefs, some participants will not embrace them.

Realistically, what you are hoping to achieve is a large core of stakeholders who share the beliefs and who are committed to the conceptual framework underlying the Self-Renewing Partnership Model and the notion of family/school/community partnerships. The leadership will need to work with those who are not initially committed to the concepts. At the very least, if you do not have commitment, you need to have compliance. Nobody should be blocking the progress. Figure 10.2 presents some examples of shared beliefs.

The following are examples of shared beliefs that have been identified by various groups:

- The parent is the child's first and most important teacher.
- The whole community should be involved in the education of the children.
- Families care about their children and want them to succeed.
- Most families want to be involved in the education of their children.
- Families need to be involved in the home and at school in their children's academic and social development.
- Some family members need help to enhance their parenting skills and knowledge.
- Partnerships with families need to be built on trust, caring, respect, and equity.
- Through a partnership between the families, school, and community, the families will be more involved in the education of their children both at school and at home.
- Family involvement is necessary to fully develop a child's potential.
- The involvement of the family is appreciated because it benefits all members of the learning community.
- Family involvement helps to shape, as well as differentiate, various kinds of support both in and out of school.
- Family involvement emphasizes the value of education and ultimately perpetuates the child's lifetime investment in communities and their education.

Figure 10.2 Beliefs about Parent Involvement and Family/School/Community Partnerships.

STEP 3. ASSESSING LEVELS OF PARENT INVOLVEMENT IN THE HOME AND AT SCHOOL

It makes sense to find out where you are now, before you decide where you want to go. The intent of Step 3 is to determine "what is" with regard to the involvement of the families in the education of the children in the home and at school. This assessment provides baseline data on which to plan the direction and focus of the interventions.

Perceptions of the Planning Group Members and Other Stakeholders

When making an assessment, it is a good idea to begin by gathering data from those who are involved with the planning before gathering data from other groups. Ask the group members to share their perceptions about the families, faculty, administration, school, and community.

These data will reveal the respondents' sense of reality. The planning group's data are compared with those obtained from the parents, faculty and staff, and members of the community. The comparisons will reveal the differences between groups. The following questions are posed to the planning group members and other stakeholder groups:

- What are the parents' lives like?
- What are the teachers' lives like?
- What are the principals' lives like?
- What is the school like?
- What is the community like?

A composite of the baseline data from the different groups can indicate the needs of different family populations and of the school and community. The information can be combined with other assessment data to develop family, school, and community profiles that describe the characteristics, similarities, and differences within and between the different entities.

Comparing Data within a Group

One way to gather and compare a group's data is to ask each member to put his or her answers on newsprint paper and post them on the wall. Discuss and compare the responses after the members circulate around the room and look at the answers. See if the data suggest barriers, issues, strengths, and other issues.

Parent Involvement at School

The school and community may already have some empirical data available to help determine the nature and degree of parent involvement at school. A good place to start is to study the history and experiences of past events, programs, and activities. For example, it should be fairly easy to estimate the number of parents or family members who have participated in such activities as PTA/PTO meetings, open houses or back-to-school programs, athletic, drama and music events, parent/teacher conferences, and volunteer programs. Besides the attendance numbers, it is important to identify which segments of the school or center's family population are represented at the events, or more important, which segments are consistently "missing."

A survey of the faculty can provide some information on the effectiveness of the activities and events. While faculty and staff perceptions and observations, are somewhat subjective, the combined data should paint an accurate total picture of what is and what is not happening.

The surveys can also produce some interesting surprises. At one school, the general perception was that there was a lot of parent support. However, when the teachers were asked how well the families were performing their roles, the survey indicated that the teachers did not think the parents were doing a very good job. At the same time, the results showed that virtually no resources were being used to reach out to the families. These data were revealing and helped the faculty and staff to develop a partnership program that eventually reached and involved more of the families.

Parent Involvement in the Home

A faculty survey can also be used to obtain insights about the families' involvement in the home. Teachers, guidance counselors, and principals can usually make good guesses about the nature and degree of involvement based on anecdotal data coming to school via the children. Keep in mind the hypothesis posed earlier, that a prerequisite to parents being involved at school is being involved at home.

Some estimates can be made by combining the survey results with such demographic data as the number of students on free lunch, parents receiving food stamps, single-parent families, and families with both parents working outside the home.

Family/Parent Surveys

A survey of the parents can provide insights about the kinds of involvement, barriers, and needs of the family population. Data are also collected when the partnerships are being evaluated. The survey questions seek information concerning many aspects of family life, perceptions about the school, and the academic and social development of the children.

While this method can be helpful, one must be cautious. The willingness to answer the survey and the accuracy of responses is affected by such things as degree of alienation felt by some families, the ability to read the surveys, the time available to answer the questions, and the degree to which the parents think that responding to the survey will make any difference.

In most situations, the questions will need to be very short and simple. Not only do some parents have trouble reading long and complicated questions, but they will lose interest very quickly. This is true of anyone. On occasion, I have read the questions to a group of parents and gathered their responses orally.

Parent Involvement Grids

Parent Involvement Grids can be used to show the degree to which the total family population or certain segments of the population are involved with their children's education in the home and at school. The data and the perceptions gathered from the different groups are used to develop involvement patterns for the different family populations. The grids are composites of data that relate to the particular family populations. The nine compartments in the grid are shaded to indicate the amount of involvement in the two settings: home and school. The shading is darkest where there is little or no involvement. Considering that the premise is that "the parents involved in school are also involved in the home," then Q2 and Q3 are rarely shaded.

Figure 10.3 shows the involvement pattern of a school's total family population. As shown, the involvement levels vary a great deal. One segment (Q9) is involved in the home and at school while another is not involved in either setting (Q1). The Q4 and Q7 quadrants show that some parents are involved in the home but not at school, and Q5 illustrates that a segment of the population is involved somewhat in both settings. The darkest compartments indicate the "missing" family populations.

Q7 LITTLE OR NO INVOLVEMENT AT SCHOOL AND MUCH IN THE HOME	**Q8** SOME INVOLVEMENT AT SCHOOL AND MUCH IN THE HOME	**Q9** MUCH INVOLVEMENT AT SCHOOL AND MUCH IN THE HOME
Q4 LITTLE OR NO INVOLVEMENT AT SCHOOL AND SOME IN THE HOME	**Q5** SOME INVOLVEMENT AT SCHOOL AND SOME IN THE HOME	**Q6** MUCH INVOLVEMENT AT SCHOOL AND SOME IN THE HOME
Q1 LITTLE OR NO INVOLVEMENT AT SCHOOL OR IN THE HOME	**Q2** SOME INVOLVEMENT AT SCHOOL AND LITTLE OR NONE IN THE HOME	**Q3** MUCH INVOLVEMENT AT SCHOOL AND LITTLE OR NONE IN THE HOME

Involvement at Home (vertical axis)   **Involvement at School** ⟶

Figure 10.3   *Parent Involvement Grid. Involvement Pattern of a Family Population with a Variety of Levels.*

STEP 4. DEVELOPING A COLLECTIVE VISION

A vision is an inspiring declaration of a compelling dream. It is what the planning group and other stakeholders believe should and can happen. It is the genesis of the partnership focus. The collective vision is "a statement of philosophy that goes beyond mere words to become an ideal of what a [partnership program] is striving for" (Whitaker and Moses, 1994, p. 14). When discussing visions, Deal and Peterson (1994) state, "A vision is a mental image of a better and more hopeful future. Visions engage people's hearts as well as their heads—especially when widely shared. Because visions are ephemeral, they are generally expressed in mottoes, phrases, or symbols that arouse passion as well as communicate direction and purpose" (p. 101).

These authors say the mental images are the assumptions, perceptions, and stories we have in our heads and that affect how we view the world and how we behave. Even the most astute pragmatic insights can be overshadowed by deeply ingrained mental images.

The collective vision evolves from the personal visions of the planning group member and the school or center's faculty and staff. If an individual's personal vision is not part of the shared vision, it is hard to achieve commitment. Peter Senge (1990) says: "A shared vision is the first step in allowing people who mistrusted each other to begin to work together. It creates a common identity. In fact, an organization's shared sense of purpose, vision, and operating values establish the most basic level of commonality" (p. 208).

A Chair's Vision

Claude Taylor, Chairman of Air Canada, is quoted as saying: "Certainly, a leader needs a clear vision of the organization and where it is going, but a vision is of little value unless it is shared in a way so as to generate enthusiasm and commitment. Leadership and communication are inseparable. You can't have one without the other."

People focus on long-term goals when they want to, not when they are required to. By combining a strong sense of personal direction held by the various individuals involved with the planning, a powerful synergistic force can emerge that helps to create the collective vision. The difference between the collective vision and the current reality produces a creative tension that moves the partnership planning process forward.

The set of shared beliefs generated earlier in the planning process and the conceptual framework of the Self-Renewing Partnership Model are used to develop the collective vision. The success of the partnership program may hinge on setting a vision that "grabs" and motivates people into action. Nancy Feyl Chavkin (1995) contends that the importance of a common vision held by key people cannot be overstated. The key people promote and support parent and community involvement and develop a common vision with others in the school's social system. She says that: "The common vision must include a broad view of the school that includes the community as an important part of the social system" (p. 82).

The Discrepancy Model

The Discrepancy Model is a method for clarifying the mental images leading to the collective vision. The model asks two fundamental questions: "What could be?" and "What is?" The shared set of beliefs identified in Step 2 will help answer the first question. These beliefs and key values help form the mental images that guide us toward our goals. The results from Step 3, the assessment of the present nature and degree of parent involvement in the home and at school, will provide the answers to the second question. The differences between the answers create the "discrepancy." The collective vision should inspire the stakeholders to reduce the difference between "what is" and "what if."

The collective vision should reflect the notion that the families, school, and community are all equal stakeholders in the education of the children, and that we must work together. The African proverb, "It takes a village to raise a child," is a vision statement.

STEP 5. DEVELOPING A SHARED MISSION STATEMENT

A mission statement is a description of the ideals toward which everyone associated with the partnership program should strive. It is an outgrowth of the collective vision, which in turn, evolves from the shared beliefs. The mission statement needs to address the following questions:

- Where are we going?
- How will we be able to tell when we get there?

The mission statement clearly defines what the project is trying to accomplish and is used as a benchmark for appraising progress. Joel Barker (1990) describes the importance of moving from a vision to a stated mission, "Vision without action is merely a dream; action without vision just passes the time; vision with action can change the world."

The mission statement provides direction for the partnership, as the school and community endeavor to foster collaborative relationships, change behavioral norms, and enhance skills and knowledge. Developing a mission statement is not a single episode. Likened to the phenomenon of metamorphosis, the emergence of a mission is an act of "unfolding" and the mission will continually need to be reaffirmed or redefined as things change. A mission statement should:

- motivate and inspire
- give clear purpose and direction to the partnership project
- support the faculty, staff, parents, and community members' own sense of purpose
- guide the development of family/school/community partnerships and the academic and social development of the children

For those districts, schools, and centers that already have a mission statement, rather than developing a new one, it may be appropriate to reaffirm or modify the existing statement. For example, a school may have a mission statement that encompasses parent involvement, but does not directly address the idea of partnerships between the family, school, and community. The school mission statement can be revised and expanded by using a set of shared beliefs, an assessment of current family involvement, and a collective vision.

Operationally, adhering to the mission should be the overriding duty of every stakeholder in the partnership. In reality, however, it is unlikely that everyone in the school and planning group is truly committed to the mission. There will be some who are committed, some who are not committed but will comply, and a few who do not share the mission. The complainers will accept the mission statement for reasons other than those expressed in the collective vision (e.g., to keep their jobs, to get tenure, obtain resources, etc.). Naturally, you would like the "core of the committed" to be large as possible. Ultimately, the value of the mission statement and level of commitment can be determined by the degree to which the statement is "institutionalized" and becomes an integral part of the organizational culture of the school, district, and community.

Preparing a Mission Statement

In the publication, *Senior High School Improvement* (National Study of School Evaluation, 1993), the authors emphasize the importance of consolidating words and phrases into the mission statement that reflect your main values and ideals. Once a draft is prepared, the partnership planning group reviews the mission statement and decides if it:

- gives a sense of direction for the partnership
- encompasses the total partnership program
- provides an insight into the future
- will be understood by the faculty, staff, parents, and community members
- is useful in setting desired parent involvement outcomes and priorities for achieving these outcomes
- suggests a variety of needed strategies or interventions, best practices, staff development activities, and evaluation plans

Distribute the draft of the mission statement the school or center's faculty and staff and other stakeholders for their consideration. After receiving feedback, use the comments and suggestions to make revisions. After a consensus is reached, the planning group presents the mission statement to the faculty and staff and distributes it to the families and the community.

Based on the steps taken in the planning process, an example of a mission statement is: The families, school, and community will be active partners in the education of all children. The school and community will reach out to the families to help them be involved in their children's education in the home and at school.

A Gem of an Idea

The mission of an elementary school in North Carolina is, "Every student will be successful and each child is a jewel in our learning community."

At the beginning of each school year, a ceremony for the children, parents, faculty and staff is held at the school to reaffirm the mission. To symbolize the mission, all of the children are given a "gem" (a rhinestone) which they ceremoniously place in a large glass bowl. The bowl resides in the hall near the entrance to the school.

When a new student enrolls in the school, the parent and child are told about the mission of the school and the importance of each student. To welcome the student into the learning community, the child is given a jewel, which he or she places in the bowl with the other gems.

Intervention Planning: Setting the Direction

During the Intervention Planning Phase, the family populations to be targeted and the barriers to be overcome are identified, and goals and objectives are developed. This phase sets the direction and focus of the interventions designed to create partnerships.

STEP 6. IDENTIFYING THE FAMILY POPULATION OR POPULATIONS TO BE TARGETED

Before the goals of the partnership program can be determined, the planning group needs to identify which segments of the school's family population are to be the focus of the interventions. The results from the assessment conducted in Step 3 will help to determine the involvement of the different segments of the population and the data will likely point to the family populations to be targeted. The focus of the partnership will depend upon the present involvement levels of families.

In many school communities, there is only a small group of parents who are actively involved in the school. The majority of the families are marginally engaged at school and in the home, and a certain segment of the population is not involved very much. In this case, the planning group may decide to target the majority of the families who are somewhat involved and then focus on the family population that is not involved in the home or at school.

If the involvement levels for the total family population are low (both at school and in the home), as it is in some school communities, then all of the families are targets for intervention. The intervention strategies would focus on overcoming barriers, connecting with all the families, and beginning to build collaborative relationships.

Once the families to be targeted are selected, the barriers to be overcome are identified. Who is to be targeted, and when, is determined by the nature of the barriers and the readiness of the school and community to intervene.

STEP 7. IDENTIFYING THE BARRIERS TO OVERCOME

The purpose of Step 7 is to identify the barriers that have to be overcome to reach the targeted families. The planning group determines what obstacles are preventing the targeted populations from moving from "what is" to "what if?"

Chapter 4 describes and discusses many of the potential barriers that can keep families from being involved in their children's education at school and in the home. Many barriers are centered around the family's lack of knowledge and the skills needed to play their Parent Partner Roles, as well as psychological barriers that include the parents' fear and alienation. There are also logistical barriers such as lack of transportation and child care, inflexible work schedules, and time constraints.

Other difficult barriers are those that deal with negative attitudes and beliefs held by teachers and principals. Some schools even have a legacy of adversarial relationships with the families.

The barriers will differ depending upon the population being targeted. This is why assessment of the present nature and degree of parent involvement is so important. The barriers for different segments of the school's parent population can be identified by studying the cultures and circumstances of the families and the characteristics of the school and community.

The barriers originating from the school may be indicated when the faculty and staff, community leaders, and members of the planning group work on developing a set of shared beliefs in Step 2. This can be tricky because, as mentioned before, saying that you don't really want parents in the school, even if you believe it, is not "politically" acceptable. It is up to the planning group to ascertain the restraining forces that are preventing the changes.

STEP 8. DETERMINING THE PARTNERSHIP PROGRAM GOALS

Goals are statements of expected results that are specified in general measurable terms. The goals show you "where you want to go."

The goals should be based on the foundation created in the first phase (e.g., the conceptual framework of the Self-Renewing Partnership Model, the set of beliefs, and the collective vision and the mission statement). If the goals are not built upon the beliefs and aspirations of the school and community, they will not be embraced by the stakeholders. Deal and Peterson (1994) contend that planners often make a tactical error when they fail to "infuse goals with passion and meaning [derived from the vision and mission statements]" (p. 101).

Goals should be broad enough to encompass the need, problem, or concern, but specific enough to focus on the issue. Some parent involvement programs are not successful because the goals are too broad and the resulting objectives are not easily measured. For example, a goal to "increase parent involvement" is very general.

The partnership program goals are indicated in the Self-Renewing Model and the School/Community Strategies are based on the desired outcomes of the partnership process. The goals of the partnership program include:

- All families are connected with the school.
- Families and school are communicating effectively.
- School and community resources reach the families in need, and the school receives support from the families and community.
- All parents are effectively playing their Parent Partner Roles.

Which goal is featured depends upon the barriers and the levels of involvement. The focus will change progressively as the collaborative relationships develop. For example, initially, the goal may be to connect the families and the school. Eventually, the goal will be for the parents to effectively play the Parent Partner Roles.

STEP 9. DETERMINING THE SCHOOL/ COMMUNITY COLLABORATION STRATEGIES TO BE EMPHASIZED

Once the goals are determined, it is easy to decide which School/Community Collaboration Strategies to emphasize. The four strategies, Connecting, Communicating, Coordinating, and Coaching, are described in Chapters 6, 7, 8, and 9 respectively.

Chapter 5 explains that the intervention strategies are progressive and hierarchical and that they are implemented in sequence. The idea is that the families need to be connected and communicating with the school before school and community services and resources can be coordinated. The Coaching Strategy is implemented after the relationships are established. Therefore, the initial School/Community Collaboration Strategy to be emphasized will depend upon the level and degree of involvement by the targeted family populations, the barriers that are keeping the parents and the school apart, and the goal that is the focus. For example, The Connecting Strategy is used when the goal is to make connections with the targeted family population, the Communicating Strategy emphasized when the families are connected and the goal is to establish two-way communications flows between the targeted families and the school, and so on. The functions of the School/Community Collaboration Strategies are the objectives that relate to the corresponding goal.

The next section presents a summary of the objectives of a partnership program. These are directly related to the goals of Self-Renewing Partnership Model. For example, a function of the Coaching Strategy is to "Enhance the parents' ability and capacity to effectively play the Parent Partner Roles." When the function is restated as a goal, it becomes, "All parents will effectively play the Parent Partner Roles." In the next section, the goals of the partnership plan are presented.

STEP 10. DETERMINING OBJECTIVES

Objectives are specific statements that describe the desired and expected outcomes of the intervention. The objectives should provide answers to the following questions:

- What are the results to be accomplished?
- How will the results be demonstrated?

The objectives "operationalize" the partnership program's goals and state in measurable terms "What is wanted and expected."

The assessment of the present nature and degree of parent involvement (Step 3) will help to identify the source of the barriers that have to be overcome. For example, the results from parent surveys and interviews could indicate that many families cannot attend evening events because they do not have, or cannot afford, child care. Since the goal is for these families and the school to be connected, an objective would be to "overcome physical barriers that are preventing the families from working with the school." Similarly, if the assessment suggests that the parents perceive the school as impersonal and unapproachable, an objective would be to "Create an inviting and helpful school environment," to help make connections. Once the objectives are determined, best practices are selected and implemented "to get you where you want to go."

With the example of the school community described earlier, where the families are involved to some degree and are not alienated from the school, the objectives would be to build collaborative relationships by strengthening connections with the parents and establishing two-way communication flows. After this, the objective would be to enhance the family members' Parent Partner Role skills and knowledge.

The objectives are based on the concept that in order to get the families fully involved, (a) they have to feel more connected with the school, (b) there needs to be a better communication flow between the home and the school, and (c) the parents' skills and knowledge need to be enhanced. The following is a list of objectives based on the Self-Renewing Partnership Model.

When the goal is, "All families are connected with the school," the objectives are to:

- prepare the school and community to reach out and connect with the families
- create an inviting and helpful school environment where the family members and faculty/staff can comfortably interact with each other
- overcome any psychological or physical barriers that might be preventing the families from working with the school
- initiate two-way communication flows between the families and the school

When the goal is, "Families and school are communicating effectively," the objectives are to:

- build collaborative relationships with the families
- establish two-way communication flows between the families and the school
- begin to increase family support for the school's programs and activities
- begin to increase school and community support for the family's partnership activities

When the goal is, "School and community resources reach the families in need and the school receives support from the families and community," the objectives are to:

- increase family awareness of the availability of school and community services and resources
- ensure that school and community services and resources are accessible to all families in need
- facilitate the creation of new services and resources
- organize family and community resources to help support the school's curriculum and programs

When the goal is, "All parents are effectively playing their Parent Partner Roles," the objectives are to:

- enhance the parents' ability and capacity to effectively play the Parent Partner Roles
- enhance the parents' general sense of well-being, knowledge and skill level

Intervention: Implementing the Changes

During the Intervention Phase the best practices are selected and implemented. After the programs, activities, and events are implemented, the planners mdnitor process to determine if the objectives are met. A Partnership Action Plan is developed for each targeted population.

Whereas the first two phases set the stage for the interventions, this is probably the most exciting phase of the partnership program plan—this is when the "fruits" of the planning process are harvested. During this phase, programs and activities are used to reach out and involve the "missing" families. Because this is the stage where the "action" occurs, there can be a tendency to skip over the earlier phases. However, without the conceptual framework developed in the earlier steps, the school and community will have to use a "hit-or-miss" method to implement the intervention strategies. It has been my experience that when the planners are "flying by the seat of their pants," the best practices are often implemented without knowing why. I suppose the Cheshire Cat would argue that, "you need to know which way you are going, before you start out."

In some situations, the school, center, teacher, and so forth, may have a pretty good idea what they want to accomplish and may feel they are ready to implement the intervention strategies. If the planners are clear about the families they want to target, and the desired outcomes, it is likely that they can begin the Intervention Phase, once they follow the first step. However, I believe that all planners should know and understand the nature and functions of the Self-Renewing Partnership Model.

A Partnership Action Plan Worksheet (Figure 10.4) has been designed to help the planners during this phase. Under the worksheet heading, the targeted family population is described, the barriers identified, the goal and objectives are listed, and the School/Community Collaboration Strategy to be emphasized is indicated. The best practices are listed under the heading.

Description of the Targeted Family Population: _____

Barriers to Overcome _____

Goal _____

School/Community Collaboration Strategy to Be Emphasized:

_____ Connecting _____ Communicating _____ Coordinating _____ Coaching

Objective _____

Best Practices to Be Implemented: _____

Figure 10.4 Partnership Action Plan Worksheet.

STEP 11. SELECTING AND IMPLEMENTING
BEST PRACTICES

After determining the objectives and the School/Community Collaboration Strategy to emphasize, select the best practices to meet the goals. An array of programs, events, and activities that can be used to intervene with the families is presented for each strategy in the corresponding chapter.

The school and community should be cautious and not attempt to implement too many best practices all at once. As you intervene and attempt to make significant changes in the families' cultures, you must be careful that you don't get overwhelmed. As the saying goes, "When eating an elephant, you eat it one bite at a time."

As mentioned earlier, often a "shotgun" approach is used to implement best practices because there is not a comprehensive partnership plan. The implementation of the best practices should be a planned intervention activity. The programs and activities are used in such a way that they impact on the targeted family population.

The creation of a family/school/community partnership is a process, not an event. Because it is developmental, it often takes time to meet the long-range goals. However, as you follow this path, it is important to have some early successes to maintain the momentum and "fuel" the program. Therefore, be sure to celebrate these successes along the way.

It is also prudent to use limited resources and personnel very carefully so that you get the "biggest bang for the bucks." This makes sense, and it helps to calm the critics.

STEP 12. EVALUATING THE EFFECTS OF
STRATEGIES AND BEST PRACTICES

The final two steps are very straightforward. After a stated period of time, data are gathered to determine the effect of interventions on the targeted family populations. The data should indicate if the partnership program's objectives were met and how the best practices impacted on the families. For example, for an objective to "create an inviting and helpful school environment," the parents can be surveyed to see how they feel about the school. If the objective is to, "establish two-way communication flows between the families and the school," and procedures to increase family participation in parent/teacher conferences were implemented, the school can determine if the best practice worked by counting the number of conferences and surveying the parents and teachers. Examples of parent surveys are presented in Step 3.

It is important to maintain good records of attendance and participation in partnership activities, events, and programs for evaluation and future planning. It is a good idea to ask participants to evaluate the different programs, activities, and events.

STEP 13. REDEFINING GOALS AND OBJECTIVES

The evaluation results will indicate if the partnership program's goals and objectives need to be redefined. The data will show which goals and objectives were met, and which were not. After reviewing the data, the planning group makes any necessary adjustments to the goals and objectives. Appropriate best practices are chosen and implemented.

SUMMARY

As stated several times before, creating and maintaining a family/school/community partnership program is an ongoing process. As conditions change and the partnership develops, it will be necessary to reassess the program and reset the direction accordingly.

Creating partnerships does not happen quickly, because it usually requires changes in the families' cultures and expectations. It takes a planned, sustained comprehensive effort to effect social change. When implementing a partnership program, it is important to be patient and keep things in perspective. Try not to get discouraged, celebrate your successes, and learn from your mistakes.

The next chapter presents a case study that describes how an elementary school used the Self-Renewing Partnership Model and the Strategic Partnership Planning System to develop and implement a family/school/community partnership program. The case study discusses how the school intervened with the targeted family populations. Partnership Action Plan Worksheets are presented that summarize the Intervention Phase.

Getting Through the Door

I acknowledge that the phrase, "changing behavior is very difficult," is a cliché and a major understatement. Changing roles and relationships can be frustrating, threatening, and even "painful." It has been my experience that people often enter into a change project with great enthusiasm, but when they are required to make fundamental shifts in the way they are accustomed to doing things, dismay and anxiety can replace the initial excitement. I call this phenomenon "Hitting the Door." When this happens, commitments to the program are threatened.

To "get through the door," the partnership program needs to be designed to produce short-term and long-term results for the children and other stakeholders. As the definition of a family/school/community partnership states, it is a relationship designed primarily to produce positive educational and social effects on the child, while being mutually beneficial to all other parties involved. The goal is to improve the academic and social development of all students.

Of course, this does not happen overnight. Therefore, as you work toward this goal, all of the stakeholders, teachers, parents, and students need to be able to celebrate the short-range successes along the way. Implement some best practices that have immediate positive impact. This way, the commitment and enthusiasm will remain high.

CHAPTER 11

A Case Study: How Does It All Work?

This chapter presents a case study that describes how the Self-Renewing Partnership Model can be used to reach out and involve a school's family population in children's education. In this case, the planning group has worked through the Pre-Intervention Planning Phase of the Strategic Partnership Planning System, so only the last two phases (Intervention Planning and Intervention) are discussed.

While the setting for the case study is an elementary school, the Self-Renewing Partnership Model is designed for middle and high schools as well. The procedures and processes that are discussed in this chapter can be used in all settings. Granted, most parent involvement programs are located in elementary schools, but family/school/community partnerships are needed at all levels. Older children require as much involvement and support as the younger ones do. Some of the best practices that are used with the families of middle- and high-school students are a little different, but the purposes of the intervention strategies are the same. For example, middle-school students may not want to eat lunch with their parents, but they do like to see them at school in some capacity. The intent of the interventions is to involve the parents in their children's education, and the programs and activities need to reflect the needs of the students and families.

APPLE HILL ELEMENTARY SCHOOL

Apple Hill Elementary School is located in a lower socioeconomic area of a large metropolitan school district. The school includes pre-K through sixth grade and has an enrollment of 484 students. There are 22 teachers, a principal, assistant principal, and a family/school/community coordinator. The coordinator position is new and is funded by the Community-in-Schools project.

About sixty percent of the children live in neighborhoods near the school; they walk to school, ride a bus, or are transported by their parents. The other forty percent are bused in from neighborhoods located about twelve miles from the school. Most of these students live with their families in two federal housing projects. The ethnic composition of the students that are bused in is seventy percent African-American and thirty percent Hispanic. Eighty percent of the students living in the neighborhoods near the school are Caucasian, the remaining twenty percent are African-American. The school population is "transitional," with families moving in and out on a regular basis. Most of these students are from the population that is bused in, but not entirely.

The school has been designated a "priority school," which means it is not reaching its benchmark goals set by the district. End-of-the-year test scores in reading, writing, and math are low; attendance is below standard; and discipline has been a problem with some students. A disproportionate number of the students who are having difficulties with the end-of-the-year tests are part of the bused in population.

The principal has recently been assigned to the school with a mandate to work with the faculty, staff, families, and community to improve the children's academic and social development. Most of the teachers have been at the school for some time. They are concerned and are interested in working with the principal to turn things around, but they are unsure how to do it. A small group of parents is actively involved with the school. These families live in the neighborhoods near the school, and have indicated they want to help improve the school.

The principal and faculty created a School Improvement Council. The council is chaired by a faculty member and is composed of teachers, parents, community members, the principal, the assistant principal, and the coordinator. The group decided that forming partnerships with the families would help the children, parents, and the school. The Strategic Partnership Planning System is being used to develop the family/school/community partnership program plan. As indicated in the introduction to this chapter, the first phase of the planning system has been completed and the council and faculty are now ready to plan and implement the interventions.

Involvement-Level Patterns

The assessment of the levels of parent involvement in the home and at school showed that about twenty-five percent of the families participate in traditional parent involvement events and activities such as parent-teacher conferences, open houses, PTA meetings, holiday programs, and fund-raising projects. The perception is that the same families are usually involved. Historically, there has been a smaller core group of parents that organizes and runs the programs, events, and activities.

When the population data are separated into two segments—the neighborhood families and the families of the students that are bused in—the results indicate that the involvement levels for the two groups are quite different. The parents who are involved with the school live almost entirely in the neighborhoods near the school. Very few of the parents living in the housing projects come to school for any events or activities.

After comparing other data such as student test scores, attendance, and

Involvement at Home ↑		
Q7 LITTLE OR NO INVOLVEMENT AT SCHOOL AND MUCH IN THE HOME	**Q8** SOME INVOLVEMENT AT SCHOOL AND MUCH IN THE HOME	**Q9** MUCH INVOLVEMENT AT SCHOOL AND MUCH IN THE HOME
Q4 LITTLE OR NO INVOLVEMENT AT SCHOOL AND SOME IN THE HOME	**Q5** SOME INVOLVEMENT AT SCHOOL AND SOME IN THE HOME	**Q6** MUCH INVOLVEMENT AT SCHOOL AND SOME IN THE HOME
Q1 LITTLE OR NO INVOLVEMENT AT SCHOOL OR IN THE HOME	**Q2** SOME INVOLVEMENT AT SCHOOL AND LITTLE OR NONE IN THE HOME	**Q3** MUCH INVOLVEMENT AT SCHOOL AND LITTLE OR NONE IN THE HOME

Involvement at School ⟶

Figure 11.1 Parent Involvement Grid. Involvement Pattern of the Neighborhood Family Population.

Q7	Q8	Q9
LITTLE OR NO INVOLVEMENT AT SCHOOL AND MUCH IN THE HOME	SOME INVOLVEMENT AT SCHOOL AND MUCH IN THE HOME	MUCH INVOLVEMENT AT SCHOOL AND MUCH IN THE HOME
Q4	Q5	Q6
LITTLE OR NO INVOLVEMENT AT SCHOOL AND SOME IN THE HOME	SOME INVOLVEMENT AT SCHOOL AND SOME IN THE HOME	MUCH INVOLVEMENT AT SCHOOL AND SOME IN THE HOME
Q1	Q2	Q3
LITTLE OR NO INVOLVEMENT AT SCHOOL OR IN THE HOME	SOME INVOLVEMENT AT SCHOOL AND LITTLE OR NONE IN THE HOME	MUCH INVOLVEMENT AT SCHOOL AND LITTLE OR NONE IN THE HOME

Involvement at Home (vertical axis)

Involvement at School ⟶

Figure 11.2 *Parent Involvement Grid. Involvement Pattern of the Bused in Student Family Population.*

so on, the planning group concluded that most of the families of the students who are bused in needed help in playing their Parent Partner Roles. For the families living in the neighborhoods around the school, the involvement levels varied. For example, the parents who are involved with the school are involved at home as well, and some of the families are involved in the home and not at school. A segment of the neighborhood family population is not involved at school or in the home. Figures 11.1 and 11.2 show the involvement patterns of the "neighborhood" and "bused in" family populations.

Identifying the Family Populations to Be Targeted

The School Improvement Council members and the faculty determined that there were two family populations that needed to be targeted for interventions: The parents of the students that were bused in, and the parents who lived in the neighborhoods who were either marginally involved or not at all. It was agreed that the neighborhood family population would be a good starting point, because it is likely that with a moderate amount of intervention many of these parents could be engaged as partners. Once programs and activities were under way for the neighborhood families, strategies and best practices would be implemented to reach the parents of the students that were bused in and the segment of the neighborhood families that were not involved.

It was acknowledged that creating partnerships with the families is an ongoing, lengthy process. The council knew the strategies and best practices had to be implemented sequentially, and be commensurate with the availability of resources.

Interviewing with the Neighborhood Family Population

Identifying the Barriers to Be Overcome

Based on the data gathered during the assessment step, it was determined that two barriers were keeping the neighborhood families from being involved. One barrier was that many of the neighborhood parents perceived the school as being cold and impersonal, and as a result did not feel very connected with the school. The other barrier was closely related to the first. After assessing the school's environment, it was decided that the school could do more to make it inviting and welcoming. Also, there was not a good communication flow between the families and the school, so it was decided that after the connections were made, best practices would be implemented to correct this problem.

Determining the Partnership Program Goals

The faculty and staff decided the first goal was to "Strengthen the connections between the neighborhood families and the school." The next goal would be, "The families and school are communicating effectively." Meeting the first goal would lead to the second.

It was acknowledged that best practices selected to meet these goals would probably not benefit the hard-to-reach families in the other targeted family population. However, when possible, these parents were invited to participate in any activities and events so they would not be alienated further. The Action Plan to reach the more disenfranchised parents is discussed next.

Determining the School/Community Collaboration
Strategies to Be Emphasized

Since the School/Community Collaboration Strategies are progressive
and interactive, the Connecting Strategy was used first to strengthen the
connections between the families and the school. The Communicating
Strategy was then used to increase the two-way communication flows
between the school and the parents.

Determining Objectives

The council members and the faculty and staff decided on two objectives to meet the first goal. The objectives were to:

- create an inviting and helpful school environment where the
  family members and faculty/staff can comfortably interact with
  each other
- overcome any psychological or physical barriers that might be
  preventing the families from working with the school

The objectives for the second goal were to:

- establish two-way communication flows between the families
  and the school
- build collaborative relationships with the parents

Selecting and Implementing Best Practices

A Partnership Action Plan Worksheet to meet the first goal is presented
in Figure 11.3. The two objectives are "to create an inviting and helpful
school environment . . . " and "to overcome any psychological or physical
barriers. . . . "

The worksheet listed the various best practices that were implemented
to meet these objectives. For example, to meet the first objective, the
warning signs at the entrances to the building were changed to "welcoming" signs. While the notices still requested that visitors come to the
office, it was to be helped rather than checked. Also, some of the parking
spaces in front of the school were designated for "Parents/Visitors." And,
a session was held to teach the faculty and staff to greet and interact better
with parents and community members.

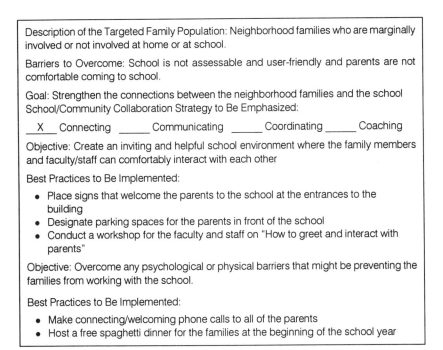

Description of the Targeted Family Population: Neighborhood families who are marginally involved or not involved at home or at school.

Barriers to Overcome: School is not assessable and user-friendly and parents are not comfortable coming to school.

Goal: Strengthen the connections between the neighborhood families and the school
School/Community Collaboration Strategy to Be Emphasized:

__X__ Connecting _____ Communicating _____ Coordinating _____ Coaching

Objective: Create an inviting and helpful school environment where the family members and faculty/staff can comfortably interact with each other

Best Practices to Be Implemented:

- Place signs that welcome the parents to the school at the entrances to the building
- Designate parking spaces for the parents in front of the school
- Conduct a workshop for the faculty and staff on "How to greet and interact with parents"

Objective: Overcome any psychological or physical barriers that might be preventing the families from working with the school.

Best Practices to Be Implemented:

- Make connecting/welcoming phone calls to all of the parents
- Host a free spaghetti dinner for the families at the beginning of the school year

Figure 11.3 *Partnership Action Plan Worksheet.*

To meet the second objective, the best practices include connecting and welcoming phone calls to all of the parents and a free spaghetti dinner for the families at the beginning of the school year.

Later, to meet the second goal, "the families and school are communicating effectively," and the objective to establish two-way communication flows between the families and the school, a newsletter describing what was happening in their children's lives at school was sent to the parents. Also, a program to increase family participation in parent-teacher conferences was implemented. The families were notified about the purpose, expectations, and desired outcomes of the parent-teacher conference by mail or over the phone. Later, being flexible about the dates and times, the teachers called the parents to schedule the meetings. Following the suggested guidelines for parent-teacher conferences (Chapter 7), the teachers planned and conducted the meetings. The teachers evaluated the results of the conferences. They contacted the parents who did not attend the conferences and attempted to remove any barriers that prevented their participation.

Intervening with the "Bused in Student" Family Populations

Identifying the Barriers to Be Overcome

The faculty and staff recognized that the school-based barrier alluded to earlier would affect some of the targeted families, but there were also major family-based barriers that were keeping the parents and the school apart. These were both physical and psychological. Time and distance were factors and many of the families were apprehensive about making contacts with the school. They were uncomfortable with the school and afraid of the teachers. It was concluded that most of the parents wanted to help their children but did not know how. Their sense of being "out of place" with the school and society was intensified when the frustrations that resulted from their lack of skills and knowledge was combined with their feelings of not being "connected."

Determining the Partnership Program Goals

The faculty and staff decided that reaching and working with this family population would take a sustained and intensive effort. The various School/Community Collaboration Strategies would have to be sequenced and the goals would need to reflect the developmental nature of the process. That is, all of the goals suggested in the Self-Renewing Partnership Model would have to be met. The goals were:

- All families are connected with the school.
- Families and school are communicating effectively.
- School and community resources reach the families in need, and the school receives support from the families and community.
- All parents are effectively playing their Parent Partner Roles.

Determining the School/Community Collaboration Strategies to Be Emphasized

With this "disconnected" family population, the School/Community Collaboration Strategies were emphasized in order, beginning with the Connecting Strategy and ending with the Coaching Strategy. As the collaborative relationships developed, a different strategy would be emphasized.

The focus of the interventions at first would be to make connections with the families. Once the families were connected, the focus would shift to the Communicating and Coordinating Strategies. The Coaching Strategy best practices would be implemented when the family members felt comfortable with the school and saw themselves as equal partners with the school.

Determining Objectives

In order to meet the first goal, "All families are connected with the school," the faculty and staff decided on the following objectives:

- to prepare the school and community to reach out and connect with the families
- to overcome any psychological or physical barriers that might be preventing the families from working with the school
- to initiate two-way communication flows between the families and the school

Selecting and Implementing Best Practices

The Partnership Action Plan Worksheet presented in Figure 11.4 lists various best practices that were selected to meet the first goal. To prepare the school to reach out and connect with the families, a bus trip was organized for the teachers to tour the neighborhoods where the targeted family population lived. As part of the tour, arrangements were made for the teachers to have lunch at a neighborhood church. The parents were also invited to come to the church and have lunch with the faculty and staff. The teachers socialized with the families and answered questions. As a follow-up to the luncheon, the faculty sent appreciation notes to the minister, parents, and the church volunteers.

To help overcome the psychological barriers, the teachers made "connecting" telephone calls to the parents and visited the homes of some of the most "hard-to-reach" families. (Guidelines for making connecting telephone calls and conducting home visits are presented in Chapter 6.) The calls and visits were intended to establish positive relationships with the parents.

Social events were also held in the neighborhood and at school so the teachers, parents, and other community members could get acquainted. To begin to establish two-way communication flows between the families and the school, family forums were held in the neighborhoods to

Description of the Targeted Family Population: Families of the students who are bused in to the school.

Barriers to Overcome: Psychological barriers (e.g., feelings of alienation and "being out of place") and physical barriers (e.g., distance from school and programs, events, and activities).

Goal: All families are connected with the school.

School/Community Collaboration Strategy to Be Emphasized:
__X__ Connecting _____ Communicating _____ Coordinating _____ Coaching

Objective: To prepare the school and community to reach out and connect with the families.

Best Practices to Be Implemented:

• Faculty bus trip to the neighborhood and lunch with the families.

Objective: To overcome any psychological or physical barriers that might be preventing the families from working with the school

Best Practices to Be Implemented:

• Make connecting phone calls to all of the parents.
• Visit the homes of the most "hard-to-reach" families.
• Hold social events (e.g., spaghetti dinner, pizza party, etc.) at the community center in the neighborhood.

Objective: To initiate two-way communication flows between the families and the school.

Best Practices to Be Implemented:

• Hold family forums in the neighborhoods so faculty, staff, and parents can discuss needs, issues, and concerns.
• Continue to make phone calls to the parents and begin to focus on ways to communicate.
• Continue to make visits to selected homes and build relationships.
• Schedule meetings with neighborhood ministers, business owners, housing authority representatives, police officers, and others.

Figure 11.4 Partnership Action Plan Worksheet.

discuss the needs and interests of the children. Meetings were held with neighborhood ministers, business owners, housing authority representatives, and police officers. More phone calls and visits were made to help with the communication process.

Once the connections were made, the school began to send the parents welcoming letters and positive notes, established a family room in a community center, and conducted parent-teacher conferences in the neighborhood. The school made sure that school and community resources reached the needy families (Coordinating Strategy).

When the families and the school were communicating and relationships were established, the Coaching Strategy was used to enhance the family members' Parent Partner Role skills and knowledge. Workshops and classes were offered at the community center and eventually at the school. Transportation and child care was provided. Field trips to the library, museums, parks, zoos, and so on, were conducted for the parents and children. The home visits continued, and the parents were helped with their parenting roles and home learning activities.

SUMMARY

This case study describes how an elementary school's faculty and staff reached out and involved the parents from two segments of the school's family population. The way the Self-Renewing Partnership Model and the Strategic Partnership Planning System was used to plan and implement the interventions was discussed and Partnership Action Plan Worksheets presented for each targeted family population.

Although each school or center's situation will be different, and the parent involvement level patterns will vary, the case study provides a template for creating partnerships with the family, school, and community. The procedures for using the Self-Renewing Partnership Model are the same. The model is used to reach out and work with all families, especially those parents deemed to be "hard to reach." By using the model to create family/school/community partnership, the "missing" families can be reached and the dilemma described in the first chapter solved. The goal to have the parents fully involved in the education of their children can be met.

REFERENCES

Amundson, K. J. 1988. *First Teachers: Parent Involvement in the Public Schools.* Alexandria, VA: National School Boards Association.

Barker, J. 1990. *The Power of Vision.* Charterhouse Learning Corporation, New York, videocassette.

Barth, R. 1990. "A Personal Vision of a Good School, *Phi Delta Kappan*, 71(7):512–516.

Bauch, J. P. 1989. "The TransParent School Model: New Technology for Parent Involvement," *Educational Leadership,* 47(2):32–34.

Brandt, R. 1989. "On Parents and Schools: A Conversation with Joyce Epstein," *Educational Leadership,* 47(2): 24–27.

Carroll, L. 1946. *Alice's Adventures in Wonderland.* New York: Random House.

Chavkin, N. F. 1989. "Debunking the Myth About Minority Parents and the School," *Educational Horizons,* 67:119–123.

Chavkin, N. F., ed. 1993. *Families and Schools in a Pluralistic Society.* Albany, NY: State University of New York.

Chavkin, N. F. 1995. "Comprehensive Districtwide Reforms in Parent and Community Involvement Programs," in *Creating Family/School Partnerships.* Barry Rutherford, B., ed. Columbus, OH: National Middle School Association, pp. 77–106.

Child Development Project. 1994. *At Home in Our School.* Oakland, CA: Author.

Chrispeels, J. 1985. *Home-School Relations Planner.* San Diego, CA: San Diego County Office of Education.

Chrispeels, J. 1988. *Home-School Partnership Planner.* San Diego, CA: San Diego County Office of Education.

Chrispeels, J. 1995. "School Restructuring to Facilitate Parent and Community Involvement in the Middle Grades," in *Creating Family/School Partnerships.* Barry Rutherford, ed. Columbus, OH: National Middle School Association, pp. 107–135.

Chrispeels, J., Boruta, M. and Daugherty, M. 1988. *Communicating With Parents.* San Diego, CA.: San Diego County Office of Education.

Clark, R. 1983. *Family Life and School Achievement: Why Poor Black Children Succeed and Fail.* Chicago, IL: University of Chicago Press.

Coleman, J. S. 1991. *Policy Perspectives: Parental Involvement in Education.* Washington, DC: Office of Educational Research and Improvement, U.S. Department of Education.

Coltoff, P. 1996. "Community Schools: The Next Stage," *Conversations: Supporting Children and Families in the Public Schools*, a newsletter published by the National Center for Social Work and Education Collaboration, 3(1,2):4–6.

Comer, J. P. 1980. *School Power: Implications of an Intervention Project.* New York: Macmillan Publishing/The Free Press.

Comer, J. P. 1986. "Parent Participation in the Schools," *Phi Delta Kappan*, 66(2):442–446.

Comer, J. P. 1988a. "Connecting Families and Schools," in *Drawing in the Family*, S. F. Walker ed. Denver, CO: Education Commission of the States.

Comer, J. P. 1988b. "Educating Poor Minority Children," *Scientific American*, 259(5):42–48.

The Committee for Economic Development. 1994. *Putting Learning First: Governing and Managing the Schools for High Achievement.* New York: Author.

Covey, S. R. 1992. Principle-Centered Leadership. New York: Simon and Schuster/Fireside.

D'Angelo, D. 1991. *Parent Involvement in Chapter 1: A Report to the Independent Review Panel.* Hampton, NH: RMC Research Corporation.

Davies, D. 1988. "Low-Income Parents and the Schools: A Research Report and a Plan of Action," *Equity and Choice,* 4(3):51–57.

Davies, D. 1990a. "Schools Reaching Out: Family, School, and Community Partnerships for Student Success," *Phi Delta Kappan*, 72(5):376–382.

Davies, D. 1990b. *Schools Reaching Out: What Have We Learned? Final Report.* Boston, MA: Institute for Responsive Education.

Deal, T. and Peterson, K. 1994. *The Leadership Paradox: Balancing Logic and Artistry in Schools.* San Francisco: Jossey-Bass.

Dryfoos, J. G. 1994. *Full Service Schools.* San Francisco: Jossey-Bass.

Dryfoos, J. G 1996. "How to Implement Full-Service Schools: Observations from the Field," *Conversations: Supporting Children and Families in the Public Schools*, A newsletter published by the National Center for Social Work and Education Collaboration, 3(1,2):1,13–15.

Epstein, J. L. 1987. "Toward a Theory of Family-School Connections: Teacher Practices and Parent Involvement," In *Social Intervention: Potential and Constraints,* K. Hurrelman, F. Kaufmann, and F. Losel, eds. New York: DeGruyter.

Epstein, J. L. 1988. "How Do We Improve Programs for Parent Involvement?" *Educational Horizons,* 66(2):58–59.

Epstein, J. L. 1992. "School and Family Partnerships," in M.C. Alkin ed. *Encyclopedia of Educational Research* (6th ed.). New York: Macmillan, pp. 1139–1151.

Epstein, J. L. and Becker, H. J. 1982a. "A Survey of Teacher Practices," *Elementary School Journal,* 83(3):103–113.

Epstein, J. L. and Becker, H. J. 1982b. *Teacher Practices of Parent Involvement:*

Problems and Possibilities, Report No. 324. Baltimore, MD: The John Hopkins University, Center for Social Organization of Schools.

Epstein, J. L. and Connors, L. 1995. "School and Family Partnerships in the Middle Grades," in *Creating Family/School Partnerships.* Barry Rutherford, B., ed. Columbus, OH: National Middle School Association, pp. 137–165.

Fruchter, N., Galletta, A. and White, J. L. 1992. *New Directions in Parent Involvement.* Washington, DC: Academy for Educational Development.

Henderson, A. T. 1987. *The Evidence Continues to Grow: Parent Involvement Improves Student Achievement.* Columbia, MD: National Committee for Citizens in Education.

Henderson, A. T., Marburger, C.L. and Ooms, T. 1986. *Beyond the Bake Sale: An Educator's Guide to Working with Parents.* Columbia, MD: The National Committee for Citizens in Education.

Johnson, V. 1993. "Parent Centers Send Clear Message: Come Be a Partner in Educating Your Children," *Research and Development Report, No.4.* Baltimore, MD: Center on Families, Communities, Schools, and Children's Learning.

Kagan, S.L. 1984. *Parent Involvement Research: A Field in Search of Itself.* Boston, MA: Institute of Responsive Education.

Krasnow, J. 1990. *Building Parent-Teacher Partnerships.* Boston, MA: Institute for Responsive Education.

Kussrow, P. G. 1988. *Community Education Resources Infusion Module for K–12 Instructors.* Boone, NC: North Carolina Center for Community Education.

Lareau, A. 1989. *Home Advantage: Social Class and Parental Intervention in Elementary Education.* London: Falmer Press.

Lareau, A. 1987. "Social Class Differences in Family-School Relationships: The Importance of Cultural Capital," Sociology of Education, 60(2) 73–85.

Lareau, A. and Benson, C. 1984. "The Economics of Home/School Relationships: A Cautionary Note," *Phi Delta Kappan,* 65(6): 401–404.

Laswell, H. 1936. *Politics: Who Gets What, When, and How.* New York: McGraw-Hill.

Leler, H. 1983. "Parent Education and Involvement in Relation to the Schools and to Parents of School-Aged Children," In *Parent Education and Public Policy,* R. Haskins and D. Adams, eds. Norwood, NJ: Ablex.

Levy, J. E. and Copple, C. 1989. *Joining Forces: A Report from the First Year.* Alexandria, VA: National Association of State Boards of Education.

Lightfoot, S. L. 1978. *Worlds Apart: Relationships Between Families and Schools.* New York: Basic Books.

Lindle, J. C. 1989. "What Do Parents Want from Principals and Teachers?" *Educational Leadership* 47(2):12–14.

Lueder, D. C. 1989. "Tennessee Parents Were Invited to Participate and They Did," *Educational Leadership* 47(2):15–17.

Lueder, D. C. and Bertrand, J. E., "Implementing Family/School Partnerships in Distressed Communities: A Critical Analysis of Four Successful Programs" (Paper presented at the *Annual Meeting of the American Educational Research Association,* San Francisco, California, April, 1989.

Lyons, P., Robbins, A. and Smith, A. 1983. *Involving Parents: A Handbook for Partici-pation in Schools.* Santa Monica, CA: Systems Development Corporation.

Moles, O. and D'Angelo, eds. 1993. *Building School-Family Partnerships for Learning: Workshops for Urban Educators.* Washington, D.C.: U.S. Office of Education.

National Study of School Evaluation. 1993. *Senior High School Improvement: Focusing on Student Performance.* Schaumburg, Illinois: Author.

Rich, D. 1987a. *School and Families: Issues and Actions.*Washington, D.C.: National Education Association.

Rich, D. 1987b. *Teachers and Parents: An Adult-to-Adult Approach.* Washington, D.C.: National Education Association.

Rich, D. 1988. Introduction in *Drawing in the Family*, S.F. Walker ed. Denver, CO: Education Commission of the States.

Rich, D. 1988. *MegaSkills: How Families Can Help Children Succeed in School and Beyond.* Boston, MA: Houghton Mifflin.

Rioux, J. W. and Berla, N. 1993. *Innovations in Parent and Family Involvement.* Princeton Junction, NJ: Eye on Education.

Whitaker, K. S. and Moses, M.C. 1994. *The Restructuring Handbook: A Guide to School Revitalization.* Boston: Allyn and Bacon.

Omaha Public Schools.1992. *School and Department Resources.* Omaha, NE: Author.

Peck, M. S. 1978. *The Road Less Traveled: A New Psychology of Love, Traditional Values and Spiritual Growth.* New York: Simon and Schuster/Touchstone.

Rioux, J. W. and Berla, N. 1993. *Innovations in Parent & Family Involvement.* Princeton Junction, N.J.: Eye On Education.

Rutherford, B., ed. 1995. *Creating Family/School Partnerships.* Columbus, OH: Na-tional Middle School Association.

Seeley, D. S. 1985. *Education Through Partnership.* Washington, D.C.: American Enterprise Institute for Public Policy Research.

Seeley, D. S. 1989. "A New Paradigm for Parent Involvement," *Educational Leadership*, 47(2):46–48.

Senge, P. M. 1990. *The Fifth Discipline.* New York: Doubleday/Currency.

Swap, S. M. 1990. *Parent Involvement and Success for All Children: What We Know Now.* Boston, MA: Institute for Responsive Education.

Swap, S. M. 1993. *Developing Home-School Partnership: From Concepts to Practice.* New York: Teachers College Press.

Tangri, S. S. and Moles, O. 1987. "Parents and the Community," in *Educator's Handbook*, V. Richardson-Koehler, ed., New York: Longman.

U.S. Department of Education. 1994. *Strong Families, Strong Schools: Building Com-munity Partnerships for Learning.* Washington, D.C.: Author.

U.S. Department of Education. 1995. *Employers, Families, and Education: Building Partnerships for Learning* (Introductory Letter by Secretary Richard W. Riley). Washington, D.C.: Author.

1991. *The Vital Connection,* a newsletter published by the Parent Involvement Depart-ment of the San Diego Schools, San Diego, CA, 2(3):1.

Walberg, H. J. 1984a. "Families as Partners in Educational Productivity," *Phi Delta Kappan,* 65(2):397–400.

Walberg, H. J. 1984b. "Improving the Productivity of America's Schools," *Educational Leadership,* 41(8):19–27.

Williams, D., Jr. and Chavkin, N. F. 1986. *Teacher/Parent Partnerships: Guidelines and Strategies.* Austin, TX: Southwest Educational Development Laboratory.

Whitaker, K. S. and Moses, M. C. 1994. *The Restructuring Handbook: A Guide to School Revitalization.* Boston: Allyn & Bacon.